Seasons in Sanctuary

Zach,
Hope you enjoy the
book.
Happy Birthday

Danny Lopriore

Feb. 7, 2013

Outskirts Press, Inc.
Denver, Colorado

Seasons in Sanctuary
Based on a true fantasy
All Rights Reserved
V3.0

Outskirts Press
http://www.outskirtspress.com

ISBN-10: 1-4327-0277-7
ISBN-13: 978-1-4327-0277-9

Outskirts Press and the "OP" logo are trademarks belonging to Outskirts Press, Inc.

Printed in the United States of America

Acknowledgements

Writing a book is easy.

Writing a *good* book is next to impossible.

Getting anyone to tell you the difference may be the key to any success an author might have.

"Seasons in Sanctuary" is now more than 10 years old -- from conception to print – an eventful decade that began with a simple story idea and has evolved into a labor of love, with the help of a few very important people.

Dianne Vasquez Lopriore, my wife, inspired my first foray into professional writing in September of 1989, handing me a classified ad for a part-time sports reporter's job at the Gannett Newspapers in White Plains, N.Y. That high school sports reporter's job began a late-blooming career in journalism that has lasted until today.

I am grateful to the all the coaches, players, parents, school administrators and fellow reporters and editors – and they know who they are – whose lives, on the field and off, provided the backdrop for the book and constant encouragement for me to continue writing good stories.

A special thanks to Yonkers high school coaches and

good friends John Volpe and Don and Tony DeMatteo for their inspiring dedication to young people and for choosing to be coaches; to writer/author and former co-worker Maury Allen for his encouragement, to newspaper editor Marc Hoffman for hiring me and not firing me when he found out I had no journalism background; and to my good friend Henry O, who was one of the first people to tell me I should be a writer.

The idea for this book germinated for several years before my hands ever hit the keyboard. A chance meeting with television producer/writer Scott Williams, a fellow Yonkers native and Gorton High School alum, ignited the actual writing of the book. Scott has been a constant encouragement over the last two years, faithfully reading several adaptations of the manuscript.

To my editor and first agent Sammie Justesen, who showed me where to put the periods and apostrophes, wrote proposals to publishers, sent out manuscripts and stuck with me through dozens of rejections. Sammie's expertise helped make the book a better read.

A special thanks to Angelo Pizzo, Jason Cerbone, Rose Davi and Kevin Snow who read first drafts and added their support of the book.

And to my family; my mother Catherine, father Angelo, brothers; Joe, Dominick and Frank, sister Rose, sons; Jared, Michael and Danny Jr., and daughters; Keanna and Kathy -- many of whom are probably as surprised as I am that this work is in print -- thanks for listening to years of long stories, bad jokes and promises to "write a book someday."

I also want to thank Mama Rose and her son, "The Coach", whose "Seasons in Sanctuary" inspired the book. You know who you are Coach. Thanks for having the courage to believe that your talent could be greater than your pain, then for having the guts to share that talent with your players and with me.

You'll coach again.

And to God – thanks for everything else.

Introduction

Seasons in Sanctuary is a novel based on a true fantasy – written somewhere between fact and fiction, good and evil and faith and failure – a tribute to those who are brave enough to uncover, express and share their God-given talents. The story is loosely based on real people, places and events covered by the author over his 15 years as a journalist. This tale of a troubled mobster, who would rather be a baseball coach, and his miraculous, redemptive journey back to his first love, is true enough to have happened and fantastic enough to make us want to believe that it could happen again and again and again.

CHAPTER 1

A man cannot serve two masters, He must love one and hate the other or he will be loyal to one and despise the other. Matthew 6:24

The game was an important division scrap between my Redemption High School basketball team and our biggest rival, Blessed Mary. Tip-off was scheduled for 4 p.m. in our gym, but I had another job to do at 10 that night—a little business with a guy at the Bronx Terminal Market who couldn't decide which trash collection provider best suited his company's needs.

Between the game and that other "thing", I planned on taking a couple of hours to shower, change, and have dinner with my girlfriend Melissa at Louie's Seafood Place in Yonkers. Then I'd meet some of my associates in the Bronx.

The game took forever.

We jumped out to a 6-point lead, extended it to 10 by halftime, and then got into foul trouble late in the second half. With only four players on my bench and two starters fouled out of the game, Blessed Mary went on a run and tied the score at 48 to 48, with 10 seconds

1

remaining in the game.

Shit! Overtime.

I kept glancing at the little black beeper attached to my belt to make sure it was turned on. I always kept the beeper on vibrate and made sure I had the use of a vacant office in the school, with a private telephone in case I had to reach someone in an emergency. I couldn't risk missing a call from my boss, Bernie "Big Ben" DeLeo, or my crew captain Ronny "The Kid" Cappelli if they needed to update me on a job or straighten me out on an upcoming deal.

Our crew did its "business planning" at obscure locations, constantly moving from restaurants to parks to department stores, even at Yankees or Jets games, always making sure to avoid being seen, followed, or phone-tapped by the feds or police. I knew when and where I was supposed to be way ahead of time, but I always carried extra AA batteries in my pocket and made sure my little black beeper was on and working, just in case. That little black beeper had saved my ass a hundred times already. If I'd been forced to hang around near a phone waiting for the word on some deal, I wouldn't be able to coach at the high school every afternoon. Cell phones were a big upgrade to mob business, but we didn't have the technology in 1992.

But no matter what I was doing in my "business life", once I hit the front door of Redemption High, walked past that statue of Mary holding Jesus in the front hallway and entered my office in back of the boys locker room, no one or nothing could distract me. I was a coach for those few hours each day and nothing else mattered – nothing. The beeper was only there to warn me that when the game was over I had to go back to my other life – regretfully.

We went back and forth against St. Mary's, trading free throws and looking for opportunities to score. Every time the damn referee blew his whistle and extended the game another 30 seconds, drops of sweat gathered at

2

the top of my head, dripped down the front of my nose, and fell with a tiny splash onto the court in front of our bench. But I loved the energy of close games.

Joey Larkin, "Sweet Pea," my point guard, dropped two free throws, giving us a 55-54 lead with 30 seconds to play in the first overtime. I took a deep breath, thinking we were okay. Our tight man-to-man defense picked up at half court and Joey slipped under the Blessed Mary point guard, reached in with his left hand, and stole the ball with a couple of seconds left on the game clock.

"Yes!" I shouted, as Joey called a time out to protect the ball.

"No! Are you kidding me?" I shouted again when the ref whistled Joey for a reach-in foul.

"That's a horseshit call," I muttered. "You can't make that call just because the kid reached in near the guy. He never touched him!"

The Blessed Mary kid hit one of the two free throws and the game was tied again at 55.

Another OT. Shit! Shit!

Not only was I gonna be late for dinner with Melissa, I'd have to rush like crazy to get back down to the Bronx for that "thing." If I screwed this up and the guys found out I was at a basketball game for three hours, I might never coach again. Hell, I might never walk again.

This was getting bad, but I had to forget about the time and concentrate on the game. Calling the next play had to be the only thing on my mind.

"What time is it?" I asked my assistant, Bobby.

"There's 24 seconds left." Bobby said, looking at the game clock.

It was 60-59, Blessed Mary, we had the ball with 24 seconds left, and I was running out of time.

Should I go inside to Trey and try to get a foul call?

Should we hold the ball until the last couple of seconds, score, and leave them with no time left to beat us?

3

Could I trust Sweet Pea to take a jumper?

And what kind of offer would I make to the market owners who were sweating it out in the middle of our mob territory garbage wars? "How about two weeks free pick-up and you tell the other company, Tommy's crew is now picking up our trash?'" Or, "How about your market goes up in flames because you don't have any protection against sudden fire?

Screw the garbage shit! No time for that now.

"Timeout!" I yelled, making a T with my hands above my head so the ref could see it. "I need a T."

Now I was really sweating and digging deep for an answer to St. Mary's defense.

Father Mike Troccoli, the school principal, stood near the exit door with his arms crossed, watching the game along with a hundred or so fans in the bleachers. He glanced over at me and I worried that he could read my mind, knew why I was sweating, and where I was headed after the game. I figured maybe someone had told him who I was, what I did. Yes, I was paranoid—but that was part of "the life"; always worrying about who was watching, who was behind me, who I could trust.

Troccoli placed his hands in front of him in the prayer position, looked toward heaven, smiled and mouthed in my direction, "We need a win"! I guessed it was his way of trying to get me some backup from *his* boss. Father Mike was a pretty good guy. A tall, red-headed and freckled former basketball player at Redemption himself, he overlooked a lot of my faults – language and temper tantrums -- because he wanted his teams to win and he didn't think I was really a bad guy. Little did he know.

No one at Redemption would have suspected I was involved with wise guys – deeply involved. As a cover story, I told the monsignor and the administration that I was in the construction, demolition, and salvage business and had a lot of time to spare. After two years of coaching baseball and basketball, nobody really knew exactly what I did. They didn't seem to care, either—

4

especially because I got the job done on a third of the salary other public and private high school coaches pulled down.

Sometimes I'd give back part of my meager coaching salary so the kids could have new uniforms or equipment. Redemption had little money in the sports budget. They didn't really push the athletic programs or recruit top high school players like other parochial schools had become famous for doing. You know—the 6-foot, 8-inch kid who plays ball like a pro and just happens to have "friend" who pays his tuition. Other Catholic schools in the New York area, in fact all over the country, would bring in the most talented kids to play ball and win titles, to pump up the alumni so they could brag about their alma mater and contribute big bucks to the school. In fact, one coach told me that his state Catholic school championship basketball team included 10 Baptists, one Methodist, and a Pentecostal kid. There wasn't a Catholic player in sight on his team—not even on the bench. The fact that we won in both baseball and basketball was like a miracle for the school. No one seemed to care about what I did away from school, as long as I got the job done.

As the game dragged on, I turned to our scorekeeper Keith O'Hara to get a check on the time. A nerdy, pimpled-faced junior, O'Hara sported black Buddy Holly glasses and wore his school jacket and tie even after school was out. I knew I could depend on this kid; he always had a wrist watch that kept perfect time, a sharpened No. 2 pencil for scoring, and a fat spiral notebook with all the team's statistics for the three years he had scorekeeper's job. O'Hara could spout the correct temperature and weather forecast, Dow Jones average, updated pro or college sports scores, and the correct time in four time zones. He looked up from his score book, glanced at his watch, and said matter-of-factly, "It's 6:30, Coach. That's Eastern Standard Time."

I paced back and forth in front of the bench, trying to

control my breathing. The pressure was getting to me and I didn't know how much longer I could play games with my own life—basketball or baseball in the afternoons, night work until three or four in the morning, sleep like a bat until afternoon, then back to the school. I didn't mind the weird schedule or lack of sleep, but I struggled with my double life. I was scamming at my no-show union job, which was like stealing from the union, and then donating the money to the school so my kids didn't have to run a car wash to raise cash for uniforms. Double-dealing took a lot of energy. Double-dealing could lead to double trouble.

And now the game moved into double-overtime and I was exhausted from thinking about how to pull us out of it.

We needed this win to gain momentum for the upcoming Catholic League playoffs. I stood there holding the ball with 10 seconds left and a team full of kids looking at me, and did what I always managed to do: I put the rest of the shit out of my head and concentrated on the game.

"We'll go inside to Trey," I said out of instinct as the kids huddled around me. "If they double team, we throw it back out to Sweet Pea for a jumper or a move down the lane. Got, it? Let's go!"

Billy Nitkowski, my shooting guard, in-bounded to Sweet Pea from just inside half court and Sweet Pea flipped it in to Trey, who faked a shot, eluded the double team, and passed it back to Sweet Pea on his way to the hoop.

Bang, bang. Sweet Pea's lay-up rattled off the backboard and through the net, with the buzzer following a split second later.

We won 61-60 and I was outta there!

The crowded locker room smelled like nine teenagers who hadn't showered in a week. Danny Lorusso, a local sportswriter from the Daily Herald, came in and headed right to Sweet Pea and Trey, who talked over each other, trying to grab a headline. I just wanted to congratulate my kids, schedule a practice for the next day, and get home.

"Hey Coach V!" the writer shouted as he tried to escape from the other seven players he hadn't interviewed. "Got a second?"

Shit!

Lorusso wasn't your ordinary knuckle headed sports writer trying to find a story where there wasn't one. He was a good Italian guy from a middle-class family – a lot like some of the guys I grew up with -- but without the prison records. He'd been covering Redemption sports for a couple of years and reported on our two CHSL baseball championships. But this basketball team was a surprise to everyone and Lorusso had been writing some nice things about me and the kids.

"Big win?" Lorusso asked.

"Big win," I replied. "We might be ready for the playoffs if we can stay healthy and out of foul trouble."

"What's next for this team? Can you win some playoff games? Are you healthy enough to make a run at the Class C title?"

"Yeah, Danny boy," I answered. "We're okay right now. We have some nicks and bruises, but we're playing well and I think we can make some noise if we execute. These kids have balls. But don't quote me on that balls thing, okay? Let's say this group has fortitude."

My locker room time was nearly spent. Lorusso asked a few more questions about practices and game plans and I answered as quickly as I could. I had to get home and change clothes. Melissa was waiting to eat and she did not like waiting; she always thought I was maybe with another woman or something. I wanted to stay and talk basketball, but I had to go.

"Talk to the kids," I said. "But don't let them say anything too stupid. I don't want the other coaches getting anything to put up on their locker room walls. We're trying to be cool right now."

I could trust Lorusso not to embarrass the kids. He'd played high school and college basketball and understood he was covering high school kids, not pro athletes. He never really slammed anyone in print unless it was a story that had to be told. He'd done a few tough stories on kids who screwed up in school and with the law. He'd also exposed some bad coaches and problems with youth sports—like the Little League coach in New Jersey who taught kids to throw curve balls at 10 and ruined the arms of dozens of kids before they could ever play high school ball. But he mostly cared about giving the kids positive press, which really made a difference with the inner city kids and those from small schools like ours who didn't always get noticed. My kids really liked the guy; they seemed to know he was about helping them.

I took full advantage of Lorusso's nice-guy approach to reporting and made sure he didn't find out what I did in my "other job." He was too good a reporter to pass up that kind of story. When he asked about my occupation or personal life, I told him I had a contracting business (somewhat true) and did carting and demolition work. Because I wasn't a noted mobster or reputed "organized crime associate" as the media says, I guess he never considered investigating me. If my name had been Genovese, Gotti or Gambino, it might have been tougher to stay anonymous.

Why would he suspect me anyway?

I was like a lot of guys in Yonkers. I had my own business, I coached recreation sports, and I played softball on Sunday mornings. Believe me, there are a lot of guys involved in "things" nobody knows about who are ministers, teachers, coaches and businessmen. Just take a look at the headlines.

Everyone knows that mob guys have always given big bucks to the church, just like they were businessmen doing charity work, but you never talked openly about who you were or what you did. Even in confession, a guy

8

might ask forgiveness for adultery, lying, or even some petty crime, but you never told a priest about "the life." It just wasn't done.

Being a coach at a Catholic school came with a sort of protective shield because the priests and teachers were ready to overlook little indiscretions in the name of Christian love. Hey, there was even a rumor a couple of lesbian ladies taught and coached at Redemption. They lived together and nobody questioned it. Nobody checked them out. Why would they? Don't ask, don't tell was invented in the church.

The only other people who knew about my double life were my "friends," and that was another story that would play out later.

With the post-game interviews over, I got past Lorusso and the team as we all left the locker room in a bunch. I sprinted into the cold February air and sped home in my gold Acura. I jumped into the shower, fed my dogs Blackie and Lucky, and ran out to meet Melissa. My wet hair, moussed to hold its comb, froze as I hit the street but I was moving, making time. The trip to south Yonkers was only two miles and I pulled into Louie's parking lot in less than five minutes.

"I guess we're going to eat and then you're going to run out on me after you pay the bill," Melissa said when I walked up to our table in to the main dining room. "What am I, like third on your list of priorities today? Basketball first of course. Then, where will you be going tonight; a meeting, a card game, or out with some bimbo?"

I didn't need this. Another pissed off woman.

Why couldn't women stay the same as when you met them? Why did they come on like you were the best thing that ever happened on the first five dates and then revert to suspicious, possessive, self-centered nags after they hooked you? And after you married them, things got worse. Not only did they nag, but they got bored. Melissa was the cutest, smartest, easiest-going girl when we met. After a few dates I thought she could be the one I wanted to stick with.

But between coaching and my night work, I didn't have a lot of time to pamper her, and man she really needed pampering. She was coming off a bad marriage where the guy had abused her physically and mentally and she wanted someone to take care of her. I didn't mind taking care of her, especially in the first few months we were seeing each other, but I did have other things to do.

"I got some business to take care of later tonight and then I'll meet you back at the apartment," I said as I looked at my watch. "I'm sorry. I'll make it up to you on the weekend. We'll go to the Atlantic City or something. We'll go shopping in Paramus."

"Yeah, right," she said. "Go do what you have to do. I'm just your girlfriend. Choke on your food. I'll see you later."

I ate like I was starving, kissed Melissa and ran out of Louie's. It took me 20 minutes to get to the Bronx.

Lenny and Squiggy waited for me in their van outside the market. These two guys helped out with the some of my dirty work and backed me up when a job required more than one person. They came along to show force while I convinced the market owner to take our new deal. We made our way past the night security guards and the hookers, who were always in the market after hours offering their talents to truck drivers, and knocked on the back door of Tropicana Fruits. The owner, Jackie Sherman, opened the door and invited me in.

"What can I do for you Mr. Vitale?" Sherman said nervously as beads of sweat popped out of his forehead.

"We want to offer you an alternative to your refuse removal contract with Cut-Rate Carting," I said, referring to the possibility of dumping his current "family-owned" garbage company. "We can give you two free weeks and guarantee your own container and a very clean pick-up." I pointed to the Cut-Rate decal on his door.

"You have a problem with them, just call me and we'll take care of it, no problem."

I could see that Sherman, a short, fat guy with a bad toupee and an obvious perspiration problem, was uncomfortable with the proposal because he would have to tell the Cut-Rate guys, a rival company owned and operated by a rival crew out of the Bronx, that he was going over to us at Rite-Way. But it was midnight in the Bronx and he could see I was serious and tired, so he wasn't about to challenge my offer. He accepted, signed a contract, and politely said good-night. I'm sure he didn't get any sleep that night, thinking about how he'd tell the Cut-Rate guys he no longer needed their service.

Another notch for Rite-Way and another businessman we could manipulate in our on-going garbage turf war. In a week or two, we'd return Sherman's business to Cut-Rate after a sit-down to settle territory, and things would be back to normal, our crew handling our area and Cut-Rate moving out of our stops and staying on their turf. It was like any business; we were always making moves to maintain the balance of power. Every once in a while these games would lead to violence when young guns would meet and haggle over customers and territory.

But not this night.

This was just a show of power to keep the other crews in their place. For each stop I secured, I got a percentage of the take. Our garbage routes brought in at least $100,000 a month. I wasn't getting rich on garbage, but I took in maybe $400 to $500 a week if things were going good. If they asked me to rough a guy up, like smack a guy around and collect gambling money, I'd get 10 percent of whatever I collected. That could mean a couple hundred a week too.

I felt like a fool every time I did one of these jobs. I was like a bad kid who never grew up, bullying some poor slob who just wanted to run his business but knew the mob was going to pick off a little piece here and

11

there. But it was all about maintaining the company's rep and instilling just enough fear and respect to keep the businessmen paying. I thought of it like Con Ed sending a poor sucker a cutoff notice.

"Pay the bill or your service is shut off," Con Ed threatens.

"Pay your bill or get your nose broken," we'd say. Hey, what would you rather have – a broken nose, or a wife yelling at you when they turned off the lights or repossessed the car?

I started my car and moved slowly down the rough cobblestone pavement of the Terminal Market, knowing the place would soon be filled with truckers and farmers bringing in their goods. Lenny and Squiggy jumped into their van and headed back to the north Bronx. There by my side on the front seat was the basketball score book, still open to the game we'd had played earlier that evening. Sitting under the streetlights, I scanned the list of player's names on the roster. These were kids who depended on me, looked up to me, and trusted me. They were innocent, trusting kids who had made me their role model. Kids who were back in Yonkers telling their friends in the park how we'd just beaten St. Mary's in double-overtime, bragging to their parents about the game, and thinking that playing basketball in high school was just about the best thing in the world to be doing.

And where was their coach?

I felt a little sick to my stomach. Maybe it was the smell of the uncollected garbage in the market or the fumes from the trucks idling under the thruway, or maybe it was the idea that only a few miles and few short hours separated me from my great life as a coach and my bad life as aaah .... well... whatever the hell I was.

It was almost midnight now. I drove slowly onto the Henry Hudson Parkway and headed north toward the Cross County Parkway, trying to decide if I wanted to see Melissa before she went to bed or just give her a break and avoid another argument about where I'd been. I still had to get back to Yonkers and report to my friends. They'd want to hear what happened with the garbage deal, have a couple of drinks, and eat some Italian food. We'd sit around and tell war stories about jobs we'd done and things we were planning. It was always about the next deal, the next problem, the next thing they needed done. The late nights would spin into early mornings, capped off by more bullshitting and breakfast at an all-night diner. Our bacon and eggs came right before going to bed. Sometimes I'd look over at the diner counter and see truck drivers and businessmen having breakfast, too. But they were on the way to work, not coming home from another break-night.

After our big overtime win and with the garbage account a done deal, I could only think about my 4 p.m. practice later that day. Then I'd get to do what I loved, even if only for a few hours.

Emeralds victorious in opener

YONKERS -- Sean Mannion scored 24 points and grabbed 12 rebounds to lead Redemption High School to a 54-48 victory over Scanlan High School in the opener of the Catholic High School Association Class C season. Mannion, a junior center/forward got support from Joey Larkin and Trey Walton, two juniors who keyed the Emeralds' inside/outside game. Larkin had 12 points and 7 assists and Walton grabbed 12 rebounds and scored 12, in baseball coach Tom Vitale's debut as varsity basketball coach.

The victory was the first for 1-4 Redemption after opening with four straight losses to Class A and Class B opponents.

CHAPTER 2

Honor thy father and mother that your days may be long upon the land. Exodus 20:12

My father was a hard-working guy, but not what you'd call the *Father Knows Best*, pipe-and-slippers, help-with-the-homework, play-catch-with-the-kids type of dad. He coached Little League for a season or two and I got a chance to play for him one summer. Other than that, I remember him as a fairly good provider who liked to flirt with the neighbor women on the block and had a wacky sense of humor—especially when picking on his friends or going head-to-head in chop fights.

"You're ass is so big the people at the Bronx Zoo thought you were a hippo from the zoo in Italy, visiting your cousins in America," he'd say to his fat friend Mario.

"Hey, your hair's growing back...way, back. Make sure you wear a hat if you go out so you won't get sun stroke," he'd say to anyone who was bald or losing some hair on top.

Both sides of my family came from Naples, located in the southwestern part of Italy on the Tyrrhenien Sea. My grandparents landed in the Lower East Side of

14

Manhattan right off the boat, then moved uptown in stages to the West Side of Manhattan and finally up to East Harlem. Eventually they made it across the East River to Fordham in the Bronx, which was like a suburb of Manhattan in the early 1900s. In Fordham, a neighborhood where Fordham University and the Bronx Zoo and Bronx Botanical Gardens were the points of interest, we lived on Hoffman Street, Cambreling Avenue, and then Prospect Street, where Da and Ma found a basement apartment. I liked the basement move, because it meant we didn't have to drag our asses up five flights of a tenement stairs several times a day. None of the buildings in Fordham had elevators back then, and no one wanted to live on the top floors, especially in the summer when we had to lug groceries upstairs in the heat. Going downstairs in the morning was great – we'd race down three or four worn marble slab steps at a time and jump a railing or two, making it down four flights in a noisy, rumbling 30 seconds. But coming home was a bitch. The only good thing about climbing the stairs was that some of the old Italian ladies who lived on the lower floors would feel sorry for us and sometimes hand out a cookie or a candy as we passed their doorways on our way up. You could tell what each family was eating for dinner by the aromas that emitted from each apartment. The basement was cooler in the summer, more than a little chilly in the winter and easy to sneak into when we came home late.

After moving into the basement apartment, we learned to identify people by their feet or their walk as they moved by our kitchen window. Sometimes we'd even cop a look at the legs and possibly the panties of a pretty girl – that is if Ma didn't catch us peeping.

My brother Joe was the oldest in the family, then came my sister Lori, and finally me, Tommy, the baby. I was always the baby, which helped me get away with stuff when I was young. But it drove me nuts when my mother or grandmother would pinch my cheeks and show me off, telling people "how handsome the bambino (baby boy) was".

My mother's father died at 43 and her mom, Grandma Sabini, lived with us, which made our meals always worth coming home for, no matter if my mother or my grandmother cooked. We could smell Grandma's gravy—that's tomato sauce to Italians—or her roast chicken, egg plant parmigiana or pasta fagiolia, a block away. Food was the bookmark of each day. We always ate three good meals even if we weren't rich, because most of the Italians I knew could produce a good meal from a bunch of dandelions, beans, and pasta and could feed a family of five for under $5 a day. We ate potatoes and eggs for breakfast, peppers and eggs for lunch, and pasta of some kind every night. Who knew we were eating poor people's food? We thought it was all top shelf cuisine.

I was born in 1958, so I was too young to understand the world-changing shock of President Kennedy's assassination in 1963, but I was old enough to understand a few things about life when the Age of Aquarius hit in the late 1960s. While some of the more radical kids in our neighborhood secretly followed the new wave of liberal thinking and moved toward long hair and Hippiedom, most of us clung to the traditional Italian-American ethic of respect for God and the flag, with a little larceny on the side. By the age of 12, most of us Arthur Avenue kids knew a little something about sex, drugs, and drinking and how to find, obtain, and keep things that didn't belong to us.

Da was a tough guy, but so were most of the working class Italian-American fathers around Arthur Ave. At least it seemed that way to us kids who were always trying to avoid a beatin.' "An Arthur Avenue beatin'" might include any type of corporal punishment, from an open-handed smack to the back of the head to a full-fledged whipping with a belt or a hairbrush. It all depended on how pissed your father was and how quickly your mother

16

got him off you. I usually got the message when my father gave me "that look"; the look that made you feel like you were a low-down thief who'd snuck into the apartment and stolen the Sunday meat sauce. When Da exploded in anger and yelled something like, "I'm gonna beat your brains out!" or "Now you're gonna be sorry!" us kids could feel the heat of his breath from ten feet away, even on the coldest winter day. Da didn't have to knock the shit out of me -- he scared the shit out of me.

But Da's words did more damage than his hands could ever do. When he yelled things like, "You're worthless," or, "you're an idiot" or "I wish we never had you" I'd curl up in a ball and cry. I think most kids, like me, would rather have a smack than a putdown from their fathers. I slowly grew distant from my dad because of the way he talked to me. He always had a criticism, never a compliment. It got so I expected him to be disappointed in me and I didn't have much self-esteem. Anyway, I sometimes wished he'd he hit me instead of calling me names. My father's hands were small and meaty, like the rest of him. At five and a half feet tall, he was stocky and weighed maybe 175 pounds, with a wide face and a big Italian nose that looked like he'd taken a few punches in his heyday. He wasn't a big guy, but he yelled like a big guy.

My mother, Rose, handled most family matters during the day and spent the better part of at least three days a week warning me, "Da's going to take care of you when he gets home if you don't behave." Most kids didn't fear their mothers, who'd maybe smack us or try to punish us in some small way to keep us in line. But the phrase "your father's gonna kill you" was not an idle threat and usually deterred us from any major disobedience. After Ma warned us, the waiting time before Da got home was terrifying. In fact, waiting was usually worse than the beatin' itself.

Luckily for us, Ma's threats were usually enough and she hardly ever followed through when the old man came home from work at five in the evening for dinner. He was always hungry, happy to be home, and not looking for aggravation. Most times Ma would let the fear be the punishment and I was saved—at least until the next day. I think Da smacked me at least 50 times before I was 12, but he never hurt me real bad. I dreaded the waiting and got tired of thinking the only attention my father might pay to me that day was a beating. One day, when I was 14, I cracked under the pressure. When my father came through the door, I jumped up and exploded, "I got in trouble in school today, so why don't you let me have it and get it over with!"

He smacked me hard, more for my arrogant move toward him than for what I'd done in school. But that was the last time he hit me. I guess he realized I was getting too old to be scared of Ma's "wait until Da gets home" shit. Either that or he just thought I was getting old enough to handle my own problems. Maybe he just didn't know how to deal with a teenager. I know one thing for sure. He didn't know how to talk to me about things that were important to me. Never did. Still doesn't.

I don't remember being real close to my mother when I was young; never talking to her about things and sharing my troubles and fears. But my brother Joe was killed in Vietnam in 1968 and Da left Ma for another woman a few years later, when I was about 16. At that point, my older sister had gotten married and I was the only man there for Ma, so we grew much closer. We were real close till the day she died. Maybe my older brother dying and my father leaving stole the fun of being a kid for me. Maybe that's why I always wanted to be older than I was, felt older than my peers and got tired of school so quickly. Without an older brother or father to guide me I thought I had to take on the world, make some money, and be somebody strong for my mother's sake.

Ma was a simple saint; a woman who cared about everyone in the family and would drive you crazy asking

18

five times a day how you were doing or could she help you with something. Her side of the family was connected to the mob world through my uncle, her brother, Mario Sabini, who's dead now. Ma had a nice smile, a quick wit and everyone in the neighborhood liked her. She was just like most of the moms—a homemaker, or a part-time seamstress at a neighborhood dress shop, or a clerk at the local Woolworth's or a drug store. She'd work a morning shift to make some money to help out with the bills and have some left for her own personal needs, like an occasional permanent, new underwear or maybe a lunch at Howard Johnson's on Southern Boulevard with her girlfriends once a week. After work, she'd come home to cook, sew, and do whatever else most working class moms did in the 50s and 60s. She wasn't a PTA or soccer mom like the ones we see today, driving SUVs and joining committees to raise money for a new playground. She didn't have the time or money to jog, join clubs, do Pilate's, or take classes at the local college. She barely finished high school and got married a year later. No career, no profession, no higher education—just hard work, a pain-in-the-ass husband, and some kids she tried her best to take care of.

In the dark, you couldn't really tell the Arthur Avenue Italian ladies apart. They all smelled like Italian cooking at home or Jean Nate' when they were going out somewhere, and they all had that unmistakable Bronx accent that could not be denied, especially when they shot expressions like "Ya fatha's gonna kill ya" or "eat all ya food" or "wanna meatbawl?" The older ladies who came off the boat had Italian accents that became thicker when they got mad and lapsed into the broken English we all know from Pat Cooper comedy routines. "Ats-a no good" "Stop-a fight" and "I tella yu mama wadda u do."

When one of the old Italian men in our neighborhood died, even if you didn't know him personally, you'd know he was dead because his wife immediately put on a long black dress, black nylons, and a pair of those clunky, black shoes. The ladies of our neighborhood always walked around the 187th Street and Arthur Avenue shops in packs, arm in arm, especially on Saturday and Sunday nights. The men would sit in the park and bullshit and play cards while the ladies talked and walked—mothers and daughters, aunts and cousins, family and friends. The ladies in black—and some kept wearing black clothes for years after their husbands died—always had friends and family to walk with them. It seemed like they had a special club, The "Black Widows", and the ladies whose husbands were still breathin' couldn't join. I used to think that every lady in the neighborhood must have had a black mourning dress tucked away just in case a family member died all of a sudden so they wouldn't miss a beat when their time came to join the Black Widows.

My mother was tight with her mother and sisters. When they got together, which was every day, they'd all talk at once, laughing and cackling like a hen house full of chickens, which use to drive my father crazy. Grandma lived with us, like many widows or widowers who moved in with their families. I don't ever remember any grandmothers or grandfathers going to nursing homes or even living alone. It would've been disgraceful to send a parent off to be taken care of by strangers. The elderly just stayed around the neighborhood, with an apartment next door in the same building, or living with their kids, until they died or their kids dragged them to the north Bronx, Mount Vernon, or Yonkers to live in a nice house with an in-law apartment. And I thought that was fine. Family took care of its own. Even poor people made sure they took care of their family members.

Growing up in "Little, Little Italy" (Arthur Avenue near 187th Street was the Bronx version of Lower Manhattan's famous tourist attraction, Little Italy), was all you might have heard about—and more. *Marty, Bronx Tale, Raging*

Bull, Serpico and other books and movies describe the old neighborhood pretty well. Wise guys, cops and crooked politicians ruled, and non-Italians (African-Americans, Hispanics) were as welcome on the block as Yassar Arafat would be at a Steven Spielberg movie premier. Blacks and Puerto Ricans were interlopers and we'd often hear a storekeeper or resident point out a stranger in the neighborhood and use politically incorrect ethnic slurs like, "Niggas", "Molenyams" (egg plant), or "Spics."

Kids in my neighborhood were tough and you had to fight for your place in the Italian food chain. Not many young boys on the block reached the age of five without receiving at least one black eye or having to wrestle or fight a recognized bully to gain respect. We had all sorts of gangs in the Bronx. The Fordham Baldies were the best-known during the late 1950s and 1960s, but their influence had diminished by the mid 70s. The Italian Aces, the Puerto Rican Ching-a-Lings, the Black Spades, and others ruled different neighborhoods. Us little guys, beginning at about 10 and 11 years old, had our own gang called the Little Aces. We wore black tee shirts with cut-off sleeves and we had the local tailor sew "Little Aces" on the front of the shirts. We younger guys imitated the Aces in every way we could, even getting into gang fights with junior gangs from other neighborhoods. We mostly fought other Italian kids from nearby blocks, until the black and Puerto Rican gangs started growing in strength. We fought with fists, sticks, small knives, and even zip guns when we reached our early teens. We often met our rivals at Grace Dodge Elementary school to fight it out.

In one such battle, I earned a scar that still hasn't faded away completely when I reached through a fence to grab a black gang member and he slashed my arm with a razor blade. It burned, oozed blood, and scared me a little, but the wound taught me I could take pain and keep fighting. I was proud of that cut and that scar for years.

The teenage boys around Arthur Avenue seemed to use most of their testosterone on hazing and harassing the younger kids, threatening outsiders, or battling for the attention of girls on the block. Those of us who weren't attracted to the macho street mentality—Bronx guys like Dion DeMucci of Dion and the Belmonts fame, Calvin Klein the designer, and Robert Klein the comedian, used music, art, and academics to escape the working class and the allure of the streets. But many of us fell in line with the idea that being tough was more important than being smart. And being tough in our neighborhood was a strong resume point.

Arthur Avenue could be heaven or it could be hell.

We suffered through stifling hot, humid summers with smelly garbage cans lined up like condemned robots on the sidewalk, especially during the big garbage strike in the late 1960s, when garbage was piled two stories high for days. When the wind blew in from Pelham Bay, the smell of elephants from the Bronx Zoo on Southern Boulevard crept through the neighborhood, providing an early education in zoology and a lesson on how far the smell of animal waste could travel with the right wind velocity. And there were the nasty, cold winters when it seemed like the dirty piles of city snow would never melt. Cars were snowed under and the already narrow side streets became impassable, causing more than a few fender benders and fistfights over car parking territory. We had to play inside our apartments or congregate in schoolyards like Grace Dodge Park, a cold, hard, blacktop playground where we played touch football and an ice-less, skate-less, and stick-less form of hockey game we invented. To score a goal we kicked an empty can or a crushed milk carton into a doorway that served as the goal. The game was murder on your sneakers, whose soles you could wear away in a couple of weeks on the blacktop. Arthur Avenue parents hated kids who destroyed their sneakers prematurely by using them as a way to stop our bikes instead of brakes or grinding away the rubber on playground cement. A good pair of gym sneakers were supposed to last until the end of the school year at which time we would throw them over the telephone wires and expect a new pair for the summer.

Among the most important games in our neighborhood was stickball. A derivative of baseball, the game could be played by as few as four guys and a major contest scheduled as quickly as a kid yelling, "Stickball at Dodge!" out of his apartment window to anyone who was willing to join him. And nothing stopped the stick ball games—neither, snow, nor rain, nor heat, nor gloom of night. All we needed was a broomstick, a ball, and a painted or chalked box scratched on a wall for a batter's box. Each schoolyard had its own rules depending on the measurements of the park, height of the fences and distances from home plate to a home run. At some parks, hitting the ball over a fence might be an out because the act of macho might lose a ball or delay the game. When one field of play was shortened by the existence of a school building or fence, that area was considered out of bounds. Windows on apartment houses or school buildings were especially difficult to navigate. Many a Spauldeen (the pink rubber ball of choice in the Bronx) disappeared through a tenement window in our neighborhood never to be found. Some of the schools utilized heavy mesh screens to protect windows that faced our makeshift stickball fields just to limit the number of broken panes. We imitated our favorite pitchers and hitters describing plays as the game progressed.

"I'm the Mick," one kid would say as he replicated Mickey Mantle's swing at bat.

"Here's a Sandy Koufax's curveball," the pitcher would say as he hurled the rubber ball toward Mantle just like Koufax did in the 1963 World Series. Stickball was a haven for fantasy and a real game we mastered in our own Yankee Stadium or Shea Stadium behind Grace

Dodge. Each big strikeout could be bragged about for days and each home run hit high off the school wall became longer each time we described it -- days, weeks and even years later to anyone who might listen.

Stickball was the king, but we also played any form of basketball or football we could manage. Sometimes we'd throw the ball through the lowest space on a hanging fire escape ladder or nailed a milk crate to a telephone pole. We even used peach and tomato baskets we stole from the market, knocked out the bottoms, and hung as hoops. Lack of money to purchase the necessary equipment was never an obstacle. Balls weren't difficult to shoplift; just one quick move in the 5 & 10 store and a tennis ball or a Spauldeen dropped into the front of a guy's pants where we were too young to have anything big taking up space. Once in a while we'd get tagged by a store manager, but they'd only check our pockets. No store clerk wanted to search near *your* balls to try to find one of *their* balls stashed in your underwear. It wasn't worth being called a fag.

One time, when I was about 7, I stuffed a tennis ball, a Spauldeen and a box of those snappers—the ones you'd throw at the sidewalk and they would go off like tiny firecrackers—all down my pants. I thought I'd gotten away with a big score until the snappers slid down my pants leg and dropped on the floor as I slipped outside the neighborhood Woolworth's. The manager saw me and I ran. I guess he thought I'd dropped my stolen merchandise, so he didn't follow me. But I wasn't taking any chances, so I pressed my legs tight around those two balls and my two balls and ran like a fag down 187th Street until I was safe in an alleyway behind my house.

We played stickball for three weeks on that heist alone, until the tennis ball split in two and we lost the Spauldeen down a smelly sewer. It stunk so much no one wanted to play with it after we finally fished it out with a plastic cup attached to the end of a stick.

24

But the Arthur Avenue neighborhood wasn't all sticks and stones and urban tension.

There were the heavenly aromas of fresh-baked bread in the morning from Cardella's, Addeo's and Prince bakeries, the inviting waft of pizza baked in the ovens of the Half Moon, Mario's and Capri, the noisy buying and selling at the Arthur Avenue indoor market where my grandparents had a spot selling fruit and vegetables, and the constant, overpowering smell of Italian cooking falling to streets from tenement apartments that stretched from Cambreling Avenue to Fordham Road and from Third Avenue over to Southern Blvd in a ten block area where you couldn't go ten feet without hearing Frank Sinatra or Dean Martin music coming out of the Italian social clubs.

Great food cooked on a thousand stoves or the aroma of elephants in the zoo. It all depended on which way the wind was blowing.

And the girls were beautiful, especially to a hormone-filled pre-teen. They were untouchable in most cases, but extremely hot. My friends were fun to be with, the Italian ices from Colavolpe's tasted like heaven, and the Feast of St. Anthony at Mount Carmel Church was unforgettable every year.

And then we had the Yankees. We had the New York Yankees, (or Mets in my case) and even when they sucked through the late 60s and early 70s, they came back with Reggie, Thurman, Sweet Lou Pinella, Catfish Hunter and the Arthur Avenue favorite, manager Billy Martin (a crazy, hot-headed genius whose mother was Italian) to reclaim the World Series in 1977 and 1978.

The Bronx of my childhood provided lessons in life, all of life. Unlike the suburbs, where we moved when I was 13. We got no protection on the streets from rain, snow, life, death or even the perils of a five-block walk to P.S. 32—where you might be clipped by a bus, hustled by a bully, or hit by an errant rock meant for someone else— all on the way to first grade.

But I loved it there. Maybe I just loved the Bronx because it was home and maybe I loved it because the streets gave me a sense of freedom and license; the license to be good or bad, strong or weak, rich or poor.

I chose to be good at sports and not so good in school. I was good at chasing girls and not so good at chasing long-term employment. I was good at scams and not so good at staying out of trouble.

My father worked hard. His main job was an iron worker for Perlman Iron Works on Washington Avenue, and he also worked part-time for my uncle in the pizza business for awhile. But my Uncle Mario, on my mother's side, was "one of the boys;" a respected and feared Wiseguy who specialized in a variety of businesses, including loan sharking, gambling, and union business. He wasn't opposed to an occasional murder for the right person and the right price.

I wasn't particularly attracted to the mob lifestyle as a kid, but I soon noticed how people responded when they heard Uncle Mario's name. It was much like E.F Hutton in the TV commercials: people listened, and that was impressive to a young kid. One summer night when I was about ten, I found out how big Uncle Mario really was. I was strolling down 187th Street on my way home and this older guy, maybe he was 40 or 45, stood on his front stoop drinking beer with his friends and acting the fool. I paused to watch. He was stumbling on the steps and talking loud, so I laughed because he looked so stupid. The guy came off the stoop, called me a "fuckin' punk kid," and kicked me in the ass. One of his drunken buddies called out, "Hey, that's Big 's nephew's ass you just stuck your shoe into!" The man almost shit his pants right there. He sobered up in less than five seconds at the sound of Uncle Mario's name, then apologized four times and gave me a dollar to forget he'd had kicked me. Uncle Mario had juice. Real power.

But at 10 years old I was still too young to start thinking about the mob life. Baseball was the prime attraction for me in those days. The sport seemed easy after hundreds of hours playing stick ball, wiffle ball, and baseball games, not to mention endless stoop-ball sessions where I stood alone throwing a ball off my front stairs and catching it to hone my hand-eye coordination. I grew to love the sheer comfort of having a ball in one hand, a glove on the other, and a bat within reach. Baseball was my first love, my occupation, my hobby and my best chance to find fame and fortune, although I didn't know it then.

Uncle Tommy honed my interest in pitching by playing catch with me almost every afternoon before dinner. Before long I could hit the strike zone pretty much when I wanted to. I clearly remember my biggest Little League moment on the mound. I was ten years old, playing for my father's Cardinals team in the Fordham-Tremont Little League. I could throw the ball pretty good by that time, and even though the rest of the team was made up of eleven and twelve year-old kids, I got the chance to start a game one summer Saturday morning when one of our older pitchers didn't show up for a game.

Pitching for your father is a Little League tradition. Every kid—and every parent who has had a kid playing youth sports—knows that one of the kids on the team is that "special" kid. He's the kid whose father is the coach. He's the pitcher/shortstop/best hitter/he-can-do-no-wrong kid who plays whatever position he wants. He bats cleanup, he gets the big hit in every game and he pitches all those Little League no-hitters, striking out almost every kid on the opposing team while his father does that, "I think I'm Bobby Valentine managing the Mets" bullshit on the bench. That's the father-son Little League tradition everyone envies and secretly hates.

"He's pitching because his father's the coach," the disgruntled and jealous parent mutters under his breath while he chomps on a hot dog sitting in a lawn chair down the left field line.

27

"Yeah," another parent says. "My kid can pitch as good as the coach's kid, but the coach won't give him a shot because his kid's got to be the star."

It's weird how even at the Little League World Series, whether the team is from Kentucky or Thailand, the best kid on the team always seems to be the manager or coach's kid. But it's inevitable, because the parent who spends the most time living the Little League life usually has the best kid. That coach is the one who has a batting cage in his yard and knows the names of every boy in town between the ages of ten and twelve. He sends his kid to baseball camp, or runs a camp himself, and makes sure little Johnny has the best glove, aluminum bat, and sunflower seeds.

But I wasn't that kid and my father wasn't that coach.

"Let Tommy pitch today," my father said, and I thought I was dreaming. "He's ready for a shot. What the hell? If he gets bombed we'll take him out."

I was starting a Little League game. I stood there with my mouth open, halfway between wanting to throw up and thinking this was a dream, just like the thousands of dreams I'd had since I started playing baseball. Me on the mound, striking everyone out, with my father smiling on the bench, turning to tell everyone who'd listen, "That's my kid Tommy. He's got an arm like a rifle."

But I was pitching, not dreaming, and I had to get my head into the game or I'd be sitting on the bench fighting back tears in less than an inning. I suddenly realized there was a big difference between me and the eleven and twelve year-olds coming to the plate to face me. All of a sudden they seemed like adults – bigger and stronger and more mature than me. Some of them had hair on their balls already. One kid, Ronny Masacoli, was so much older looking that people said he already had a wife and kids. I think he forged his birth certificate so he could play Little League until he was 18. Everything Masacoli hit went over the fence or was lined so hard the infielders dove out of the way when the ball came at them.

But for some reason, I wasn't scared. Somehow I felt at home when I climbed the high mound and looked down at the roughed-up, spike-marked white slab where I'd kick off my pitching career. In that moment, I knew I belonged there. I felt secure, knowing I could throw the ball hard and straight. When I turned to look at home plate, it seemed only 5 feet away instead of the regulation 45 feet from the mound. Everything else in the world disappeared in that split second; the batter, the backstop fence, the fans, the umpire, and even my father, who was busy making up the lineup card while I warmed up.

All I could see was that big, brown, round catcher's mitt hovering a couple of feet above the white home plate. All I could see was my hand letting the ball go right into that glove. I don't even remember who held the mitt. I just knew it was there for me, like a big leather target with a bull's eye.

"You okay?" my father said, breaking me out of my pitching trance. He was standing behind me with the scorer's book in one hand and the other on my head. "Don't worry. If you get banged around, I'll come out and get you. Just try not to hit anyone."

Was he kidding? I could hit a flea in the ass with a baseball from 45 feet away even at ten, and he was worried about me hitting a batter by accident? My father had no confidence in me, but Uncle Tommy knew what I could do. He was always telling me I'd get a chance to pitch someday. Now he was over there in the stands, watching and smiling. I guess my father just thought I'd screw up and embarrass myself. But he hadn't spent much time with me and he had no idea what I could do. Like I said, he wasn't a typical Little League father. He wasn't Ward Cleaver, the father in "Leave It To Beaver" who always had time for his sons Wally and Beaver. But then again, I wasn't the Beaver, either.

The first big play of my Little League pitching career is still a vivid memory. That moment compared in importance to my first sexual experience, my first car, my first beer, and the first time I held a $100 bill in my hand.

It was an infield pop-up that rose from the batter's swing. The ball looped up into the summer sun and seemed to stay in the air for an hour. I waved to my infielders and yelled "I got it!" But when I lifted my face to find the ball, the morning sunlight and the heat of the day hit me square in the forehead. I felt the sweat under the headband of my hat, felt the drops thicken and race down my face and all of the sudden, the ball, floating between the sun and the sky, looked like one giant uncatchable balloon.

"I got it. I got it!" I yelled again with renewed confidence. And the ball fell right into my glove, nearly knocking me over as I stepped down the slope of the inclined pitcher's mound.

The crowd applauded and I was officially a pitcher with my first out on my first pitch to my first batter. What could be better than this? Sex? Beer? A car? A hundred dollar bill? Nah. To a ten-year-old rookie Little League pitcher, that looping fly ball that landed in my mitt was the first step to Yankee Stadium. I could play with the big kids. I was ready for the next step in my baseball life. I was the man!

I pitched a two-hitter for about five innings and as I gained confidence with each strikeout, ground ball, and pop fly, my father seemed to lose faith in my ability to finish the job. The story goes like this, according to Da.

"The league president Ralph Ferrigno said your pitches are letting up and you're getting tired," Da told me when he came out to the mound to get me. "Are you tired?"

"Nah" I took off my cap to wipe my forehead. "I feel good. I can pitch more."

"Nah, you're tired and I don't want you to lose the game," Da said.

"Take a seat on the bench and get a drink."

Our reliever was a bigger kid with a good fastball, but he didn't have it that day. He was wild and walked four or five guys. He lost our lead and lost the game—my game. And Da was pissed. I was pissed too, and the ride home wasn't fun.

"That fuckin' Ferrigno," Da kept saying. "I shouldn't have listened to him. He's supposed to know about baseball. I wanted to leave you in, but he said you were tired. Fuckin' idiot, asshole, rat bastard."

I didn't know whether to be mad at my father or that asshole Ferrigno. To this day I don't know if my father was trying to save me from the embarrassment of a loss, trying to save the game for us, or trying to impress Ferrigno by agreeing with him.

I prefer to blame Ferrigno.

My father wasn't an experienced coach and he listened to the wrong advice. But he should have left me in. I was ready to be a player. That moment in the sun on that hot summer morning in June, my first experience on the mound holding the game in my hand, motivated me. I worked harder and harder on my game and got better every day. But my father never really involved himself in my baseball career after that. I guess he just didn't feel qualified. I thought he didn't care.

CHAPTER 3

Now, set your heart and your soul to seek the Lord your God... therefore arise and build the sanctuary. I Chronicles 22:19.

It was St. Patrick's Cathedral, St. Peter's Basilica, and the Mormon Tabernacle rolled into one perfect vision of spiritual and architectural bliss. Warm summer sunlight touched the vivid emerald-green grass and stark red-brown clay baseball diamond; the field was accented by three white pillow bases and the five-sided home plate, the altar of my childhood prayers. A scalloped, white overhanging facade draped that hallowed temple in symmetrical purity that separated my baseball heaven from the noisy, hard, and dirty South Bronx neighborhood surrounding it.

It was fuckin' beautiful.

My mundane black-and-white childhood world was forever changed by the colorful majesty of Yankee Stadium—a baseball field to some; a historical relic to others. This marked the beginning of my deep and abiding love affair with the game and places where the game was played. Yankee Stadium became the prototype for the future "green pastures" of my life, where God would "make me to lie down" and where he would restore my soul."

My sanctuary.

I've never found a more comfortable place to play or to pray than the sandlots, the high school fields, the gymnasiums, and especially my first sports haven—a narrow sun-dashed alleyway just off our basement apartment in the Bronx where my Uncle Tommy trained me as a Little League pitcher. The steps in front of the four-story tenements along Arthur Avenue were my childhood confessionals, where I repented each of my youthful sins to the rhythm of a dirty, hollow, pink Spauldeen ball rapping off the stairs, over and over, into my praying young hands.

The concrete playground ball field at Dodge High School, with its chain link boundaries and painted white markings designating our baseball diamond, was more sacred to me than Mount Carmel Church in my Fordham parish neighborhood. To me, stepping inside our "real" church meant facing arcane spiritual things I didn't understand. The masses were all in Latin. The holy smoke, candles for the dead, and statues with blood dripping from their hands and feet seemed vaguely threatening. I actually feared going to confession. I didn't want to tell the priests about lying to my parents, stealing baseball cards from the newsstand, or fighting in the street. What did they know about me anyway? What did they care?

I preferred a game of stickball or touch football or pick-up basketball, in parks where I felt at home with myself and the games. I'd pray for a big hit in a big spot and often God would answer, blessing me with a majestic double high off the school wall or an opposite-field single that would score a winning run. I think God heard all my prayers when I was playing because he knew I was doing something that I loved, something innocent, something he gave me as a gift to enjoy. In church, you had to go through another person—a priest—and some mysterious translation of the scriptures to get to God, who was easier to interpret right there on the vast cement outfield at Dodge playground every afternoon. Prayers should be direct, personal and easy to send. Answers should come quickly, even if the answer is no. Church prayers came with candles, dogma and a bad history of religions that killed and frightened people into good behavior. I preferred the God I knew who lived in the park much better.

The most distinct and lasting memory of my early childhood was an 8-year-old's summer baseball visit—led hand-in-hand by my father Joe Vitale—to Yankee Stadium. It was 1964 and the Yankees were still in their glory years, despite being swept 4-0 by Sandy Koufax and the Los Angeles Dodgers in the 1963 Series. Mickey Mantle was still the biggest name in New York sports and the team still had Yogi Berra and Roger Maris. It would turn out to be the last pennant-winning year for the Bronx Bombers until 1976, but Yankee fans, especially little kids like me from the Bronx, didn't know that at the time. The team was in first place and I was going to see my first game – with my father.

My heart pumped like a teenager anticipating his first French kiss when I was led through the turnstiles. An scruffy, unshaven old guy with a ruffled Yankees cap and a Yankees usher's shirt ripped our tickets and my father handed me the torn piece and a warning, saying, "If you get lost, tell an usher or a cop and show him the ticket. He'll find me."

I didn't really understand why Da was giving me instructions about getting lost until I looked up and saw the crowd, like a moving mass of humanity, shuffling to buy beer, going to the rest rooms, purchasing souvenirs; men, women, a lot of kids like me, holding parents by the hand, walking up long inclined ramps that looked like driveways, to their seats. People were walking in all directions, all smiling, all with one team to root for, all carrying baseball gloves, programs, hot dogs and beer.

There were more than 40,000 people at the game I learned the next day when I read the newspaper, but it looked like a million to an 8-year-old kid.

Da grabbed my hand and practically lifted me off the ground, walking through the crowd toward where we would be sitting. We walked past the old vendor hawking programs, under the darkened catacombs of the stadium's walkways and eventually out into the light of baseball salvation. Who knew the Bronx could look like heaven? Sure, the Bronx Botanical Gardens and the Bronx Zoo were in my backyard and we'd go to both places a lot, but this was different. This was a place you'd see on television in gray and white shadows or in pictures on the back of newspapers. Seeing it and being inside it was like when Dorothy gets to Oz and suddenly the world turns to color. I couldn't wait for the game to start and the peanuts, Cracker Jacks, and soda to start flowing.

"Whadda ya think, Tommy?" Da asked as he lifted me up so I could see the whole field. "You know they got 20 or 25 guys who just take care of the grass here. Imagine that? We can't even get the super to fix a stinkin' leaky faucet and the Yankees have 25 friggin' guys working just to make the grass perfect and keep the dirt smooth. It must be a good job, probably union. Maybe someday you can be a groundskeeper and see all the games for free. You'll work six months in the baseball season and then take off. Nice friggin' job."

Watching those baseball players, dressed in those white uniforms with pinstripes and that NY on the hat and shirt, I wasn't thinking about being a groundskeeper or even a rich guy who could afford box seat season tickets. I was thinking about being a baseball player. I could see myself running around on that field, catching fly balls and hitting the ball over the wall. "I'm going to be a Yankee or a Met someday, Da," I said as he sat me down in my own seat to watch the game. "I wanna be a baseball player, Da. Can't I be one?"

Da laughed and said, "Sure Tommy, and I'm gonna be Mayor of New York. I'll come in with all my body guards and sit in the box seat near the dugout and watch you play, right?"

It sounded good to me. Me playing centerfield for the Yankees or the Mets and Da and my mother and sister sitting in the box seats. I'd run in from the outfield and tip my hat to them and everyone in the stands would know they were my parents and be jealous of them for having such a great kid. Dreams start like that, with one vivid day at the ballpark, when you can close your eyes and almost see it coming true. At 8, I was a believer. I had no idea that dreams only come true if you work hard, get the breaks, and help make them happen. Otherwise, that first baseball game in the Bronx, with Da, was as close to perfect as you could get.

But God would snatch that perfect moment, the way he has repossessed other brief successes in my life. (I don't know why). Out of nowhere, dark green thunder clouds formed like a shadow of death over the Bronx Courthouse over the centerfield wall and rain fell in buckets, dousing the field and prompting the grounds crew to cover the field with the biggest canvas I ever saw. The game between the Yankees and the Red Sox was postponed. As I left the stadium with my father, crushed by nature's cursed interruption of my visit to heaven, a sign of hope, the summer sun broke through and a rainbow appeared across Macomb's Dam Park outside the House that Ruth built.

My first professional baseball game was cancelled due to the rain and I had to wait for the rain checks to be redeemed weeks later when my father could take me gain. I really don't remember if we ever went that summer. Da was always busy working or doing something, so I can't recall when we went again.

It has been that way for me over the years, and it may continue to be that way for me as long as I'm still on this earth. Bright days and rushes of success and glimpses of heaven, followed quickly by that infernal storm that would steal my faith away. But those successes always brought me back to the field. Any field would do. And many of those dirt and grass fields and wood floor courts have held my prayers, my faith, and my love for the games that have often saved me from my demons.

I always seem to be looking for another season of sanctuary, like the one where I hid my soul for four years, from 1992 to 1996, at Redemption High School in Yonkers.

We moved to Yonkers, or should I say my parents moved me to Yonkers, in early 1971. I migrated with them to the suburbs, screaming and clawing, away from my Bronx roots, where garbage cans and city buses served as playground equipment and streetlights and neon signs kept vigil through the night in neighborhoods that never really slept. Our's was a neighborhood where we were often awakened in a moment by a screaming couple next door, a police siren, or the grind of an early-morning garbage truck digesting our trash.

I was transported to a foreign land and although the place was less than five miles away, it seemed more like a thousand miles. Yonkers was a place where nightfall meant complete darkness and nothingness, where they pulled in the sidewalks at 10 p.m. and nothing would happen until the suburbs reopened the next morning. Stores closed at 9 p.m., kids deserted the playgrounds at 7 p.m.—unlike in the Bronx, where we had ownership of the parks by age groups. Little kids ran the Bronx blacktops by day while their moms sat and talked on wooden benches until 3 p.m. Grade school kids took possession of the parks right after school and played games like scully, boxball, Johnny on the pony, or spent hours trading baseball cards or flipping them against the schoolyard walls and curbs. The games ended when hundreds of impatient mothers, exiled to their third-and fourth-floor walkups without the luxury of cell phones or beepers yelled out their windows like a fractured choir, "Tony, Mario, Dominick, Frankie, Salvatore. Come home and eat—your father's home!" You hardly ever heard mothers in our neighborhood calling for their daughters. The girls stayed close to home, helping with housework or cooking, or babysitting while their mothers worked.

Teenagers and young adults owned the park after dinner, sneaking beers, sharing smokes and making out in dark corners, until midnight when the cops would come by in squad cars or walking a beat, flash their high beams or flashlights around the schoolyard, and throw everyone out.

In Yonkers, a Bronx kid could get lost trying to get from Bronx River Road on the east side of the city to downtown Getty Square on the west side—if you didn't know the bus routes. Yonkers had a downtown that was like a small version of the Bronx, with walk-ups, stores and an Italian neighborhood on Park Hill that was called, "Little, Little, Little Italy" because it ranked after the Little Italys on the Lower East Side and in the Bronx at Arthur Avenue. But we lived on the quieter east side of Yonkers, where the nearest noise came from the Fleetwood Metro-North train station, the stores on Yonkers Avenue and Bronx River Road or the mall at Cross County Shopping Center. I don't think I ever heard a cricket until I moved to Yonkers. If there were crickets in the Bronx, like in Bronx Park or Pelham Bay Park or places like that with trees and grass, their "cricketing" was probably drowned out by subway trains, buses and things like that.

I found my suburban sanctuary at local baseball fields and parks in Yonkers. The place was greener and there was more room to play and more open space in which to run. I missed the concrete playgrounds of the Bronx and the chain link fences, cool alleyways, and quick trips to the candy store. Some south Yonkers schools had fenced-in concrete playgrounds, but most had fields. I'd see more people in a 10-minute, one-block walk down Arthur Avenue than I would see all day in Yonkers.

Yonkers had its good points, like the Tibbetts Brook

Park swimming pool, Nathan's Famous on Central Avenue where they had pinball games, Adventurers Inn, an amusement park at Cross County, and Yonkers Raceway, where you could watch the horses trot around through the fence and laugh at the old guys with funny hats and cigars who came out every day to toss their money away on the trotters, two dollars at a time.

But, Yonkers wasn't the Bronx. Growing up in the Bronx and moving to Yonkers was like dating Marilyn Monroe, getting dumped, and then hooking up with Madonna. You could dress her up in a tight, form-fitting dress and dye her hair the same color blonde, but Madonna just ain't Marilyn Monroe. You could open a pizzeria and a deli in Yonkers, but the people who moved up to the suburbs still traveled to Arthur Avenue every Saturday and Sunday to find real Italian food.

A lot of things were different in Yonkers, like the Italian restaurants, the schools, the parks and the people— especially the people. The kids my age were sort of protected, if not spoiled. And to me, not anywhere near as tough as the kids on Arthur Ave. I would find Yonkers duller and the challenges easier.

Getting along and making my youthful "bones" in the new neighborhood was a priority. My first fist fights came at the urging of my Cousin Mario who preceded me to the suburbs. I was told I had to gain the respect of the locals, but the ground rules were as different as the turf. Dealing with the natives was a little confusing.

"Let's go over to the grass to fight," my first Yonkers opponent, an Irish kid named Donny McHugh, said. "We don't fight on the concrete."

I was stunned.

These suburban people had rules for everything. No kicking, no biting, no pulling hair, and stuff like that I understood, because it was faggy to fight like a girl. But this was a place protected by rules and regulations I hadn't heard of before.

"Okay," I told my adversary. "Let's go over the nice,

39

soft grass and when I knock you on your ass it'll be padded."

I proceeded to whack the kid around with a few shots to the head, gaining instant respect and taking over the No. 2 spot behind Mario as the toughest kid on the block, or should I say "in the neighborhood." We rated the toughest guys in the neighborhood numbers 1-5. Why we didn't go deeper into the count, I don't know. I guess once you got past the knuckleheads and bullies down to the normal kids who valued their teeth and bones, there weren't too many others who wanted a ranking bad enough to fight for it.

From there on in I was respected by the other kids, but I never really found a place for myself in school, where I felt like a foreigner and misunderstood by the teachers and the straight-type kids from the get-go. My final years of grade school were fine, playing sports and being admired by the gym teachers who saw me as a budding athlete. But when I hit adolescence, with my parents not really able to handle me and no older brother around to guide me, things changed.

The next step up from neighborhood tough is teen troublemaker, but that role had to be put aside for awhile because I was too busy playing ball. There would be plenty of time later in my life to find trouble. My crime career, which began as a little kid with petty theft from local stores, would eventually flourish under the guidance of my Uncle Mario when he showed me the underworld I had only known from newspaper stories about mobsters or movies. Between the ages of 5 and 19, sports and girls kept me busy most of the time. Basketball, football, baseball, any ball -- and chasing skirts were in line of priority over school. But baseball was my first love. The ball and the bat, the smell of fresh cut grass on the baseball field, the feel of leather on your hand, pounding your fist into your mitt while you waited for the ball to be hit to you.

I played in any league I could find right up through

my high school years, 1974, and 1975. I dropped out before my junior year, but ended up playing with some of the best players in the New York City area in sandlot leagues. All little kids start out hoping they'll be able to master the art of hitting a baseball, but by the time you're 10, you kind of know if the brain function that tells the hands and eyes to coordinate, then move a bat toward a spinning, round ball to make contact, is working right. Squarely hitting a curved ball with a curved bat ain't easy. Most kids can make the bat-ball connection often enough to have fun, but very few can make that leap from Little League play to being a real grown-up hitter. I got it early. And when you find out you can accomplish that skill, man it's like an orgasm each time you find the sweet spot on a fastball coming at you at 60, 70, 80 and 90 miles per hour.

I truly believe that if Frank Sinatra could have hit a baseball with any skill at all, he would never have become a singer. If President John F. Kennedy could have hit a Major League curve, he would never have yearned to be president. If Albert Einstein had ever picked up the American pastime and been able to rock a fastball, the world might never have learned that $E=Mc2$.

Every kid—well at least before basketball and soccer took over the American world of kids' sports—grew up hoping and praying he or she would have a chance to hit a baseball over the fence at Yankee Stadium one day.

By the time I was 16, I could.

I was that one-in-a-million kid who really had the talent and the drive to make it. The only thing missing was the opportunity and a little guidance.

And I loved every hit, run, and catch I made growing up and learning the game. When I was on the field, I forgot everything about school, family, problems, girls or my fears. Once I found that sweet peaceful place, where the world faded away, I was addicted. I spent

41

most of my early life hiding on the field.

When my short and unsuccessful high school days ended, baseball stuck with me. In the Bronx or Westchester, a kid who wanted to play baseball almost year round could find leagues in summer, fall and spring, and a good bat usually found a spot on several teams.

My bat was in demand, so I played for three teams, weeknights and weekends, and I made a name for myself in the sandlots leagues where pro scouts investigated young players like they were the FBI and the kids were suspected criminals. They used binoculars, speed guns, stopwatches and charts to track the best players in the New York area. Most times the scouts would find their prospects in high schools or junior colleges—kids who weren't looking to get a college degree but were using school to be seen and evaluated for the Major League entry draft. Since I didn't have a high school resume, the scouts had to find me in the amateur sandlot leagues.

I heard about an open tryout at Yankee Stadium in the spring of 1975 when the Yankees had rebuilt their team and were on the verge of winning their first American League pennant since 1964. The tryout was more than a dream come true. For me, it was the kind of day you'd want to have right before you died. Forget about making it to the Major Leagues. I just wanted to run around that plush Yankee Stadium outfield where you didn't have to step over glass and rocks to make a catch. I wanted to slide into that perfect infield dirt and take some home on my uniform pants. I wanted to look out from the batter's box at the giant scoreboard and the Bronx Courthouse beyond the wall, listen to the No. 4 train rattle along the elevated tracks out past the right-field wall, and hear the echo of my bat hitting a nice white baseball, just once in Yankee Stadium, just the way DiMaggio, Ruth, Gehrig and Mantle heard their hits.

A kid's dream of playing at Yankee Stadium is just that, a dream. Maybe a thousand kids over 20 years ever get to try out for the Yankees and I was one of them. I would romp around that Disneyland of baseball in the South Bronx for one perfect afternoon, like I was born to be there. And after experiencing that daydream, if I had to die the next day—I was ready.

CHAPTER 4

And my elect shall long endure the work of their hands. Isaiah 65:22

I remember seeing Ricky Henderson on television one Saturday afternoon. He was about 43 years old at the time, poised on the top step of the Boston Red Sox dugout on a bright Boston autumn day during the 2002 season. This all-time base-stealing champion and Hall of Famer, who played for the Oakland As two different times over his career and sold his talents to the Toronto Blue Jays, the New York Yankees, the New York Mets, and the San Diego Padres during a 20-year career, was now a part-time player with the Sox late in his playing days.

Ricky, who never seemed to lose a step of his blazing speed or the desire to play, gazed out onto the field between innings with a look in his eyes that's born when you first start playing baseball as a little kid. It's the same look you have when the kids in the neighborhood are choosing up sides and you're waiting to see which captain picks you. It's a look composed of equal parts fear, anticipation, and dreaming.

"I'm gonna play short today and hit a home run to win the game. I'm gonna catch every hard grounder they hit to me and steal a couple of bases too. I can play with these guys."

The best two players were usually captains in a kid's choose-up game, whether it was baseball, football or basketball. Pick-up games are where you learn to compete in the real world. No parents, no refs or umpires, no coaches; just the guys wheeling and dealing players in a quick-draw draft—and then the game begins. There's no celebration, hugging the family, meeting the commissioner, or doing an interview with ESPN about how happy you are to be chosen by the Oakland Raiders or the Sacramento Kings.

And there's no bonus or big-bucks contract; just the recognition of your peers, the people you have to deal with in the growing up world where every day is a struggle to belong.

Maybe that's why waiting for sides to be chosen is so important to a ten-year-old kid. Being chosen in the first few picks gives you some juice. Being picked low makes you mad enough to want to prove yourself to the asshole who didn't pick you earlier.

Being picked last, after all the nerds and lesser talents are chosen, is the ultimate embarrassment. It means you're only on the team because there's no one else to pick. It means you suck—and sucking when you're ten is worse than not being picked in the NBA or NFL or Major League Baseball drafts. That's because the schoolyard draft isn't for money; it's for honor, respect, and a place in the social strata of your very small and selective world.

Being picked first, or somewhere close to first, means everything when you're ten. I think most guys who turn out gay were probably kids who were always picked last in pick-up games. Being picked last is humiliating. If it happens enough at a young age, it can make you want to take up fashion design or dancing.

When you get picked in a choose-up baseball game

you may be on a "slaughter-sides" team. That means one side is obviously better than the other, which can happen if one of the captains is stupid and picks his friends before choosing the best players. In such a case, you'll either be on the side of the big winner or have to wait until another day to win.

In basketball, being picked on a good team can guarantee you'll play for a couple of hours, because winners keep playing and losers sit, leaning against the fence or dribbling a ball on the sidelines, until you get picked by whoever claimed "next" (a NY playground term for the person who challenges the winning team). Waiting for "next" is like waiting for a girl to let you touch her tits. You have to be patient until your opportunity with the right girl comes, then you jump in, hoping you don't get rejected.

I was always picked first, or else I was one of the guys doing the picking.

I was the kind of kid who had a mustache at 14 when the other kids were still looking for that first curly pubic hair to appear. "I'll take Tommy V," a guy would say. And with me to lead the way, you could be sure that team had a shot to win.

I could rule and reign in the unorganized sandlot pick-up games and schoolyard leagues, but the structure and discipline indoors was a different story. My gym coaches loved the way I played and led my gym class squads, but none of them cared to deal with the way I handled the rest of the school day. Class after class of problems with teachers, low grades, truancy and a bad attitude you'd expect from a guy who'd been incarcerated for 12 years instead of being enrolled in public school. I considered my time in school a long-term sentence—12 years in public school with no parole. And they wouldn't let me play on the prison baseball team unless I toed the line.

School sucked -- alot.

Don't get me wrong, I enjoyed learning things like

history and war, or unusual people who'd done great things. I admired intelligence and accomplishment, and great men like Thomas Edison, Leonardo DiVinci and General George Patton. But I couldn't deal with the authority that came with school. I guess back then they didn't know about attention deficit disorder (ADD). That's when they take kids who can't stay still and give them some drug like Ritalin to keep them from tearing up the classroom and driving the teacher crazy. Schools are filled with dozens of those kids nowadays; hyperactive kids who can't sit and listen. These are the kids who play video games, watch TV, or sit at a computer for hours, but can't sit still for ten minutes in class.

Well, I had ADD all right. Asshole Delinquent Disorder.

I just didn't want anyone telling me what to do and I would spend my time daydreaming about playing ball or being outside, free. I still don't know why I couldn't deal with school, but I guess it was my nature. Occasionally I showed them I had a brain. Once we were studying "Catcher in the Rye" and I listened to the class discussion while I had my head down on the desk. The teacher expected me to flunk, but when we took the test on the book I felt I could handle it. I related to Holden Caulfield, the main character; a kid who was alienated in some ways from people and hated school, but was intelligent. He didn't like the phony standards the schools went by. He was also sensitive and a loner—things that caused him real problems. Thinking I understood the guy made the book easier to read.

"Miss Trabert, can I move to the back of the class to take the test?" I asked. "Someplace away from everyone?"

"If you're more comfortable, sure," Miss Trabert said with some interest. "Do you think you know the material?"

I guess she'd noticed my lack of attention during class – sleeping and doodling on the desk might have given the impression I was not paying attention—and I knew she thought I was an idiot because she sort of gave up trying to include me. For once, I wanted to prove I wasn't a dope, so I made sure no one sat near me during the test, just to be sure they didn't get me for cheating off another kid. I aced the test and was done way before anyone else. I guess Miss Trabert told the administration about what had happened and they gave me some IQ tests right after that. When I achieved a really high score, they told my parents that I had a high IQ and the teachers started trying to get me to do more work. But I'd made my point, so I went back to being a slug in class and I never realized any kind of academic potential. They gave up on me after that, realizing I just didn't care. My books stayed in my locker and I just floated through ninth and tenth grade without doing any work.

I didn't love many of my teachers, but I loved my coaches because they held a carrot—the games—in front of me and I respected men who were tough and in control. But I couldn't stand wimpy teachers; the ones who whined, "Tom, you're not living up to your abilities," and "Tom, you could succeed academically if you just gave the same effort you do on the field."

After a series of failures in biology, geometry and Shakespearean literature, I developed a sophomore jinx that led to more cut classes and confrontations with teachers and administrators. My grades in several subjects dropped below the freezing point, because I would get docked three grade points for cutting a class and two for not doing homework assignments. With class averages of 30, 27 and 29 in my three worst subjects (I did have a 90 in American History for some unexplainable reason), it became obvious I wasn't going to pass any of my tenth grade classes, so I just stopped going to school. The truant officers called and came to my house a few times until my sixteenth birthday and tried to get my mother to make me attend school, but that didn't work either. She'd get me up and out and I'd go straight to the local playground and play ball with anyone who had a game going, baseball or basketball.

At sixteen, it was legal for me to drop out, so I just never went back to school. I think I left a pack of cigarettes, a Playboy magazine and an old pair of smelly sneakers in my gym locker which had a combination lock on it. I always thought maybe the custodians left the locker sealed as a kind of memorial to my high school career. Over the next few years, every time I saw a clock and remembered a class I was supposed to be in at that time, I thought about going back, opening that locker up, finding everything intact and trying it again. But I never set foot into that school again until 20 years later. I was 16, free of any responsibility or possibility of failure (in school) and ready to play ball, which I thought was my ticket to fame and fortune.

By the time I was 19, I'd become such a good baseball player that people were encouraging me to go back and finish high school, then attend college to play. I had so few credits that I knew it would take more than a year to get my diploma and I hated school so much I wouldn't consider going back. As I said before, my father wasn't the type of guy to give advice and had no clue about my playing ability, so I didn't get much encouragement from him. I was kind of on my own, but the coaches made sure I kept playing. All that time on the field made me a standout player in the Central Park League in New York summer league baseball. Scouts from all over the country came to our games and it wasn't unusual for them to single out a player like me. I was hitting about .450, with 16 home runs and about 50 RBI over 50 games in the summer of 1977, and a scout for the New York Yankees told my coach about the tryout at Yankee Stadium.

About 15 players were invited from local high schools and colleges. I went to the tryout without any real expectations, but once I was there and saw I could compete with the other guys, I knew I had a chance to play pro ball. But I was shocked when the Yankees called and came to my house to sign me to a minor league contract. My father didn't know much about baseball and tried to get more money because he thought that if the pros were making close to a million dollars a year I should get at least $250,000 to sign. But my Uncle Mario and my coach calmed my father down and told him that any deal to get a chance at the major leagues was a good deal.

"Hey Joe, the kid ain't Mickey Mantle yet," Uncle Mario told my father in a closed door bathroom conversation I heard about later. "The kid has no high school diploma, no scholarship to college and no job right now. This is his chance to get outta Yonkers for a while and play ball. Don't go askin' for a million bucks and blow the deal."

"But they're gonna take the kid and not pay him and I'm gonna have to support him while he plays ball," Da told Uncle Mario. "When's he gonna make some money with this? He needs to get a job or get paid for playing."

"It takes time Joe," Uncle Mario said. "Give the kid a shot at this and if he don't make it I'll get him a job when he comes back. C'mon, let the kid have a shot."

"Okay, Da said. And the bathroom conference was over. My Uncle Mario, aside from being a made man in the mob, had a knack for convincing people to do things. I think he really wanted me to have my dream and maybe have a life. Maybe he was thinking ahead, seeing my future like his own, a guy in the rackets, chasing scams and hiding from the law all the time. Uncle Mario was a legend in the neighborhood because years back, in the late 1940s, he was connected to a bar room murder. The story goes that he had to disappear to Florida for four years until his mob ties got him a plea bargain with a district attorney they paid off. He did a few years in Sing Sing, taking the rap for the mob. And when he came back he was rewarded with a "button", which is like getting a mob diploma. He was made and

50

the rest of his life was sealed. He lived the life until he died of cancer in 1990. Uncle Mario may have remembered himself as a young kid with no formal education and no prospects and predicted that my life might turn out like his. Maybe he didn't want his sister's only boy to be a mobster.

Thanks to Uncle Mario's intervention, my father backed down from his demands and we signed a two-year minor league deal for a $5,000 bonus that included more money if I made it through two years in the Instructional League and Rookie League. Plus, I got a plane ticket to Florida in March of 1978.

As I entered the Yankee farm system, I quickly realized that being the best player at home in the Bronx or Brooklyn didn't mean a free pass to the big time. A thousand guys just like me came from all over the country and even places like Puerto Rico, the Dominican Republic, Venezuela, and Mexico; all of them young, strong, fast and ready to take on the world. Only one in a million would make it to the Major Leagues.

At the time, 24 teams made up the American and National leagues and each time had 25 players their roster. That added up to about 600 major league players, so being first picked on Arthur Avenue didn't have the same juice here. We entered the Instructional League first, then moved up to the rookie League, where we learned the finer points of the game while the management people evaluated us and decided if you were worth paying more than the $125 a week and the meal money we were getting. Free agency had taken over the game, with guys like Reggie Jackson making millions, so getting a contract meant at least one big payday, a bonus, and possibly a chance to play for a Major League team. I did well strictly on talent, but talent wasn't always enough. I was the guy out on the field with the dark cloud over my head.

Playing the minor leagues should have been heaven for me, but it wasn't. Once the excitement of being

51

signed to a pro contract faded, the real work began. And I mean work. I was never fond of working for a living and avoided doing so at every opportunity. Even the thought of getting a job, going to college, and building a career of some kind made me shudder. From the time I realized how much fun sports were, I fully expected to be a major league baseball player, with about three hours each day set aside for playing the games and the rest of the time spent partying and sleeping. That's the way I perceived it after watching and reading about guys like Mickey Mantle and Tom Seaver. I knew a lot of practice was involved, but I thought that would be as much fun as playing in the school yard or in all the youth leagues I played in coming up.

I was sent to Florida for training camp and later to the Instructional League in Florida. I thought the trip to the Sunshine State would be like the vacations New Yorkers took during spring break. Baseball, beach, broads and beers—not necessarily in that order. What I found was baseball, baseball, baseball, bus rides, bad meals, and more baseball. We played nearly every day, and on the days we didn't play, we were stuck on overnight or day-long bus trips, traveling from one small, minor league town to another. I'd never been away from home for more than a few days and I was desperately homesick after two weeks. The games weren't bad, but getting along with different kinds of people, most of who were competing for the same job as a major leaguer, was horrible. These guys weren't like the teammates I'd known, all for one and one for all. They were all talented and hungry and didn't care if you did well. In short, this baseball fantasy was a like a job.

The minor league team I landed with had a roster full of rednecks who didn't like anyone from New York, anyone of color, or anyone who spoke Spanish. The black guys stayed with the black guys and the Latin players hung with their amigos. Me and one other guy were from the northeast part of the country but he was a fuckin' jerk from Maine who didn't like anyone but himself. I missed my mother's food, my girlfriend, soon to be my child bride, the friends I'd go drinking with every weekend, and the polluted air of New York. I even missed Yonkers. I'd already gotten into some scrapes for fighting and drinking and just plain actin' like an asshole and I was close enough to my Uncle Mario to know that if I wanted a union job or a spot in "the business" he would help me. I thought about going home every day. I started to realize that loving the game wasn't enough. You had to love working *at* the game and that the game had to come first. It came before your love life, family, and friends and even before money, which you weren't going to see much of unless you made the big leagues.

Before I could go AWOL from baseball boot camp or decide to give up the idea of being a pro and go home, the game gave me up.

I wrecked my leg.

My brief professional baseball career ended on a freak play during a game in the Instructional League with the Yankees. I was playing right field on a hot spring day in Sarasota when the batter hit a short fly ball toward the foul line. It was one of those balls you know you can't catch, but you run it out anyway, just in case the ball comes back to you. This ball just floated and floated until it was foul by about 10 feet. I let up a little, lunged forward, and felt something unnatural happen to my leg. My leg bent to the left, right in the middle of my thigh, and I heard a loud popping sound. Everyone else must have heard it too, because a bunch of my teammates ran over to me. When I looked down I could see a dent in my thigh where the muscle had ripped and separated from the bone and the bone broke in two places. I looked like a cartoon character after a fall, with my leg bent and bulging like a twisted pipe cleaner. But unlike Wylie Coyote after trying to catch the Roadrunner, I knew my leg wasn't going back into

53

place in the next scene.

Right then, I knew this was the kind of career-ending injury ballplayers dread, hoping it won't come while they're young. I've watched football and basketball players helped off the field with injuries and you just know it's real bad by looking at the people around the guy who's hurt. Everyone, especially an athlete, knows when it's bad. I didn't want to believe it then, but I was damaged goods at the age of 20. With so many healthy prospects coming along every day ready to take my place, a major injury like mine would scare off a baseball organization for the long term.

When orthopedic doctors looked at the X-rays at the hospital they said I must have had a stress fracture or a weak spot in my femur before the injury, because the normally strong bone buckled and snapped without any contact or abrupt stop. I'd done a lot of karate and kick boxing as a teenager, taking numerous shots to my legs and arms, but I never had a broken bone. The doctors said the karate could have weakened the bone. It was a freak injury, almost supernatural, like it was meant to be.

Sorry, Tom," the doctors said. "You're gonna need surgery and a year of rehab and even then you might have trouble getting your speed back. Take a year off, then come back and we'll see how you're doing."

I didn't believe them. I knew my career was over before it even got started. I knew I'd never play in the big leagues. And I knew I didn't have another dream to back it up. I went downhill from there.

As the days passed, the thought of never having a chance to play pro baseball ate me up inside.

Without baseball, my first love, depression set in. I didn't realize it at first, but I was lost without the game, and since I had no other aspirations I could see no real future for myself. I drank more alcohol and then graduated to recreational drugs like pot and coke, hanging out with my friends back home. I drowned my pain and partied to overcome the depression, and then realized I needed to make money. I gravitated to the opportunity that fit my personality. Staying out late, getting up at noon, making easy money and avoiding a regular job made organized crime a perfect fit for my aptitude. And so what if the life led me to jail or even death?

"Fuck it," I said. "Life sucks anyway. Everyone dies, my brother died, baseball died. What the fuck?"

But I did learn discipline on the farm, and it made me a better person down the line, later, when I was teaching kids to play ball.

As a ballplayer, I had an innate quality, especially on the baseball field, to sense what would happen next; the attitude of a jewel thief, able to take anything my opponents gave me. Now I fell into criminal activity like it was just another game—competing for a real score, not just a number on the scoreboard. I thought of the hustle as trying to use my skills to outwit an opponent. I enjoyed gathering all of my physical and mental prowess and channeling it toward making an easy buck.

Seeing me heading downhill with alcohol and drugs, my Uncle Mario made a place for me in his business: His family. You know. Nepotism runs rampant in the mob. The family names everyone knows, Bonnano, Columbo, Gigante, and Gambino attest to the fact that the apple doesn't fall far from the tree. Uncle Mario got me involved in collecting bets, handling his numbers pick-ups, a little gambling, and even a legit job working for a grocery wholesaler where he controlled the union jobs. I was making $400 a week at the grocery warehouse back in 1978, which was like making more than a $1,000 today. Me and my cousin Anthony went to work every day, at least for the first few weeks, then we'd think of ways to call in sick, like "my car broke down" or "my mother's sick"—anything that would get us out to the beach on a sunny day. I hated taking orders from a boss. Mob business was more to my liking. Collect a bundle of cash, deliver some stolen merchandise, and earn a couple hundred dollars for a few hours' work. I didn't enjoy hurting people, but there were times when we had to rough up a guy who wasn't paying a vig or a get he lost. My athletic skills translated well to physical violence. I was worse when I'd been drinking, because I could get mean. Although I didn't realize it at the time, my frustration at not being able to play ball fueled much of my anger.

I went to the doctor often beginning in my late 20s because I began experiencing what I thought were chest pains and heartburn. I attributed the symptoms to my lifestyle of drinking and running around all hours of the night. But tests showed I had early symptoms of anxiety and stress and that really scared me. I was fine most of the time, and then I'd suddenly explode in temper tantrums, screaming, throwing things, and even hitting people. My girlfriends, and later my second and third wives, said I was moody and had two personalities, going from the highest of highs to the lowest of lows, with flaring episodes of anger. Sometimes it got crazy.

One night, me and my cousin Anthony went to a club in Manhattan, a place owned by a made guy, Johnny Mancini. I had a few drinks and started smacking people on the dance floor, shoving and manhandling people I didn't even know.

"V, you gotta knock it off," Anthony said. "You're acting crazy."

"Get the fuck away from me," I shouted. "These fucking people better get outta my face."

As I stepped back to clear away from Anthony, two huge bouncers got me in an arm lock and dragged me downstairs toward a hidden office.

"This is 's nephew you're fuckin' with," Anthony said, following us down a dark a hallway. "You're gonna have a problem if you do anything to him."

Anthony's suggestion may have saved my life, or at least my ass from a major whuppin'.

"Let's make a call and see," the bigger guy said."

We'll call Mr. Mancini and see what he says."

The call was made while I wrestled and tried to get loose. The biggest bouncer listened on the phone without saying a word, then hung up and let me go.

"Mr. Mancini says you're with Mr. Sabini and for us to take care of you," the guy said. "We'll go back upstairs and behave, right?"

"Yeah, right, you big fuck," "Let's go back to the party."

I spent the next hour banging into people and causing all kinds of problems, but those two bouncers stayed with me like the Pips stayed with Gladys Knight. Every time I headed toward a fight, they herded me away, apologizing and making sure I didn't fuck up too bad. At the end of the night I passed out and Anthony took me home.

The next day my Uncle Mario woke me up with an ominous message on my answering machine. "Tommy, you get over here right now, you little fuck," he screamed. "Right now!"

So far, Uncle Mario had put up with my bullshit for the family's sake, but his patience was wearing thin. He smacked the shit out of me that morning and said I embarrassed him in a made guy's club and that now he owed the guy big time. You could see he felt sorry for me, his sister's kid, but he wouldn't tolerate anything disrespectful. I had to be told and told good. Uncle Mario told me a few years later, while I was coaching and looking to get out of the mob thing, that the top guys wanted to make me at various times as I was coming up, but he knew I was so messed up with drinking and using drugs that it would have been like sending me to my own execution. I would have done something really stupid that he couldn't protect me from. The problems I had dealing with my fears and failures and all the emotions that came with it, made me a risk.

When I straightened out, got married again, and had a daughter, things got a little better for me. My talent for sports translated into a talent for doing business, dealing with people, union work and other things. I was on my way back up the mob corporate ladder in the mid 1980s. For those who don't know—and after the Valachi Papers and Joe Valachi's testimony in front of the Senate committee on organized crime in 1963 everybody in the world knew—the Italian so-called Mafia organizational system went something like this:

On top of the family tree was the Capo Crimini/Capo de tutti capi, or super boss/boss of bosses. There were five of those; one each for the five New York families. Next in line to the boss was the Consigliere, or trusted advisor or family counselor and Capo Bastone (Underboss, second in command). Next came the Contabile (financial advisor) and the Caporegime or Capodecina, a lieutenant, who typically headed a faction of ten or more soldiers, comprising a crew. Next came the Sgarrista—foot soldiers who carried out family's day to day business. Made guys were sgarrista or "soldiers" and everyone below that level was scrapping to have a chance to be made one day. The Piciotto were lower-ranking soldiers, enforcers, also known on the streets as button men. Finally, there was the Giovane D'Honore—a Mafia associate, typically a non-Sicilian or non-Italian member.

By the time I was 30, I was somewhere between a Piciotto and a Sgarrista, close to being made. I handled collections, betting money, loans and interest, and stuff like that. When a guy was due to pay up, we collected— and when he didn't pay—well, convinced him it might be better for his health if he came up with the money. You know, like Rocky Balboa, the has-been fighter in "Rocky" who worked as a collector for the local loan shark. You collected and got a percentage of what you came back with, so it was like a sales job; the more you sold or collected, the more you earned.

Unlike the mild-mannered Rocky, I didn't have much patience when a guy didn't pay. Mob work is mostly stealing and making "commissions." You did a "job" and for whatever you earned you kicked something up to the guys above you. They provided protection, guidance and kept individuals or "crews" of guys from having "beefs" or conflicts. The work could include simple theft, loan sharking, gambling and extortion. On the bottom level it included union involvement, construction, money laundering, and investment and control of legitimate businesses, which was where the real money was made. Some crews were deeply involved in drug dealing, which historically brought huge profits to the mob, and also caused most of the violence and in-fighting. The old timers didn't like the drug business, but it paid so well, they allowed their people to earn and looked the other way when millions of dollars came up the ladder. And drugs were imported into the United States through Italian and other European connections, so it was sanctioned by the Sicilian end of the mob.

Low-end guys made their bones by earning wherever and whenever they could. You stole, sold the merchandise, dealt pot or coke, ran small gambling games, did collecting and enforcement work—anything you could do to earn money and impress the guys above you at the same time. Nothing impressed a captain or boss more than a big earner or a guy who would use muscle on demand. I was primed, and just crazy enough to do whatever it took to make it in this line of work. Despite having an uncle in the business and knowing what it took to be in "the life," I would quickly discover that my talent for crime was not a gift.

CHAPTER 5

Oh, death, where is thy sting. Oh grave, where is thy victory?
I Corinthians 15:55

"Get to the hospital, quick!"

I was perched on the edge of an exam table at the doctor's office, getting an evaluation on the hand I'd injured when I put some guy's head through a glass window during a bar brawl. I'd cut a couple of tendons on my throwing hand and they weren't sure I'd be able to go back to playing minor league baseball in the spring of 1976.

But at that moment I didn't care about baseball or anything else. The receptionist said it one more time: "You need to go to the hospital quick, Mr. Vitale!" and I flew out the door, not even stopping to pay my bill.

I'd gotten my girlfriend Maureen pregnant the previous summer, and now she was having our baby at St. John's Hospital in Yonkers. Maureen was only seven months pregnant, but she was in labor, and I was eight miles and a shit load of New York traffic away from the hospital.

I ran out of the doctor's office on the Grand Concourse, jumped into Maureen's 1969 silver Vega, and headed back to Yonkers. The trip would normally take 25 minutes, but I did it in 12. During my race with time, I left silver paint deposits on several cars parked along North Broadway as I bumped and banged through the streets, doing 60 mph. Maureen and I had gone to the hospital just the day before, but they sent her home, saying it was too early.

It was definitely too early.

Maureen was 16 and I was 17 when we met in the summer of 1974. She was a real Irish doll, with long blonde hair falling in perfect waves around her beautiful face. She had green eyes, a bog smile, freckles in all the right places, and a great body. I had a driver's license at 16 and my father let me use his car once in a while if he was in a good mood, so one thing led to another and our puppy love quickly turned into a heavy backseat romance. Maureen got pregnant after we'd dated about a year—no big surprise, since we never used a condom. Being from two Catholic families and too stupid to know any better, we decided to get married and make sure the baby got a legitimate start.

One afternoon a few days after the positive pregnancy test back, we went over to nearby Bronxville with our parents where the local justice of the peace did the ceremony. We should have known it wouldn't last.

I was in my first year at Sarasota in the Yankees farm system and had to be away from April until August. Neither of us graduated from high school and I didn't have a job, except playing baseball. Maureen was working as a clerk at the local A& P.

But my 17-year-old sperm had a mind of its own and could swim like a fish -- and Maureen was very good to me. She was the kind of girl any mature 25-year-old guy with a job, an education, and a brain would want to marry. Too bad I was 18 and clueless. My parents separated a couple of years before we got married, so they weren't much help in the way of advice. But my mother and sister Lori were right on top of this baby thing. They helped us get ready for the baby at our apartment, putting a shower together and all the stuff women do for each other.

The blessed event was anticipated as you'd expect from any Italian or Irish Catholic family. We worked on names and tried to deal with the responsibility as well as we could. Relatives teased us about taking the baby to school with us and asked if we had enough diapers for the three of us. Maureen's parents were good about it. Her father was nice enough not to kill me and they helped with the whole situation. They probably felt sorry for us, knowing our teen years were prematurely over and life wouldn't get any easier.

My entire trip to the hospital was a blur. People who had their cars parked on Broadway are probably still looking for the silver car they glimpsed pin-balling up the road that May afternoon. I slipped into a parking space in the emergency room parking lot and ran toward the hospital, holding the cast on my right arm so it wouldn't bounce around. I hit the elevator button maybe 100 times before the doors opened. The elevator was crammed with old ladies, nurses, and delivery guys with flowers—all staring at me. I was sweating bullets, breathing hard. I pressed the No. 4 button each time the elevator stopped at another floor.

"I'm having a baby, can this thing move any faster?" I shouted, watching the floor lights creep up to the fifth, sixth, and seventh. "C'mon you fuckin' piece of shit elevator!"

Everyone on the elevator laughed or put their heads down and tried not to laugh as the car finally reached the maternity ward. I burst out before the doors completely opened and launched myself at the nurse's station.

"I'm Tommy Vitale and my wife Maureen is having a baby," I blurted. "Is she all right? Where is she?"

"You're wife's fine," the nurse said. "She's in 801."

"And how's the baby? It's a boy, right?"

"Don't you know?" The nurse flashed me one of those looks you'd get from a teacher when you failed an exam. "The baby died."

I don't remember hitting that nurse, but they said I landed a shot across her face and then went nuts. The next thing I remember is waking up with a doctor standing over me.

His name was supposed to be Anthony, named for St. Anthony, whose day it was when we found out Maureen was having a baby. We were going to name him after St. Anthony and he came out dead. You get a kick in the stomach like that when you're 18 and you've got a lifetime big beef with God—or at least you think you do.

Maureen took it badly of course, but I think I took it harder because I'd already lost my brother in Vietnam and my grandmother. I wasn't afraid of dying, but I was deathly afraid of death and all that came with it. I'll always remember when the Army guy came to the door and told us Joe had been killed. Everyone started screaming and crying. And the funeral was worse; more crying and moaning. The idea of all that happens when someone dies was worse than death itself. Even when my grandmother died at the ripe old age of 84, the family reacted with a long mourning period.

I was already a veteran of death and people who taste death at a young age can't get the taste out of their mouths. It's like the vomit you can taste even before it comes up. It's like when you get nauseous and your stomach spins and you feel like throwing up. It's a taste you know you're gonna have again at some point in your life, so when things go good you can almost feel a bad thing coming. When things go bad you can see trouble behind you, snowballing and mounting up. People who have that taste in their mouths and don't find a way to get rid of it are allergic to success.

Later in my late teens, when I was getting into mob

stuff, I knew at some point I'd face being killed or be asked to kill someone. But I never remember being afraid, even in the most dangerous moments when I faced gang fights or the business end of a gun. The idea of being killed was never a problem for me. I just hated the idea of everyone crying and screaming at my funeral. I hated the loss I saw in people's faces when someone died. It was the most painful thing I could imagine.

That's what I felt like lying in that hospital emergency room with my sister, my mother, and the doctor looking down at me. It felt like when my Grandma Regina died. I was 8 years old and it shook me to the core that such a strong woman, the head of the family, could die. She was so strong. Everyone in the family, in the building, on the block, came to her with their problems. She was a rock. The whole family depended on her. She was always there.

When I came home from school, Grandma was there to give me something to eat—leftover meatballs from Sunday dinner in a big wedge. When I came home at night she was there to give me a hug, especially after I got a beatin' for something. When I went to bed Grandma would tuck me in, and when I woke up in the morning, no matter how early, she was already sitting in her chair sewing or doing something with her hands. I don't think the woman ever actually went to bed. She sat up in a chair all night as far as I knew.

When baby Anthony died, my Grandma, my brother Joe, and every other person I'd ever known who died seemed to be in front of me again. I saw their faces, heard their voices, and the frightening memories of loss haunted me again. I'd learned that death was the only thing I couldn't fight. Once a person was gone you couldn't reach them. I remember lying in bed as a kid, when things would go wrong or I felt lonely, and "talking" to my Grandma and my brother Joe in Heaven, but I never got an answer. I could feel them close by, but without the touch of Grandma's soft hands on my face or my brother Joe's strong hand holding mine as we crossed the busy streets of the Bronx, I felt alone.

The priests always said those who died lived on in those who remained, but I felt abandoned every time someone I loved died. Death had always stolen the people around me, and now, with the death of my newborn son, death had taken a part of me. It took my own flesh and blood and I could feel it creeping closer to me. Another piece of my heart was gone and I never even got to know him.

Something about Anthony's death made me feel guilty, sad, and angry all at the same time.

Maybe that's why I slugged the nurse.

Understanding death makes it easy to accept almost anything, because you know nothing is going to last forever. Babies die—thousands are aborted each year without even having a chance to grow inside their mothers. People get clipped for no reason; good guys, bad guys, churchgoing women, and whores. Innocent kids get diseases and die before they even start school, while fucking assholes like Stalin kill millions of people and get to live until they're in their 70s.

They say only the good die young, and it seems so true when you hear about all the babies, kids in war zones, and the innocent victims of rapists and serial killers. So, when people described mobsters as cold-hearted killers, I used to think, what's the difference? The guy was a bad guy, a loser, a rat, who didn't do the right thing. At least we don't kill innocent people. Dying is gonna happen to all of us, some sooner, some later, so what's the difference?

I was 17 years old the first time I saw someone whacked. Some buddies and I were out late in the Bronx on a Friday night, hanging at an after hours club on White Plains Road under the El train. We never had a problem being carded because we knew almost every bouncer and club attendant in the city. We'd spent a couple of hours drinking and trying to hit on girls and were headed out to look for an all-night diner.

As we left the Blue Light Club on the corner of 234th Street and White Plains Road, two guys in dark suits jumped out of a car and fast-walked to the sidewalk, where another guy was getting into his car from the passenger side. Before the victim could turn around, the two guys opened up with handguns, putting four or five shots into the guy's back and head. When he hit the ground, the two hit men shot him twice more. Then they just walked away, stepped into the back doors on both sides of a Jeep Cherokee, and then sped away toward 233rd Street.

I knew this had to be a mob hit because there was no confrontation, no talking, and no yelling. Just a business-like ballet of goons and guns, a victim who never knew what hit him, and stunned pedestrians who stopped in their tracks, watched the shooting, and then quickly continued walking. Sirens started screaming a few seconds later and we all took off so we wouldn't have to answer questions.

The next day we heard from some guys in the neighborhood that the hit was on a bagman who'd been pocketing play sheets and stealing cash from a bookie over a period of time and finally got caught. I was close enough to the life by then to understand the mob's code of justice. You don't cheat guys on top and you don't rat—even f you have to do time for a guy above you. And when you commit an infraction against a made guy or cause a beef that will hurt business, you can expect to get whacked. By that time in my life death didn't bother me, and the thought of killing someone was more like what I'd feel if I had to go to war. It was part of the job.

Mob guys understand the philosophy that showing power through violence and killing is sometimes the only way to solve a problem. Organized crime, like any big government or business, has always used the "sit-down" or diplomacy to deal with the distribution of power, major business deals, and problems between factions. But when a problem can't be solved by discussion and compromise, the mob uses capital punishment just like any government. People say we're taking the law into our own hands, killing innocent people to perpetuate criminal activity. But within the mob, we understood the death penalty was an accepted punishment for certain crimes.

The thought of killing someone was never a problem for me. Maybe I was cold-hearted, but knowing I might have to kill someone during a business deal was part of my job. When were we out in the street during the "garbage wars" or when we had to rough up a guy who owed money or needed to be taught a lesson, I never hesitated. You never knew when you'd go up against another crew, and shooting some guy wasn't personal. I even got a rush sometimes when we had to smack a guy around because he'd crossed the line somewhere.

One time we had to take care of an old guy who owed money and wouldn't pay. The guy was an elevator operator in a midtown dress factory, into us for about ten thousand dollars in gambling debts. Me and two other guys went to see him and we were set to scare the shit out of him, bang him around, and leave him praying for his life. When we got into the elevator, I could see he was scared. His green uniform started to get tighter, especially around the neck. Sweat popped out on his face and his eyes got all watery, like a kid who was going to start crying.

And then we heard something that not only broke the tension, but broke wind. The old guy farted—loud. He was terrified and about to shit his pants, but before that could happen, he let go with a warning. Me and the other two guys couldn't keep a straight face and we broke out laughing. Here's a man we were about to hang by his feet in the elevator shaft, beat the shit out of, and maybe even kill, and he was farting in the elevator.

We fell apart like grade school kids in church, doubled over with laughter.

The old guy didn't laugh. He just held his breath and tried to squeeze his ass cheeks, which made his face turn red.

This may sound morbid, but one of my favorite places to visit is the Gate of Heaven Cemetery in Valhalla, about thirty minutes from the Bronx. While some people like a stroll in the park or an afternoon beside a lake feeding ducks, I like the solitude and peace of a cemetery. For a guy who hates funerals, wakes and even the idea of someone laid out dead, you'd think cemeteries would be a problem. But no. There's nobody, no crying family members around a coffin, no black dresses. There's just grass, trees, and thousands of monuments marking the lives of people. It's walking through a library full of short biographies. You can move from one grave sight to another and try to figure out what kind of life each person had. Some graves were sad, like the ones that said, "Maria Fiorini, born November 12, 1945, Died, November 13, 1945". Those made me wonder how the parents felt about having a baby and losing it the same day. Or the ones that read: "Beloved Son, Born 1950, died for his country 1968." That was on my brother's grave, killed in Vietnam, like 500,000 other young guys, still a teenager. Those graves gave me the chills. I could almost feel like it could be me. You could fee the loss because it was a young person. My favorite graves were the ones that read, "Guiseppe Santoro and beloved wife Rosa Santoro, Guiseppe Born 1895, Died 1985, Rosa, Born 1898, Died 1986." Two people who lived until they were like 90 years old, probably married for 70 years, buried together for the next million years. It felt good to see that kind of devotion, even after death,

Located near the front entrance of Gate of Heaven is the grave of Babe Ruth, the world's greatest baseball player. Behind Ruth's grave and to the left, is the grave of former Yankee manager Billy Martin. I admired these were two guys. I knew Ruth was the best player of all time, and despite his personal problems, he was a great performer and a man who loved people—especially kids. He was bigger than life; a gifted man born in the right place at the right time to help make the game of baseball what it is today. Martin was street tough, hard-assed, and one of the best on-field managers I ever saw. He overcame his own demons, at least at times, to become a winner everywhere he managed.

I liked to visit their graves because it always touched me how people who weren't even alive when the Babe was playing would leave baseballs, caps, coins and other memorabilia at the gravesite to honor the man. Even in death, Babe inspired people. He was big guy with a big heart and big troubles, who only wanted to make people happy watching him play baseball. He died of cancer at the age of 53. Martin's grave was less popular, but people did leave mementos on his grave and headstone. People understood Billy's struggles and could relate to him. I guess visiting Billy helped remind me that I still had time to get my shit together before I died. Billy was killed in a car accident at the age of 61 on Christmas Day—way too young.

But death is like that. It doesn't ask when or how you want to go. It just comes to take you, ready or not. I've seen them come and go. Some, like the guys we knew in the mob who got whacked, weren't ready. Their last hours were filled with corruption, cheating, lying, stealing and even killing. I often wondered if they even tried to pray before they drew their last breath.

And others like my grandmother, who always took time to help others, seemed more prepared for death. Even in the casket, Grandma looked peaceful. I always thought when it came my time to die I wanted to be prepared. The big question was -- how did a person get ready?

CHAPTER 6

The Lord redeems the souls of his servants, and none of them that trust in him shall be desolate. Psalms 34:22

Nothing good ever happened to me. At least nothing good that lasted.

The three years between the death of my son, my first love and my baseball career are a blur of alcohol, Nembutal and reckless behavior that might be perceived by some – including my mother, my friends and me, after I detoxed – as suicidal. There were a couple of incidents where suicide had the goal, but I was so slammed with vodka and pills that I don't remember consciously wanting to kill myself. It was more like, "Who cares if it's crazy to drive 90 miles per hour down the Cross County Parkway at 3 a.m. with every county cop laying in wait?" Or "So what if I drive through Yonkers down one-way streets knocking over garbage cans and bouncing off cars?"

According to my cousins, close friends, mob associates and others who crossed my path from 1977-1980, I went from crazy kid to maniac after my son died and my wife decided our marriage wasn't going to work.

Each new girlfriend I had reminded me of the pain of loss and I was so insecure with my relationships, I began to dive into drugs and booze to dull the pain. I tried to be tough and I wanted to be the life of the party – always cracking jokes and wanting to party. But once the substances hit my system, I turned into – well Wolfman. You know, the guy who was bitten by a wolf and knew that when the full moon came out he would have no choice in turning into a beast. The Wolfman didn't want to become a killer, but when that "thing' hit, he was helpless. Vodka and pills were the full moon for me. They brought out a horrible creature that I didn't want to be. A creature that followed me from woman to woman, friend to friend and hung-over morning to hung-over morning.

I'd like to be able to recall all the terrible events that defined my "three years in hell" from 19 to 22, but I have to rely on the memories of my friends an family who dragged me out of bars, brawls and burning cars – yes burning cars, plural, because I just can't remember most of it.

My friend Dominick Sciano, whose family was also involved in mob activity, in fact his father and grandfather were made guys, remembers the night I was so deep into my Wolfman routine that I made a vain attempt to end my life. Dominick said we were partying at my girlfriend Laura's apartment and I proceeded to down a quart of vodka accented by some pills.

"You were shit-faced as usual but worse," Dominick said. "We were all used to taking turns watching you because you would get violent and lash out when you were drunk, not at us, but sometimes at your girlfriend or people you might meet in a club or a bar. This time you disappeared into the bathroom and we were all outside the door wondering what you were doing. Four or five of us, big guys and a couple of girls with our ears to the door listening to you piss. After a few minutes we heard a loud crash and when you didn't answer we broke the door down and found you on the floor bleeding from a crack on your head. Your belt was around your neck attached to the shower rod which was lying across your chest."

According to Dom and the other people who came through the bathroom door, I had tried to kill myself by hanging off the shower curtain rod, which couldn't hold the weight of two towels much less a guy weighing 190 pounds. Despite the stupid attempt at hanging, I did almost kill myself by cracking my head on the bathroom floor. Lots of blood, the girl friend screaming, guys smacking me and throwing cold water on me and well, I just know what they told me, it was a fucking mess.

There were other such events, not overt suicide attempts but episodes that could be interpreted as "subconscious attempts at suicide" by many mental health experts. Like the time I drove my big yellow Cadillac through a closed gate at the local VFW hall, scaring my girlfriend and making her father want to kill me with his bare hands. After I left the hall gates I gained speed, crashed into two parked cars and settled under the bumper of a big, black Lincoln. Through the haze or beer and pills I thought I was alright once the car settled. But 30 seconds later, after I had laid my head on the steering wheel to take a breath, the car I was under exploded in flames. I just got out and walked away like I had parked the car at a meter. I wasn't scared, shocked or sorry that I had wrecked a whole street. I was the Wolfman and I had no choice. I just went with the full moon. I guess just like the Wolfman who wanted someone to help him escape his monthly torture. I thought, "Well that didn't kill me, what's next?"

Benders, binges, brawls and bad relationships were the result of my not being able to deal with my losses – child, wife, baseball career – but in fact, my life hit a wall and instead of trying to overcome my injured mind and heart be replacing the losses with new loves, I bathed them in booze, hoping I could kill the pain – or myself.

A third car crash and the resulting fire helped me see that I was headed for a premature death. I was driving erratically -- at least that's what the witnesses said – across the Fleetwood Bridge across the Bronx River Parkway near my apartment one summer night, full of rum and coke, when I dozed off and rammed the guardrail that stood between the roadway and the parkway below. The last thing I remember was the car slowing down and scraping the side of the rail. But according to the neighbors who pulled me from the car, I bounced off the rail three times before knocking it down and sending my front bumper over the edge of the bridge. The drop was at least 50 feet, but the car stayed perched with the wheels hanging over the rail. I didn't know at the time because I passed out, but somehow the car's gas tank caught a spark and ignited. The car was in flames, like DeNiro's Cadillac in the movie *Casino,* and some people who were in the area had to pull me out and drag me back to my apartment two blocks away. When the phone rang the next day at about noon, I heard a familiar frightened and angry voice that I'd come to know over the last couple of years of my frantic life. It was my poor mother, who lived in an apartment above mine in our six-story building and had just heard about my near-death accident at 2 a.m.

"Are you happy that you almost killed yourself again," She screamed.

As I was trying to focus in on her voice I remembered a dream I had during the night. A dream about a car accident and a fire. Between her voice and my foggy hangover I noticed the faint smell of rubber and smoke in the room and on my clothes which I hadn't removed before passing out in bed -- like a tire burning. I remember thinking, "Hey that was some dream, so real, I can even smell the smoke."

My mother's tirade snapped me into reality.

"Are you happy you crazy idiot," she screamed. "Are you happy you almost killed yourself again? People have to drag you home at al hours drunk and almost dead. Why don't you just shoot me and get it over with. I'm gonna kill you myself someday if you don't get some help!"

I realized at that point that the car crash and fire dream was not a dream at all. The smell of smoke on my clothes, the odor of near death, was real and my mother was one step closer to a heart attack or a nervous breakdown. It wasn't the turning point for me but it made me feel terrible that I was giving my mother such grief. I gave in and opted for rehab, and a few months later, after coming out of a 30-day detox program and then relapsing a few times, I stood in front of the mirror one morning and saw the man that my girlfriend, my friends and my family had been seeing for years – a worn out, 160-pound, pale, wretched loser. Where was the tanned, funny, handsome baseball star that had left for Florida to become a Yankee just three years before? Where was the strapping Italian with hopes and dreams about having a nice family, living in a nice house in the suburbs and someday becoming a coach after my playing days? Where was Tommy Vitale?

I knew right then I was going to try to dig myself out of the hole I had dug to bury myself in. I knew I wanted to live. I wasn't sure what I was going to be or how I would change my life, but I knew I didn't want to be that drugged drunk I saw in that mirror. I stopped drinking and using drugs, except the prescribed valium to help me cope with anxiety and other issues and over the next decade I settled into the organized crime business with my uncle and cousin, married and had a child over the next 12 years. But crime replaced the drinking and despite being sober I could never escape the feeling that I was missing something in my life.

I still felt that nothing good ever happened to me. At least nothing good that lasted.

So, when my kids won 10 straight games to start the 1993 baseball season, I wasn't surprised we were winning. But I did feel a little stunned at the stretch of success I was having and the all-around good feeling that came into my messed up life that spring, when I coached my first Redemption High School baseball team.

Although Redemption High was located in Westchester County, the school played in the Catholic High Schools Association league along with several New York City schools and a couple of other suburban schools. Recent history hadn't been good to the Emeralds' sports programs. Despite being in a parish that included kids from several strong sports feeder programs (local clubs), the city's public schools got all the top athletes—especially inner-city and low income kids who couldn't afford a parochial school education. Parents who could afford the tuition sent their budding athletes to bigger and more established schools that offered a chance to develop athletic skills as well as academic success.

And those schools won games. The Emeralds lost—and we lost often. In fact, the school hadn't had a boys championship team in any sport since the 1970s, when they won baseball and track championships. Most of the kids at Redemption were there because their parents wanted them to get some discipline in a school that wasn't understaffed, under-funded, and out of control like most of the city schools.

After desegregation and busing came along, the Yonkers public schools never recovered their academic or athletic successes. Kids were bused all over to the city's four high schools, making it tough to play sports after school. Many low income kids needed after-school jobs to help support their families, so they worked instead of playing ball.

Redemption kids—a mix of all the ethnic groups in and around Yonkers and the Bronx—came from working class families who wanted to be sure their kids didn't fall through the cracks in a large public school with overcrowded classes and low funding. Catholic schools had the reputation of keeping kids in line; and with parents paying $2,500 or more a year for school, the kids usually behaved.

My friend Anthony Menci, a guy I played semi-pro ball with, took over the Redemption varsity baseball team in 1992 and I went with him as an assistant coach, because he knew I had the experience to teach hitting and pitching skills. The team was a rag-tag bunch of Irish, Polish, Italian, Puerto Rican, and black kids who were like a perpetual expansion team. We were the New York Mets of 1962, the "Bad News Bears," and the "Gang that Couldn't Shoot Straight" all rolled into one. But we also had talent.

Hidden under the undisciplined, disruptive, out-of-shape, mixed-up group of baseball wanna-bes, was the nucleus of a championship team no one could have predicted. Most of these kids had played Little League, Babe Ruth, or some PAL baseball and they knew the game. They were also pretty tough and didn't mind our "adult" brand of coaching. We treated them like grown-ups and they liked it.

I'm not much for praying, but when Anthony and I took over this crew, I casually petitioned God, who I hadn't spoken to since my leg exploded in the Yankee's Rookie League back in 1976, for help.

"God dammit," I said when I saw the first practice. "You guys are gonna need a miracle if we wanna beat anybody. What are you guys—a bunch of ladies? You throw like ladies and you run like ladies. We're gonna have to do better than this, God dammit."

Prayer, even when you don't know you're praying, sometimes works. I loved baseball and I knew I'd love coaching, because I'd done it before in youth baseball leagues. But I didn't know if I could deal with this motley group of kids, who weren't exactly blue chip prospects and not the easiest bunch of teenagers to handle. But it worked from day one. I fell in love with the whole idea of being a coach, even though I was only an assistant at first.

Something struck me during the first few days of coaching the Redemption baseball team. The more I looked at them, the more they reminded me of me. Me without the talent, that is. They were rough kids with good hearts. They'd never been winners at the high school level and some were failing academically. They came from working class families and had an urban edge to them. They were slightly cynical and completely arrogant.

Just like me.

Here I was at 35, a former New York Yankees minor league prospect with no athletic prospects because of my blown out leg. I was a high school dropout with no real formal education of any kind, divorced after two failed marriages, and employed by a questionable organization with ties to such things as garbage removal and labor unions. But I was coaching a Catholic school baseball team. Afternoons in the sun, baseballs popping into mitts and pinging off aluminum bats, and the smell of grass that's been cut to ready the field for a game.

I was in heaven.

Getting the opportunity to coach a Catholic High Schools League team wasn't as difficult a job hunt as one might think. Because parochial schools are not restricted by rules that govern public schools in New York State, finding a job can be as easy as replying to a newspaper ad.

WANTED: Coach for struggling sports team at small parochial school. Low pay, long hours, difficult kids. Some knowledge of the fundamentals of sports a must, and CPR and other basic first aid qualifications required.

First come, first hired.

And May God Bless You.

In today's world, I probably wouldn't have applied for the job even with those bare requirements. No one did background checks in those days, nor did they ask to see my resume—a good thing, because my "resume" included a couple of drug arrests and some assault stuff, and I knew the FBI had something on me, even if it was vague. But Anthony's nephew was on the team and when the team lost its coach, the kid asked the athletic director if his Uncle Anthony and I could take over for the fall and spring seasons to see if we could get the team to play. Most of the parents knew Anthony or me from recreation baseball leagues and from the neighborhood, so they vouched for us. Redemption needed a coach—and quick. We were there with nothing more important to do. We were cheap and we were willing. So without much fanfare or formality, we were hired.

A mob-connected guy coaching. What harm could it do? It would only be for a season, and I had the afternoons free. No one would bother about the assistant coach of a losing high school team. I was working a no-show carpenter's job in the Javits Center, where I had to drop in from 7 a.m. to 1 p.m. just to keep up appearances. The mob ran the Javits Center, everything from exhibits to plumbing; we had tied up with unions. My job was to keep the regular union guys in line and once in a while help cart off some stock that was on exhibit—televisions, small appliances, videos and stuff like that. At that time, back in the early 1990s, we were getting a piece of almost every inventory on cargo ships coming into Brooklyn. We'd get VCRs, watches, radios, tires, anything you could think of. All I had to do was help sell the stuff to area stores at a discount and pick up union "donations" on the docks. I also did a little loan sharking, lending money to guys in the unions who were short of cash. I could make up to $500 a week in interest on my loans.

So, doing a little afternoon coaching fit right into my daily routine. In fact, it helped keep me out of the trouble because it was a good front. Who would be suspicious of a guy who coached high school baseball?

They were too busy investigating garbage guys and gamblers and contractors to worry about me from 3 to 7 p.m. every day. As for business, mine was all done in the shadows after hours. All I missed by coaching was an afternoon nap or a manicure or an afternoon Mets game.

So, in that spring of 1992, Anthony took the head baseball coach's job at Redemption and I tagged along as his assistant and batting coach. We did a pretty good job getting the kids involved and developing players that first fall season, but in less than a year, Anthony took a new job, had a kid himself, and didn't have time to coach, so he quit—leaving me holding the equipment bag. I was suddenly the head coach, the "capo di baseball" at Redemption High.

Putting on that Emeralds' uniform and being with the kids made me feel like a ballplayer again. I was back in a place where I felt comfortable. I was a finally the coach of a legitimate team; the only legitimate thing in my life accept for my family. We didn't win anything in 1992, but that would change in 1993.

Being a coach in good standing with the baseball team had its benefits. When the varsity basketball coach Paul Moran quit the next year just before the season started, I was again the only guy available and I was already proven to be a good influence on the kids. The varsity basketball team was an accumulation of wackos and street players. Moran was a great Xs and Os guy, but not the toughest disciplinarian, so he lost control of the team and couldn't get them to adhere to his rules. The players were dictating to Moran who should play and when, like patients in a mental ward, they were running the asylum. That is until they met me. I was crazier and tougher than any of these kids and they knew it immediately. The ones who feared me stayed; the ones who didn't fear or obey my rules were cut. Within less than two years at Redemption I was coaching both the baseball and basketball teams and becoming a fixture at the school. My mob stuff was like taking candy from a baby, but the cheating, lying and stealing could wear a guy out. There was a price to be paid for being a gangster. Coaching kids was another thing altogether.

Coaching came easy to me.

It was a fuckin'' shame how easy it came. It was like I was born on a baseball field and coaching was like farming to a farmer who was born on the land.

I know I was good, because I won championships at Redemption. None of the coaches, baseball or basketball, who followed me there have been able to match that.

My first championship was in the spring of 1993 and I'll never forget the place, the time, or the weather. I remember every inning like there's a scorebook in my mind, with hits, runs, and strikeouts; each symbol written with by eternal pencil. This is evidence that I did contribute something to the world besides a life filled with crime and confusion.

We played Cardinal Spellman for the championship on June 12 at Fordham University Field on a windy, clear day that reminded me of those days when I was a kid and would run home from school to catch a Mets day game just toward the end of the school year. A right-hander named Jimmy Reilly was pitching for us and he had a nice breaking ball and a good fastball that day.

Spellman scored one run in the sixth inning when our defense let up and we made two errors. Otherwise, it was Reilly's day. He struck out 10 and walked one and we won 5-1.

"Hey coach, here's the game ball, who gets it?" Reilly said after our second baseman grabbed a grounder in the hole going toward the first-base line and threw out Spellman's last batter. "I think you should take it, for getting us here and winning your first title."

"No, Reilly, you earned it," I said, acting like it didn't mean much to me. "You take it."

After we'd packed up our gear and spent some time

80

on that Fordham Field soaking in the victory and talking trash to each other, most of the kids left with their parents. The few of us who remained grabbed the equipment bags and started for the bus. When I bent down to pick up my bag, I saw the game ball, sitting on top of my cap, signed by all of the players. It said, "Thanks Coach V. You got us where we wanted to go."

That Spellman victory, on June 12, 1993, that perfect, spring afternoon in the sun, was supposed to be my last game as a coach, because I had a big summer coming up with a new job at the Javits Center. I'd be working on a union crew and didn't think I'd be back at Redemption for fall baseball. Some of my Yonkers mob connections saw me that night at The Embers, a bar on Bronx River Road, and bought me drinks to toast me winning the championship.

"Hey, Vitale, what are you, Billy Martin now?" one guys said and a few of them raised their beers to salute me. "Maybe you can repeat next year. Maybe you can make it a career."

Everyone laughed.

I laughed.

But when I got home that morning, I put the signed baseball on top of my nightstand and spent two long summer months looking at it every morning and night. That perfect summer afternoon, June 12 at Fordham University Field, stayed with me all summer, and that baseball—the one I tried to give Reilly after the game, the ball I didn't want to keep, stayed with me too. It was like an invitation to the next season, an invitation to another chance to win, an invitation to teach and coach again.

My summer was planned and the work would be a big step in my climb up the dangerous and tempting mob ladder.

But that ball was more than a scuffed up baseball with a dozen names scratched in black and blue Bic pen ink. It was an invitation to a new life.

Emeralds take Class C title

BRONX -- Jimmy Reilly's uniform top was soaked with perspiration, but each drop of sweat was evidence of his pitching effort—a two-hit, 10-strikeout performance that carried Redemption High School of Yonkers to a 5-1 victory over Cardinal Spellman in a Catholic School Association Class C championship game played at Fordham University in the Bronx. The sophomore right-hander tossed a complete game in 85-degree, nearly-summer heat at Fordham University Field to lead the upstart Emeralds, who finished their season with a 19-3 record, to their first baseball title in a decade.

"I wanted to show everyone that we weren't some loser school," Reilly said. "We have a lot of heart and we proved that we could play with the top teams."

Redemption's first-year coach Tom Vitale was the first person to the mound to congratulate Reilly. "Jimmy really matured this year and he is just going to get better," said Vitale, who took over the team earlier this spring when coach Anthony Menci resigned. "I'm just happy to be able to get a title for Redemption. The kids played hard and let me coach them. They deserve all the credit."

CHAPTER 7

As cold waters to a thirsty soul, so is good news from a far country. Proverbs 25:25

For a reporter, covering a Redemption High boys' basketball game was an act of charity—maybe even an act of contrition; a punishment for having the easy job of sports writer.

I'd met a few newspaper people in my day, mostly guys who were hanging around police stations and city hall looking for police blotter stories or government stuff. I was even asked to comment on a strike once when our union pulled workers off the job at some Manhattan parking garages. I always thought journalists were okay, just doing their job, like cops. Some were honest and some weren't. The television news seemed slanted to the liberal left to me, and they always loved those mob-related stories.

Most of the old-time mob guys dealt with the press by shrugging off questions and pleading the Fifth Amendment. From Lucky Luciano to Carlo Gambino, all they got was a little smile and, "Fellas, I've got nothing to say. I'm just a businessman trying to earn a living. I was falsely accused because I'm Italian and I associate with other Italians."

After Joe Valachi turned rat in the 1950s and opened up the mob books for the Senate crime committee, the press had more access to our lives. Joe Colombo further opened the crack in the dam in the 70s when he started the Italian American Unity League to draw attention to contributions Italians had made to American life. But Colombo was an idiot, because he opened it too much. Gangsters started to become neighborhood heroes, with the press making them into Robin Hood types. And then moviemakers, who'd always depicted us as cutthroat killers and antisocial maniacs, started showing the other side of gangster life, with "The Godfather" being the prime example of glorified gangsterism.

When John Gotti became a boss, he really loved the press, the limelight, the attention of the community—and it got him in trouble. Most of our people tried to avoid the press because it would only bring attention to a business we wanted to keep quiet. Once the press got access to wise guys, we lost some of our power. People didn't have the same fear; and without that fear, the organization grew weak from inside. Later, in the 1980s and 1990s, when Rudy Guiliani went on his crusade to crush the mob, people weren't afraid to go to court to testify and even our own guys started to feel comfortable turning state's evidence.

I just tried to avoid reporters—at work anyway.

Lorusso had been covering the high school sports beat for about four years when we met. To be honest, I think he'd avoided attending a single Redemption High boys' basketball game because he didn't want to embarrass the Emeralds fans, parents and players by writing more than a couple of inches of copy on our frequent losses.

At Redemption, the girls' team was sort of a mini-dynasty, at least in the county. The Lady Emeralds annually won 20 games and made a decent playoff showing, before being bounced by one of the New York City parochial school teams. The girls were coached by a guy named Matty Bell, who ran the neighborhood funeral parlor and had a lock on most of the girl jocks in the area, who were recruited to play for the Emeralds. These girls weren't top players, but Bell taught them some basics and a nasty, swarming defense—enough to compliment one or two good offensive stars and win consistently.

Watching Bell coach was a study in discipline and restraint. He handled any and all conflicts with a controlled enthusiasm reflected by his players. They were cool and had a killer instinct. Once they were up by a couple of points they made sure they put you away. Bell was the picture of class after every game, whether his team won or lost. He answered each question calmly and honestly, thanking the reporter for covering the game. But his post-game approach to the losing coach exposed his vocation and was hysterically funny.

"Sorry about your loss," Bell would say with a firm and consoling handshake. "I can understand how you feel and our thoughts are with you and your team. Remember, this is just a temporary setback. Good luck in your next game and we'll see you soon."

Bell hardly ever lost, so his post game condolences were immaculate.

But the rest of the school's varsity sports programs were mediocre at best—the result of the small student body and lack of good coaching. Coaches aren't paid very well at small, neighborhood Catholic schools. The tuition wasn't high, which meant the salaries weren't either. And Redemption wasn't one of those small powerhouse basketball schools, like Rice in Harlem or St. Raymond's in the Bronx, nationally-recognized magnets for top players where sneakers companies donated shoes and coaches made a few more dollars because their teams fed the college game.

Covering local sports had to be a passion or no one

85

in his right journalistic mind would do it. Once a sports reporter built his resume doing high school football and recreation softball leagues for a couple of years, he or she could tell whether they had a future in sports journalism or if it was time to take a job doing something else.

A local sports writer is forced to stand on the muddy sidelines in the pouring rain at football games, bake in the extreme heat of Saturday baseball doubleheaders, squeeze into the stands at high school gymnasiums for endless basketball games, and wander the pool deck in the fog at local swim meets; all in the hope of finding a few stories that someone beyond the parents of the kids he was writing about would read.

The writer deals with complaining parents and arrogant coaches, smart-ass players, and irate fans, all because he someday hopes to become a beat writer or columnist for a major newspaper where pro players, managers, coaches and PR people can make his life more miserable—but for more money. Love of sports is the inspiration for most sportswriters, but the reality of a business that pays little and demands long hours and crazy deadlines can take the joy out of the game for many aspiring Red Smiths and Mike Lupicas.

For Lorusso, local sports coverage was just the opposite.

Having begun his writing career covering New York Giants and New York Jets games for a Spanish-language daily, he'd already had his fill of spoiled pro athletes and pompous pro coaches, who either wouldn't or couldn't answer a question in the post-game locker room. Yes, there were some wonderful moments he told me about, like his first day covering a New York Yankees game, walking through the pre-game clubhouse, into the dugout and onto the field where he'd watched his childhood heroes play.

And going to his first New York Giants football game.

Like thousands of frustrated others, he couldn't get

tickets to see the eternally sold-out Giants, so his first-ever professional football game was witnessed from the Giants press box, sitting next to Mike Lupica, Steve Serby and other pro writers from the major New York daily newspapers. And there were athletes who made the interview process worthwhile: Don Mattingly was a gentleman who talked with Lorusso about his kids while Donny Baseball's two young kids ran through the Yankees locker room. With patience and intelligence, he answered every question Lorusso threw at him.

And there was Carl Banks of the Giants, who sat by his locker after a win or a loss to answer questions from print and TV reporters, sometimes repeating the same answers to the same stupid questions several times. And believe it or not, L.T., Lawrence Taylor, the Giants Hall of Fame linebacker, was willing to answer questions truthfully if he was caught in his locker. Taylor once asked Lorusso to distract quarterback Phil Simms while the Hall of Fame linebacker showed his practical joking side, hiding Simms' helmet in his locker in return for the answers to a few of Lorusso's questions.

Hey, Lorusso even had the opportunity to meet one of the most infamous and important names in American history because he had access to the Giants' locker room. Seeking an interview after the Giants beat the Washington Redskins in a late-season game in 1985, Lorusso came face-to-face with none other than Richard M. Nixon, the 36th President of the United States, a Washington Redskins fan and the guy who almost got Lorusso killed during the Vietnam War. Lorusso was so shocked to see the old fart that he reacted in a way that surprised himself and possibly the former President.

"Mr. President," Lorusso said. "Thanks for repealing the draft in 1972. I drew number 56 in the lottery and was going to report for induction until they reclassified me. Sorry, I voted for Humphrey and McGovern, but it's good to see you, and again, thanks for saving my ass. How'd you like the game?"

Nixon didn't flinch. He leaned toward Lorusso's tape recorder and quickly and expertly explained why the Giants' defense had stopped his beloved Redskins. He then smiled and said. "See, I'm not such a bad guy. A little misunderstood, but not a bad guy at all."

So much for the big time. I loved hearing Lorusso's stories about pro players. He always had a big smile on his face when he talked about the games. He loved sports like I did, local high school sports in particular. That excitement about his work grew out of his love for playing the games as a kid and an adult. He said in one column, "Watching the games at the high school level is as pure an experience for a sports lover as one could find. That is until money and recruiters and sneaker companies invaded the high school campuses in the early 1980s. Parents were there to support their children, teachers came to monitor the crowd, coaches were coaching mostly out of love for the sport, and the fans wanted to see a game played just for the fun and competition."

But Redemption High was another story.

Lorusso described his coverage of me as "as good a subject as I ever came across in any high school gym."

Here's part of a favorite passage Lorusso wrote about me after a year covering our teams:

"Vitale looks like a cross between Los Angeles Lakers and New York Knicks coach Pat Riley and a character out of "Goodfellas." His jet black hair is moussed back and his matching thick black mustache is a throwback to the style of Sicilian immigrants from the early 1900s, faces I saw in pictures my grandparents had in their family album. His clothes are sharp, always pressed, always the latest style, and he has a walk, a stroll if you will, that tells you he isn't a teacher.

"When Vitale stood beside the other Catholic school coaches—many of them in sweat suits or button down shirts, ties and preppy jackets—he looked like he'd just stepped out of an Esquire magazine. He just didn't look

the type to be coaching at a small parochial school.

"The first time I saw the coach I knew he'd be an interesting story; a stylish, sartorially resplendent 35-year-old with city mannerisms leading a band of scruffy city kids dressed in baggy pants and sneakers. An odd match, like maybe Frank Sinatra and Tupac Shakur, veal parmigiana and Nathan's hot dogs; a guy with a 24 karat gold money clip and his kids with empty pockets.

"Yet somehow, the coach and the kids seemed very much alike; down deep under the slick hair and suit, this guy was a former scruffy kid with a hunger to be needed and a bigger hunger to win."

Lorusso was closer to the truth than he knew.

Some of my friends read those first articles in the local paper and I started to get some razzing. Tenants in my building, some of whom I'd never spoken a word to, began to smile and giving me a thumbs up when I passed. The guys in the gas station on the corner near my apartment would give me the daily paper for free when the game reports were in that day.

"Great job, Coach," they'd say. "My son wants to come and play for you at Redemption someday. Good win last night."

After avoiding the spotlight or any attention about what I did for so many years, having parents and grandparents, shop owners in the neighborhood, and people on the street know me was uncomfortable at first. But I quickly started to like it.

The only other times my name had appeared in print were when I signed with New York Yankees, and several times as a teenager when my name made the police blotter—the section of the newspaper that detailed arrests. The beginning of my Yankee career was chronicled by a short item in the Daily News with a small headline that read: "Bronx Ravens' Vitale inks minor league deal. "The story read: "Tom Vitale, an outfielder with the Bronx Ravens of the Metro League, signed a contract yesterday and was assigned to the New York

Yankees farm system Instructional League. Vitale, who attended school in Yonkers where he currently resides, received a $2,500 bonus."

My arrests ranged in importance from driving without a license to assault and battery, a charge that often followed one of my frequent bar brawls. My most felonious arrest was a drug possession charge when I was 22, but I never served time for it.

This guy Lorusso covered about 10 schools and most of the Yonkers high school baseball and basketball teams weren't very strong during the 1990s, so he made me into a mini-celebrity with his stories. He even got me on the local sports show he did with a guy named Nat Simpson on cable television. There I was, on television, answering questions about my teams. We talked about my coaching methods, the games, and other sports issues like steroid use and recruiting. Whenever I was being interviewed, I had a terrible fear the next question would be: "So, how do you have the time to coach two teams at Redemption with all your mob responsibilities, Coach?"

I fantasized that Lorusso might one day say, "You must be very well organized, organized, organized...."

Yeah, I was organized all right. My teams were organized and so was my crime.

But, Lorusso never came near it.

He was so into the games and the kids he never really asked much more than, "So, you do construction? That must be lucrative for you. My father was in construction. Do you know him? What do you do, build homes, do renovations? How many people do you have working for you?"

I stuck to my story.

I was a successful construction contractor with time on my hands who coached for love of the game. And the story worked. The press saw me as a successful coach with an interesting personality, my friends saw me as a odd guy with too much time on his hands and my

90

"family," well, they just thought I was nuts.

Lorusso was a preppy/athletic kind of guy, about 6-2, slim, but gaining middle-age weight in his gut, with eyeglasses and a full beard. You could see he was once a decent ballplayer and he told me he'd played Division III basketball at a little place called Valley Forge College back in the mid 1970s. When we met he was still playing basketball at 38 in adult recreation leagues, until he snapped his Achilles tendon. The guy had five kids, one adopted, and a daughter his wife Dianne had when they got married. He was a sort of a church guy, always trying to help somebody. Two of his kids were teenagers, so I guess that's why he got along with my players. He wrote stories on the games and the star players, but also found space to write about kids who rode the bench, the water boys, the scorekeepers—anything related to sports you wouldn't expect to make the newspapers.

Me and Lorusso had more than few conversations about sports, family, politics, and what he loved about his job. When he talked about why he loved newspaper work, he'd always come back to the fact that he regretted being involved in the family real estate business, where he spent 20 years renting apartments and selling houses. He wished he'd had begun his writing career right out of college instead of starting at the advanced age of 35.

"My father made you feel guilty if you weren't working with Lorusso & Sons, even from the time we were just 10 or 11 years old," he said. "He didn't like it that I wanted to go to college to become a minister or a writer and he wouldn't help me pay for college. When I ran out of tuition money, instead of going out on my own, I came back and worked for him again. Even after I got married and moved to the Bronx, got a job and had my own family, he always criticized me and found some carrot to bring me back."

Lorusso had worked in building management and real estate, drove limos, taught preschool for a church,

91

worked as a painter, and clerked at the post office before his wife handed him an ad for a part-time sports writer's job and encouraged him to try it. He hesitated at first, but then took the job and said it came so easy that he felt like he was born to write.

"I never thought I'd be able to do something I loved so much and actually get paid for it," he once told me when we were discussing how much I loved coaching. "It's like I had two hearts; one that went along with what my father and my family wanted me to do, and another that was hidden, trying to find an opportunity to come alive. I may not make as much money as when I sold real estate, but I love going to work every day and I feel like my shoes fit. I'm a writer. And you're a coach."

"You're a coach." It was the first time I heard those words said right out in the open. They sounded so natural and real. People in my world knew saw me as the up-and-coming wise guy who had his hands in every pie and was always looking for an easy score. But Lorusso, whose own talent had been smothered for years in the wrong "calling," could see something no one else, even me, had seen.

"You're a coach," he said. "You can make money in business or doing whatever you do, and I'm sure you're good at it. But what you do with these kids, the way you relate to them and get the best out of them, it's more than a job. It's a gift. It's a perfect fit. It's who you are."

It was as simple as that. I was a coach.

Just like with Lorusso and his unplanned writing career, I had somehow stumbled into the thing I was born to. Redemption—coaching—was where I was meant to be. It was my calling, my real heart. But now, what would I do with my other heart—the heart I'd devoted to a career of crime?

CHAPTER 8

Let the children come unto me and forbid them not;
for of such is the kingdom of heaven. Matthew 19:14.

I can still see their faces in my late-afternoon daydreams, just after I close my eyes, in that space between consciousness and dreaming. I clearly see the faces of my success.

Billy Nitkowski's intelligent eyes; Trey Walton's big, pearly white smile; Joey "Sweet Pea" Larkin's bumpy, shaved head; Sean Mannion's steely stare; P.J. Reagan's mussed red hair and sneaky grin; and Jason Mendicino's adolescent five o'clock shadow.

My kids.

They were part me and part someone else. They were like my long-lost children from dozens of relationships, different neighborhoods, different families, who'd grown up and moved away. Graduation stole some of my kids each year, but having them for the springs, autumns and winters during their coming-of-age teen years fit right into my search for someone who needed to learn the facts of life I'd worked so hard to discover on my own.

My own children, Anthony from my first marriage to

Maureen; Vanessa, from my second marriage to Eleanor; and Tommy from my brief marriage to Melissa, aren't with me now. Anthony died at birth and the other two went the way of so many kids of divorced parents, with their moms. I sometimes believe they would've been better off with me, but then again, maybe I couldn't have given them offered the stability a growing child needs. I was always like a big kid myself. Still am.

Coaching kids through three or four years of high school sports sort of makes them yours. It's like having shared custody—a ready-made family after school and on weekends. You spend quality time with the kids, and then they go home to dinner, homework, and their families while you go home to a dark apartment—with a big crazy cat and two yapping dogs that watch your every move, wait for you to feed them, walk them and change their litter, but never ever talk, and only listen when it's about them.

A coach can make or break a kid. They come in for tryouts—gangly, clumsy, and nervous; some uniquely gifted with athletic ability. Each has the hope of earning a spot on the team, a varsity letter, and a place in the school's jock world, where success brings the attention of the hottest girls in school, local newspapers, a quick shot on local cable television, or even the chance for a college scholarship.

My kids were nothing special. We had no 6-6 basketball players, monster home run hitters, or 95-mile per hour pitchers. My kids had zits, trouble with math, problems at home, horny daydreams, nightly wet dreams, and part-time jobs. Some of the kids were good students with college in their futures, and others couldn't wait to graduate from high school so they could go on to become cops, firemen, electricians and construction workers.

But my kids were all special to me.

Like a parent who sits on the sideline and believes his kid is the best one out there, even though he's on the bench, my kids were always the best in my eyes. At least that was my fantasy and my goal—to make them the best. When they were out on the field or the court playing some talented team with all-star players, I did everything I could to even the playing field by working the game.

My baseball teams always had one or two good pitchers, which are all a high school team really needs— and a few kids who could catch it, throw it, and even hit the ball once in a while. Hours of batting practice and hints on how to work a pitcher for a walk or steal a base or drop a bunt made my .200 hitters into .280 hitters and my .300 hitters into young Ted Williams and Mickey Mantles.

We had one kid named Bobby Podalak, a big easy-going lefty-hitting kid who played first base and could hit a ball a mile—that is if he knew what pitch was coming. I used to give him signs on what pitch might be coming. I was always skilled at guessing pitches and high school pitchers only have two or three pitches they can depend on, so the guessing was easier.

"Here we go Bobby," I'd say. Then I'd clap my hands together twice if it was going to be a curve ball. "Here we go Bobby!"

Podalak might get the sign the first time, but often he'd just shrug when he forgot the signal or wasn't paying attention. He'd jump at the curve like it was a fast ball and then look at me with that blank expression, like to say, "What, Coach?"

One day, with runners on first and second and two outs, down 3-1 in the sixth inning, I yelled over to Bobby as he stepped in the batter's box with a 2-0 count. The pitcher had been getting him out with his sneaky curve, so I guessed it was on its way.

"Here we go, Bobby!" I clapped my hands above my head twice for the anticipated curve ball.

Bobby stepped out of the batter's box and gave me that look.

"Curve ball?" he mouthed silently so the catcher couldn't hear.

"Yeah, you mope!" I yelled. "Get back in the box."

The next pitch was a the kind of curve that breaks so far you'd think it's a slow motion replay, with the seams on the ball spelling out "c-u-r-v-e-b-a-l-l" as it moved toward the hitter. Bobby waited, waited, waited, then cocked his bat, timed the break perfectly, and sent it into the woods behind the right-field fence about 400 feet away. The kid slowly rounded the bases to give us a 4-3 lead and when he reached the third-base line he looked over to me with a big smile on his face and yelled, "Good guess, Coach. Curve, right?"

Unbelievable!

We won that game and 16 more that spring on our way to our first Class B Catholic championship.

Jason Mendicino, probably the most talented baseball player I coached with the Emeralds, was my star pitcher, shortstop, and hitter that year. He went on to be county MVP, graduated, and went into construction. Jason had a girlfriend, a baby, and few prospects by the time he was 24. He had a few tryouts and showcases for major league teams, but always seemed distracted by his personal life. He was the most like me of any of my kids—a rough, talented Italian kid from the Bronx who couldn't find the discipline or focus to make it. He never went to college, although he could have played Division I baseball.

I hated Jason for being like me and loved him for being like me. It was one of my biggest disappointments as a coach—not being able to get Jason past where I left my life as a teenager.

My kids.

I thought I could get them all straight and on to college, or at least a good job. I wanted so badly for them to learn from my mistakes, go that next step, stay away from the streets, and have legit lives.

I think the success of my teams and my players

helped me justify the loss of my own baseball career.

I'll never forget the way I felt when the New York Yankees gave me a shot at my dream in 1976. I remember going to Yankee Stadium for a tryout and finding out they wanted me. I wasn't really a Yankee fan. I'd always liked the Mets, but suddenly the idea of being with a franchise where Babe Ruth, Lou Gehrig and Joe DiMaggio played was a huge deal. That feeling of acceptance, even if it was for my baseball talent, made me understand how a kid can get a major boost from doing well in sports. Since I'd blown my own high school sports career, I wanted to make sure my players didn't.

But, like a parent who's lived a less than exemplary life, asking my players to do something I hadn't done was a bit hypocritical.

I was Bill Clinton telling Chelsea not to give blow jobs to older, powerful married men.

I was Jerry Garcia telling his kid not to smoke a doobie or do heroin.

I was Roberto Alomar scolding his kid for talking back to an umpire.

I was George Bush I telling George Bush II not to raise taxes.

I was a basketball and baseball coach at a Catholic high school who moonlighted as a mobster.

And on top of that, like most of my friends in the "business," I considered myself an honest person. I hated liars, rats, cowards and people who couldn't do the time for doing the crime. In the old-time tradition of the mob, I had loyalty and was a stand-up guy. Keeping with my high moral philosophy, I never lied to my kids. I just didn't tell them anything that wasn't their business.

I led a double life that started as a natural desire to be around sports and ended with a tug of war for my soul. For four years, I moved through life in a Jekyll and Hyde manner. It was like I chugged down a potion each afternoon and turned from a heartless, cold-blooded soldier of the mob, into a hard-nosed, disciplined coach who loved teaching and educating young people.

I've watched lots of other people.

Everyone ever born who grows to adulthood wages an inner war, with at least two personalities fighting for control. Some get to be like that wacko woman Cybil, who had 16 different personalities because of the war going on inside her head. Everyone has that ying-yang, good versus evil struggle going on. I've seen church-going, family-loving businessmen going to hookers on the West Side of Manhattan. I've seen religious leaders point their fingers out of the pulpit and warn us not to sin, then wind up in jail for embezzling church funds or getting caught with hookers in the back of the church limo. I've seen the police who arrest drug dealers then take the drugs and sell them for profit. We all fight the war every minute of the day. Some people manage to win that inner war. They find a way to push away the dark side and embrace the positive side, at least most of the time.

For me, the split personality fit too well. The night had its place and the day was just as comfortable. As long as the two didn't clash, I was all right.

But when I worked with my kids, I felt every paternal urge a guy could have. I felt like Joe Kennedy grooming his boys Joe, Jack, Bobby and Teddy for the game of politics; like George Bush trying to keep his sons George and Jeb moving ahead so one of them could finish the work he screwed up.

As a coach, I used every memory of pain, failure, success, disappointment and unfulfilled dreams that marked my own athletic career, to motivate, teach and inspire better things from my players. Like most men, I didn't want the sins of the "father" to be visited on my ball-playing sons. I wanted them to be better, stronger, smarter and more successful at sports and with their lives.

And I didn't want them to ever entertain a thought of doing what I did—letting the dark side rule and steal the wonder of living a positive life. I wasn't a hypocrite. I knew my sin, my conflict, and even though I continued living a double life, working with those kids was my salvation and I wanted to make it their salvation too. I tried not to be a bad influence, although sometimes I behaved too much like the kids, talking about "getting laid" and goofing on the teachers and administrators. I was a realist. I knew these kids were into things like drinking and trying to get girls to give it up, so instead of trying to run a Boy Scout troop, I was like the head of a fraternity house. Do what you have to do in school and on the field and have fun during your off hours. But I never shared my business, asked any of the kids to do anything illegal, or brought my business into the school. I wouldn't even use the school phone to talk to my "friends."

I did make the kids accessories to one crime of my crimes. The heist was called "The Magic Quarter" and every one of my players had a hand in it at one time or another. Here's how it went: The team van would approach one of the tolls on the Westchester County parkways, like the one on the Saw Mill River Parkway near McLean Avenue in Yonkers or the one on the Hutchinson River Parkway right near Sanford Boulevard in Pelham. Just before we reached the toll booth, I'd raise my hand and say, "Sean, give me the magic quarter."

Whichever kid I asked would then reach into his pocket and come up with an imaginary quarter, show it to the team, and ceremoniously hand it to me in the driver's seat. I would then show the non-existent quarter to everyone again, slow down as we reached the toll basket, and toss "nothing" into the receptacle with a flourish. We'd drive away, having stolen 25 cents from the county. The team would applaud the "magic quarter" as we proceeded to our destination. In those days the highway department didn't use those moving barriers that rose up after you threw in a coin, and with four or five cars going through at the same time we'd just ride off with the bell ringing, a signal that no toll had been paid. No cop ever followed us because we had

"Redemption High School" written on the side of the van and toll collectors would never think we'd pass through without paying. In the event they did, I told the players the security cameras or toll takers would be our best evidence.

"Anyone who saw us would testify that I asked for a quarter, a player handed it to me, I threw it toward the basket and we rode off," I told my accomplices. "Who's going to question a bunch of nice Catholic school kids?"

In four years of baseball and basketball games, traveling to maybe 100 away games in all, we never paid one toll, thereby saving the school at least fifty dollars worth of tolls coming and going. We always believed this petty theft of services from the county might have led to the eventual removal of tollbooths on county highways. We took pride in the fact that our "scam" had given commuters a less congested path to and from New York City each day.

Nitkowski was one of those kids who'd stand out in any high school. He was a smart, good-looking blonde kid, not too big, but wiry and athletic—an excellent second baseman and a smart, tough shooting guard. Billy was the one who asked questions that made real sense. "Coach, when we switch on defense, whose responsibility, is it to pick up the wing man?" he'd ask. "When we have the bunt on, should the runner show early or wait until the pitcher or third baseman breaks to the plate?"

Players like Billy, a top student who planned on becoming an architect after college, make you a smarter coach because they help the other kids understand what you're coaching. Sometimes I'd have trouble getting a point across, but once Billy understood it, he'd "translate" for the other guys, who'd pick it up quicker. Billy was quiet, but liked to tease the younger players and always had a smart-ass comeback because he was a smart-ass kid. He'd trash talk on the basketball court or on the baseball field from the dugout, but you'd

100

swear his lips never moved. He'd say things like, "Hey, big man, Trey told me he's gonna walk all over you today. Better get ready."

Billy would piss off the opposing players and get them to lose focus. And he was always stayed as cool as the other side of the pillow. When everyone else was agitated or flustered, I'd look at Billy and he'd have a crooked smile on his face like he was taking an algebra test and had all the answers. A great kid. I knew he'd go far someday. I respected him because he knew how to make each day work for him.

Trey and I became close, which was strange because I grew up seeing black people as the enemy. In my Arthur Avenue hood, blacks owned the neighborhood south of us toward Tremont Avenue near Southern Boulevard. If they came onto our turf, they were fair game. Once, during a hot summer in 1968 or 1969, the neighborhood gangs stopped a bus full of black kids on their way to summer day camp and there was a brawl right there in the street. We didn't have any black kids in my Yonkers neighborhood and Lincoln High School was mostly Italian, Jewish, and Irish – well, white. So, the only black people I knew were guys I played ball with—and I never brought any of them home for dinner.

Trey was a lovable kid; always smiling and talking to anyone who'd listen. All the girls—black, white, and Hispanic—loved him. Talking to the girls was his favorite pastime and I kidded him about it all the time.

"Hey Trey, what are you doin' talkin' to Maria when you told me you were sweatin' Shanique?" I'd say. "I'm gonna see Shanique after third period and tell her you're cheatin.'"

"Yeah, Coach," Trey would say. "You're just jealous 'cause your datin' days are over. You're engaged now and your girl got you by the balls. Wait, I'm gonna tell your lady you're checkin' out the high school girls, too."

I made a real effort to reach out the Trey as much as I could, because he was my best athlete and I could see him getting a full ride to some college. He eventually got a scholarship to a school in Vermont and I even ragged him about that.

"Trey, you'd better learn to ski," I told him. "And you better start lookin' for some black folks up there in Vermont right now, 'cause there ain't many and it's gonna take time to find partners up there that don't listen to country music and think all black people are rappers or ballplayers."

"Okay," Coach," Trey answered. "Maybe I'll find some of those dark-skinned Si-Cilian I-talians up there, because they the next thing to being black."

Trey got better with each game and turned into one of the toughest, big-time players we had. He became a magazine and runway model after college and every time I saw his layouts in a magazine, I imagined Trey smiling and talking to some beautiful model. "Hey, what's up girl? Don't you look fine today?" just like in the Redemption hallways between classes.

One of my favorite kids was P.J. Reagan. P.J. stood for Patrick Ryan, but no one but me called him that. I called him Patrick like a father who was making sure everyone knew his namesake. "Way to go, Patrick!" I'd yell when he made a good play. "Nice shot, Patrick Ryan!" I'd say when he got a big hit. If any of the kids called him Patrick in public, they were in for a smack. But he took it from me as a way of showing respect.

P.J Reagan loved the game so much that he was willing to do anything to keep playing. And that included passing all his courses at Redemption. He was one of my first two baseball champions and a reserve on my first basketball team—a fine athlete, but a lousy student. By the time P. J. began senior year, he'd been in a two-year academic slump. His older brother Michael had been killed in a car accident before his junior year and that seemed to really mess P.J. up. It kind of took the air out of him. I could see it when he walked down the halls. He had that distant "nobody home" look I remembered

102

from when my bother was killed in Nam; the look of a guy who was daydreaming, remembering how it felt to have his brother alive to help him out or just talk to. It was a lost look. It seemed like I could relate to one or two things in each of my kids, like Trey's love of the ladies, Billy's sharp feel for the game, and P.J.'s loss. Losing a person who was a big part of your life could make or break you, especially at an age when you were looking for guidance. I tried to fill some of the gap for P.J. when things got tough early in his senior year.

"I've always had trouble in school," he told me. "I had an average of about 68 or 70 as a sophomore and junior and I was failing a subject or two. But I don't want to miss my senior season, Coach."

Instead of leaving him to sink or swim on his own the way my parents did when I was in school, I did what my brother Joe would've done for me if he hadn't been killed: I told P.J. he had to do his work or sit on the bench. He responded like a true gamer.

"I don't want to let the guys down," he told me one afternoon. "I'll do the work."

P.J. made the honor roll in the first semester and never looked back. He hit .420 to lead the team in hitting, and in his classes, he racked up a combined total of 109 points in seven subjects, finishing with a grade point average of 84.

P.J. graduated on time and I saw him a couple of times during the next school year when he came back to watch us play. Five years later, after I'd left coaching, I was coming down Bronx River Road doing about 50 in a 30 zone. I saw the flashing police lights just as I neared Yonkers Avenue.

"Shit!" I slammed both hands on the steering wheel. "I don't need this tonight."

The cop approached my car and without looking up I asked, "You want my license and registration, right?"

"Nope. I just want a hug, Coach." The cop took off his hat and put his big Irish face through the driver's side window. "Hey, Coach, wanna step out of the car?"

"P.J!" I yelled. "You fucking scared the shit outta me. What are you doing, posin' as a cop?"

"Yeah, posin'," P.J. answered. "And what are you posin' as, a Coach?"

I got out on Bronx River Road and hugged the little shit right there in the street. Cars going by slowed up to see whether I was assaulting a police officer.

"I'm one of New York City's finest," P.J. cracked. "What you been doin', Coach?"

I didn't know how to answer the kid. He looked good, a little bigger and he even had some hair on his face. His smile was exactly the same and his hair still had that Irish red color. P.J. was the first of my kids I'd seen since I left Redemption in 1996.

"Joey, Trey, Jason, everyone's been asking about you," P.J. said as his car radio sputtered a call from his dispatcher about a drunk and disorderly on McLean Avenue. "We should all get together for a little reunion. All the guys on the team. Give me a call Coach; I'm at the same number. Remember when you used to call me to see if I was doing my homework? You got me through school. You were like a brother to me after my brother Michael died in that crash. You saved me from screwing up and now...hey, I'm a cop."

"Yeah, a cop," I said. "Just what I need tonight. Better get back to work and round up that drunk and disorderly. I'll call you and we'll have breakfast or something. Maybe we'll have that reunion."

I didn't call P.J. or any of the guys I'd coached for a few years after that meeting. Mostly because I wasn't the guy they knew anymore. I wasn't a coach and I wasn't the big brother role model who'd helped them become better players and better men. I was just a guy trying to make a living and wishing I was still a coach. I do know this. I didn't do as much to save them as they did to save me.

Redemption Repeats

BRONXVILLE -- P.J Reagan had three hits, including a home run and four runs batted in as the Redemption Emeralds completed a 16-2 season with a 7-3 victory over Cardinal Spellman High School of the Bronx to earn back-to-back titles in the Catholic School Association Class championship game.

Reagan, a red-headed junior left-fielder, drove in two runs in the first inning and hit a solo home run in the fourth to give the Emeralds a 5-1 lead. "I can't believe we won another championship, but Coach V told us we could do it if we stayed focused," Reagan said following the game. "We had a good season and we were the favorites, but we had to deal with some injuries to get it done."

CHAPTER 9

Who can find a virtuous woman... for her price is far above rubies.
Proverbs 31:10

One of the things I enjoyed most in life—aside from a Bruce Springsteen concert or a long day baking in the sun—was a manicure. I loved having my hands in that warm water, with a cute girl taking care of me, polishing and cleaning each nail. It got my mind off work and anything else that was bothering me.

I'd spend hours in the sun wherever I could find a place to spread out a towel or unfold a beach chair; on tar a beach, tenement rooftops as a kid, or a stretch of grass along the Bronx River Parkway years later. I loved the sun, sucked it up like it was part of me. A deep olive oil suntan, clean fingernails, a great haircut—with a touch-up to hide the gray hair on the temples—expensive cologne, and a first-rate wardrobe; these things will make any woman pay attention.

Getting the hair thing done right was a problem. But vanity is vanity. I started seeing gray on my temples right after I turned thirty and, though it looked distinguished, I wasn't ready to have young women asking me how old I was. So, I got a black die kit at the local CVS and took it home to try it one Friday night. I thought I read the directions right; correct amount of water to the proper ratio of dye. I was perched on the toilet in my bathroom and applying the dye to my temples, frequently checking the process out in the mirror. Within seconds I started feeling a warm sensation, like a trickling stream of perspiration under my hair. I touched both sides of my head and when I looked at my hands they were jet black and dripping wet. I didn't know what to do there all by myself, so I ran to the nearest phone and called a friend of mine, Stevie, for help. Stevie was a Yonkers guy who went to Lincoln right after I did· and hung around the gyms I worked out in. We played some softball together and got to be good friends. We hit all the city after-hours clubs and good restaurants together in the late 80s and chased hundreds of women. He was a former jock like me, but bigger. He stood about 6-2 and nearly 270 pounds of muscle at the height of his body building days. He looked more like a bouncer than a public relations guy, which is what he did before becoming a cop the late 1990s.

"You gotta come over here right now," I begged when I reached him by phone. "I got a big problem and I need your help. I'm in trouble and you gotta help me."

"Tommy, I can't," Stevie said. "I got a softball game and I'm already late. What's the problem? Can't it wait until after the game?"

I was starting to panic with all that dye dripping all over the place. "Stevie, right now man!" I shouted. "Please, right now, will ya?"

I don't think Stevie had ever heard me use the word please in all the years we'd been friends. I always thought saying please was a sign of weakness. He obviously realized I was desperate.

He arrived at my apartment within minutes and knocked on the front door, calling my name like he thought I might be shot or dead.

"Tommy, you in there?" You all right?"

"The door's open Stevie, hurry in here will ya?"

The instant he saw me sitting on a kitchen chair with black die running down my face, neck and back, he started laughing. He actually almost fell over laughing, which didn't make me feel any better. I thought I would be dyed black for weeks before the stains wore off.

"Help me, you fuck!" I shouted. "Can't you see I'm drowning in dye here? What do I do?"

Stevie managed to soak up the dye with some old towels and get me pretty well cleaned up, but he didn't stop laughing the whole time. I wanted to smack the big fuck, but it was making me laugh too. The next five times I dyed my gray patches, I made Stevie come over and dab my face while the dye took. You had to see it. Two big Italian guys who looked like bouncers of football players, dying hair and dabbing. It was like a bad makeover on Oprah.

But manicures were my biggest vanity, so when I met Melissa D'Amato, a cute, blonde Italian manicurist about 32 years old, with green eyes, an adorable smile, and a great ass, I couldn't resist the combination of sex appeal and a great nail job. Melissa was married and I was on my fourth of fifth woman that year, but when she started telling me about how bad her husband treated her, I took advantage of the girl-needs-me opening and came on pretty strong. Two weeks after we met she was bouncing on my bed, riding into my world of short-term affairs. Or so I thought.

Melissa had a daughter and so did I. My Vanessa was about nine and her daughter Tina was three. The two of them hit it off like big sister and little sister, and one thing led to another—mostly because Melissa was hot and really wanted me. We dated for a few months and then decided once her divorce came through we'd get married. A secretary who worked at Redemption was pursuing me, but I didn't pay much attention to her. That

108

was just a quick fling; not unusual for me since my second divorce.

I must have been out of my mind when it came to the Melissa thing, led astray by my dick and the idea that maybe this time I'd found a woman to keep around for more than a few weeks. During my second marriage I realized I was the kind of guy who got bored being with one woman. It's not that I didn't love my first two wives. I just wasn't the kind of man who could come home every night to the same woman and keep the excitement going.

Maybe I was too insecure to really give all of myself to someone, and when the excitement of being with a woman wore off, I looked around for a way out. And forget about living with someone and having her try to organize my life. I just couldn't deal with, "Where are you going, Tom?" or "Who was that guy who called last night?" or "What time will you be getting home? or "Why don't you get a job with benefits and security?"

How do people stay married for fifty years to the same person?

I'd been married for about 11 years, but that was a combined total with three wives. My parents divorced when I was 14 and most of the people I knew got married, stayed together for about 10 years, and then split up. It was always on grounds of irreconcilable differences or adultery, but I knew what it really was. One of the two people, or maybe both, just got bored and didn't want to admit it. So, one or both of the spouses found someone to screw around with or "grew in a different direction" or "grew apart" or some other stupid excuse for just not wanting to be with the same person day after day.

I'd always had a robust sexual appetite. Like most teenage boys, I thought getting a girl to give it up was like winning a ballgame; as soon as the game ended you wanted to brag about who, what, where, when, and…well, we all knew why. The urges hadn't stopped

109

since I got my first piece of ass off Denise "The Piece" Liberati when I was 13. The Piece was the girl in every neighborhood who was willing to go further than the other girls. She learned young that doing things with boys brought gifts and attention. She was 16 and went with some of the older guys who had cars and jobs, but she also made room for guys like me she liked.

My "day" with Denise happened at the Kent movie theater on McLean Avenue one summer night when the place was almost empty.

We saw the "The Godfather" at the 10 o'clock show and right after the scene with Sonny Corleone screwing his girlfriend at his sister's wedding, The Piece let me feel her up and then put my young, willing manhood where it had only dreamed of being. We lay down behind the last row of seats and I think I did pretty well considering it was my first time and I'd been waiting to unload for about two years. I put on a condom The Piece gave me and climbed on top of her. She lifted her short skirt, pulled her panties aside, and helped me find the paradise I'd been dreaming about. I think I lasted about 10 minutes and she was breathing hard so I must have done something right. Then I fell back and it was like I'd found a new country, a place where for a few minutes you forgot everything and joined someone in an experience that was so private and good you almost felt like you were one with each other. I also found out the feeling faded and you wanted more an hour later, like Chinese food. Denise helped me get rid of the condom, asked me if I liked it, and smiled. She kissed me on the lips and said she liked me. We did it again a few times before I found my own girlfriend about a year later.

But The Piece was always a favorite. After all, she was the first, the one who was willing to let a young gun have a shot at being a man. And she didn't seem to mind when guys shared their experiences about her. I guess she was more grown up than all of us, and more realistic about life. It turns out her mother was a single woman, the father took off when she was two, and her mom had a lot of "boyfriends" if you know what I mean. A few years later I found out she'd married an electrician, had two kids, and moved to Mount Kisco. I saw Denise a few years ago at funeral in Yonkers for the father of an old friend. She came right over to me, said hello, and kissed me on the cheek. She looked like a typical suburban housewife, in great shape with her hair tinted a nice shade.

"How are you Tommy," she said. "I heard you got married and divorced. If you don't mind me saying it, the girl must be a dope, 'cause you were always a good kid."

"Doing fine, Denise," I said. "You look great. I guess I wasn't ready to get married and I got bored. But I'm glad to see you're happy."

Denise looked at me with a kind of shy smile that I had never seen from her when she was a kid. She always looked older and more worldly than the other girls her age back then. Now, with 10 years on her, she looked like a different person, almost angelic, sweet, really. Not the same hot-to-trot girl I remembered.

"It took awhile for me to even know what being happy is," Denise said. "I was crazy and mixed up about a lot of things when we were kids. I didn't know what the heck I was doing. But I got lucky and found a great guy. And he never asked me any questions about who or what I did. He just loves me. I needed that."

"Me too," I said. "I guess everyone needs love like that. Maybe someday for me too."

It amazed me how well Denise's life had turned out. She seemed really happy, even after years of being the neighborhood whore; the girl everyone thought was just out for a good time. She'd found her heart, a guy who loved her, and now she was giving him all the love she'd craved as a kid. It was like she was reborn and living the perfect life. I thought, I guess it can happen. People can change.

I'd been with so many women—between wives—that I couldn't begin to have to name each one on a bet. I had older women, younger women, black women, blondes, short women, tall women, Latin women—even a mother and daughter combo. Man, that was crazy. I started going out with the daughter and later on met the mother, who showed me mother knew best. That experience freaked me out a little, but when you're hungry, you're hungry. I guess I saw most women first as sexual beings, beautiful trophies I wanted to have, at least for awhile. But when the trophy needed dusting, polishing, or care of any kind, it got tough. I had so many issues of my own that having a woman was nothing more than release to me, like having a drink or doing drugs.

The male-female relationships distracted me from my own problems, but when I had to deal with another human being's troubles I'd get frustrated, then angry, sometimes lashing out with my wonderfully-explicit language. Being verbally abusive is sometimes worse than hitting someone, because it leaves a mental scar that can't be healed with a band-aid, stitches, or time. Time can heal physical wounds. But spiritual wounds, like when you tell someone she's a "selfish cunt" or a "lying bitch," or you don't talk to your wife for days on end when you're angry: that takes more than a little Bacitracin to fix.

Finding that one special woman was never my goal. I just fell into marriage–three times—because it seemed like the next step after romance and sex. You know: Italians get married. And I was Italian, so if I wanted to show some kind of respect for the women I wanted; it meant marrying her and having kids. I married my first wife Maureen because she was pregnant, but I loved being loved by her, so it wasn't hard to get me to make that move. I didn't get much love at home after my father left my mother, so marrying Maureen made me feel like I had a license to love. But when our baby died, we lost our reason to stay together. We just decided to give each other a break and split.

My second marriage, to a girl from Yonkers named Eleanor Marino, came in 1984 at a time when I thought I needed to settle down and prove I could be a grown-up. All the guys I knew were married, had kids, and then found goomahs—a girlfriend or girlfriends on the side to be there during the late nights and early mornings when wives and kids were home in bed. Hey, if we could justify murder it wasn't hard to justify having girlfriends. It was part of the deal and one of the parts I enjoyed. Eleanor and I got along really well; we both liked the same music—big Springsteen fans, old movies, and sex, which was the most important thing we had in common. But after a couple years of marriage, when our daughter was born and Eleanor settled into the suburban housewife thing, it wasn't the same. Even though Eleanor knew I was hustling, I had union jobs with the carpenters at the Javits Center or as a shop steward with the parking garages in Manhattan, so it was like I was a regular Joe. She'd drop hints about my lifestyle, like, "Why don't you go into a real business, like a store or a gas station, or even get a job on your own away from these people, I don't like it that you're never home at night." And she'd tell me I was moody, up one minute and down the next. She attributed the mood swings to the Valium and the "job."

"Tommy, you're not the same as when I met you," she'd say. "What's going on in that thick Italian head of yours? I never know what you're thinking or what you're doing or who you're with. What about our future? What about your daughter's future?"

That's usually when I'd take a walk, go out and meet some friends, or take a ride or something, because I didn't want to argue. When I argued I got nasty, just like when I used to drink too much. All my insecurities would rise to the surface and I'd explode with some curse-filled tirade or grab Eleanor and scream in her face. She was a

113

tough kid though and didn't take much shit from me. She'd fight back and curse me out and that would make me even angrier, not being able to control things. It flashed me back to my childhood when I heard my father screaming or cursing and be afraid he was going to hurt me or my mother. I hated hearing myself get out of control, because I sounded just like my father. Maybe I was acting out because I'd held all that fear in for so many years. And I always feared people wouldn't love me and wind up leaving, like my grandmother and brother when they died. The Valium helped calm me most of the time, but the pills made me moodier and after about three years of haggling and complaining about me, Eleanor left. We were divorced in 1989, tried to reconcile a year later, and split for good in 1991.

Eleanor remarried about a year later and moved, with my daughter, to north Jersey where they still live, happily. I stayed close to my daughter Vanessa, seeing her as many weekends as I could. Being with that kid, having her fill up the lonely space in my apartment when she stayed over, saved my life. I took her to my baseball and basketball games, where she saw me doing something positive with my life. She looked a lot like me and had my athletic skills. Everyone liked Vanessa; the players, people at school, and my mother obviously loved having her granddaughter visit. In those days she was still young enough to see me as her Daddy, perfect, big, strong, and handsome. As time went by she got more involved with school and other things, so I saw her less.

Having the coaching job and Vanessa in my life those years between 1992 and 1996 helped show me I could enjoy love with someone close to me without running away and I could contribute something positive to other people's lives. Those two things made it easier to leave the "life." Even the lure of money and power couldn't match my daughter's smile or a big playoff game with my kids playing their hearts out for me.

114

Melissa was another kind of woman, but the results of our affair and short-lived marriage were familiar.

After we met in 1994, we were together all the time. She was in therapy for problems related to her break-up and I had started getting help for my anxiety attacks. Two people with big issues: it should've been no surprise when our relationship ran into problems. We thought we were soul mates, two people who could balance our problems and help each other. But sex only goes so far. In fact, the intensity of a sexual relationship can replace the need to communicate in other ways. When it came to everyday situations, the smallest thing would set one of us off.

"Why do you talk to my mother that way," Melissa would ask when her mother made some stupid remark about me or the way I made a living. "You have no respect for my family. No respect for anyone."

"Why can't I go away for the weekend with my girlfriends?" she'd ask. "I feel like a prisoner in this apartment. You're always jealous. Do you think I'm cheating on you?"

Everything became fuel for an argument. My watching sports on television, my coaching, my friends, my leaving and staying out all night. The arguing escalated into screaming and cursing. One afternoon Melissa got really mad and picked up a vase and threw a perfect strike, hitting me low on my left leg. Two feet higher and little to the right and she'd have given me an instant vasectomy. I was ready to grab her around the neck and choke her, but I held on, pushed her aside, and took off. That was the beginning of the end.

"You're a fuckin' nut," she yelled as I walked down the hallway. "You don't love me. You never loved me. You don't love anyone."

She was probably right. I didn't know how to tell if I was in love. The only people I knew for sure I loved were my daughter, my new son, and my mother and sister. Everyone else was in question.

CHAPTER 10

Consider the lilies of the field how they grow, they neither toil nor spin, (yet God provides for them.)
Matthew 6:28

Union work is hard work.

A union delegate occupies an office with the other union officials, has lunches, makes phone calls, settles disputes between management and employee and... well that's about it. A normal day consisted of a big breakfast at 10 a.m., some meetings, lunch at a nice restaurant, some Meetings, then going home to meet some guys for a nice dinner in the Bronx.

But the money was good. And it was clean, compared to some of the other jobs we had to do inside "the business". Garbage wars, muscle jobs, collections and other stuff took some effort and a certain mean streak I never really developed. Although, I did what I had to do.

"You do what you gotta do."

I can't tell you how many thousands of times I've heard that phrase. It ranks at the top of most-used phrases in "our business" and has been reflected in so many movies and books about the world of wise guys that it has become a cliché now used by corporate magnates, professional athletes, rappers and even housewives who want to justify why they stay home and rustle kids from place to place while juggling a household.

"I can't believe all the things you do in one day and that you do them all day every day," a recently married girl tells a veteran housewife.

"You do what you gotta do," the worn out stay-home mom says.

For wise guys or wanna-be wise guys, "doin' what you gotta do" is as simple as saying "yes" to anything your are told to do, especially when you start out earning. Hijacking trucks, stealing from warehouses, busting up a guy that won't pay back his loan or can't keep up with the vig.

Here's where it gets tough.

I've done some bad things in my life -- things that most people would consider antisocial or even evil, but me and "my friends" considered it all part of daily business. The only two of the Ten Commandments I hadn't broken by the age of 16 was the "Thou shalt not kill" and the one about coveting your neighbor's ass or oxen or whatever animal that commandment says you shouldn't covet. I wasn't looking to be a shepherd, so you could keep the live stock. But I stole, I cheated, I lied, I fornicated, I masturbated -- is there a commandment against that? – I coveted mostly everything I saw and I even dishonored my mother and father. But doesn't every teenager do that?

I don't know when I stopped going to confession, but I was really young. But I was old enough to know that confessing, saying some Hail Marys or Our Fathers, wasn't going to clear my conscience or take away my sin, so I just gave up on the idea.

My first crimes were forgivable, like small-time theft, selling pot or shoplifting. The first time I realized crime could be organized, or at least a lucrative business, was when we started selling stolen stuff we highjacked from warehouses and stores. We would let people know we had something like televisions, you know that fell off a truck, and then we'd set up a deal. We'd offer the televisions for $100 and tell the buyer we had 20. That's $2,000 on delivery, and delivery meant you met us in a parking lot and we showed you the back of the truck with the televisions. Once we got the money, the buyer would back up his truck and start unloading the 20 boxes stacked in the truck or on a loading dock.

Only five of the boxes had televisions in them. The other 10 were filled with wood or some other stuff that weighed the same as a TV. Most of the time the buyer would open the first three or four boxes, then feel okay about the deal. No one wanted to stand around a parking lot in full sight and check all the goods. We'd make sure we were out of there when the last few boxes were being loaded and hoped that no one would open one of the bogus boxes to check. That scam worked most of the time until this one occasion when my Uncle Mario, who was a made guy, found out we hustled a "friend of ours". This guy described us to Uncle Mario and he went nuts.

"What's wrong with you asshole kids," my Uncle Mario said. "You fuckin' have no shame, selling half loads to guys we know. This guy wants me to smack you idiots. Now I have to give the guy back $1,000. Can't you find any suckers who aren't guys we know? Goddammit, you gotta have some professional courtesy and know who you're dealin' with."

We were kids who thought anyone was fair game, especially guys who were crooks themselves. Who knew we had to be honest with dishonest people?

One time, me and a couple of guys worked an idea that we thought was foolproof -- at least for some stupid 19-year-olds. We lured our buyer to the loading dock at Alexander's on Fordham Road in the Bronx with a deal to

118

sell them a truckload of televisions. These guys were coming from Rockland County and we agreed to meet them at about noon on a Friday in July. It was really hot I remember. The two guys met me and showed me the enveloped filled with $20 bills and I pointed out the truck with the TVs, which we parked about 100 yards away. The plan was to convince them to give me the money, give them a bogus set of keys to the truck and then take off out a back way through a fence before they found out the truck was filled with empty boxes.

Everything went perfect.

I talked one guy into waiting next to "my car", a car that I had picked out in the lot that wasn't really mine. The other guy handed me the cash and I gave him the keys to the truck.

"I'm gonna count this, so wait for me," I said. "Then we'll go check out the truck."

I walked with him to the truck while I was counting and when he was busy opening the back, I slipped around the other side of the truck and down an alley where my guys were supposed to be waiting in a car. Instead of my guys being there, the guys from Rockland had left their van parked at the end of the alley and before I could start running I heard them yelling, "He's back there. He took the money! Get him!"

What could I do? Where the hell were my guys? I had no where to run, so I jumped into their van with the keys still in the ignition, so I gassed it, trying to get out of what looked like was becoming a real bad situation. I sped off onto Jerome Avenue and under the elevator train where I knew it would be hard for them to chase me.

The next 10 minutes were like that famous chase scene from "The French Connection" movie. I took a quick glance in the rear-view mirror to see if anyone was following and spotted a van close behind me with two guys in it. I couldn't believe they found my escape hatch. They must have had a backup van waiting just in case. I didn't think these Rockland guys had that kind of smarts, but I guess I was wrong. I was weaving in and out of traffic and between the elevator train supports, watching the street markers go by. I just wanted to get up toward 233rd Street where I could get on the Major Deegan Thruway and away from these guys chasing me.

Another look in the mirror and I could see the other van on my bumper. It was so close I could almost see the faces of the two guys in the front seats. Just as I glanced back to the traffic in front of me I saw the high rear end of a big delivery truck coming at me. The truck was stopped at a light and I was headed straight for a decapitation if I didn't swerve in time. I cut the wheel hard to the right and crashed into the side of a parked car. Without even checking to if I was hurt, I opened the driver's side door and started running, but before I could take 10 steps, two guys grabbed my left and right arms and lifted my off the ground. When I turned to see who it was, I realized that the van that was following me was an unmarked police van and not the guys from Rockland. While I was making my escape, I just happened to race by a van full of cops on their way to some cop training session.

If I had just stayed calm and driven away, I would have been free as a bird, with the $2,000. The van-full of cops acted like they had made the bust of the century. I was taken to the 53rd Precinct in the north Bronx and booked for reckless driving and a number of other moving violations.

But I was smiling because I still had the envelope full of money stuffed down my pants and I was going to get off with just a few fines for speeding, running a red light and reckless driving.

"Officer, I thought someone was trying to stick me up," I began explaining to the desk sergeant who was taking the report as another patrolman started emptying my pockets. "I was down here buying some electronic equipment for my boss who lives in Rockland. I thought these two guys were going to hold me up at Alexander's.

It's my bosses van. I just stared working up there. I'm sorry I was driving like an asshole. You can call my boss and ask him. Here's the number."

I knew the Rockland guy who had sent his boys to make the deal for stolen televisions wouldn't tell the cops anything when they called him because it would be an admission of guilt. He would probably verify that I was his guy and then try to chase me down later. So, the sergeant made the call and I could see by the way he was nodding that he was getting all the right answers from the guy.

"All right kid," the sergeant said when he hung up the phone. "Here's a desk ticket for your court appearance and here's your money back. You can tell the judge what you told us and maybe he'll cut the fines a little. But just don't go crazy out there will ya?" Here's your boss's money. You van's parked out front, so let's try to keep it on the road and off the sidewalks."

I was free and clear.

My two partners were waiting for me back at my house in Yonkers for a split of the money and I couldn't help thinking about what I had just gotten away with, so I left the precinct with a big smile on my face. The smile disappeared before I could hit the Bronx sidewalk.

Just as I headed for the police station's front door and freedom, the two guys we ripped off were coming in with two cops. It seems they had reported the event to the cops, telling them we had promised to sell them a used car and not stolen televisions. They said that while looked at a car, I ran of with the money. And when they found out the car wasn't really mine, they knew it was a scam. They nearly flipped when they saw me on the way out, pointed at me and had the cops grab me again. Two minutes later, I was back in front of the desk sergeant, and he was not in a good mood. "What are you guys, assholes?" the sergeant said after listening to the other side of another bogus story. "What are you guys, little mobster wann-bes? You two, take your money and go back across the bridge to Rockland and stuck with buying cows instead of used cars from the Bronx, or whatever it is you were here to buy. And you, Vitale, get the hell out of here and stay off my streets. We'll see you in court next week. I hope they send you to Sing Sing, you little bastard."

When I got to my apartment house, my partners were waiting for me on the roof where we had planned to meet and cut up the cash after the deal. They had followed me on my escape through the Bronx long enough to watch me get busted. Then the cowards took off. They couldn't believe I was on the street so soon and congratulated me for my quick thinking after they heard the whole story. Then one of them, a guy named Mousy, who was not the brightest bulb in the box, asked the dumbest question I ever heard.

"Do you have the money," he asked.

"What are you stupid? No never mind, I know the answer to that question," I yelled at him. "I'm lucky I'm not in the Bronx House of Detention right now. You think the cops are going to let me keep $2,000 in cash after I wrecked half the Bronx and led them on a two-mile chase up Jerome Avenue? I can't believe I hang around with you fuckin' idiots. Next time, you guys can do the heavy work and I'll run and hide."

We didn't learn our lesson very well because we pulled that same scam a dozen times before my Uncle Mario, who was a street boss in the Bronx, found out we had hustled a "friend" of his. The guy was telling Uncle Mario about being ripped off and in the process of telling the story, described the guys who did it. When my uncle heard that it was three kids who looked like me and my friends, he went nuts. Within 10 minutes from the time the guy told him what we had done, we were standing in front of him in his grocery store on 187th Street.

"What's wrong with you asshole kids?" Uncle Mario said. You fucking have no shame, selling bogus loads to guys we know. This guy wants me to smack you idiots.

Now I have to give him back $1,000 and it's coming out of your asses. Can't you find any suckers who aren't people we know. Goddammit, you gotta have some professional courtesy and know who you're dealin' with. Someday, you're gonna come back from one of these deals dead. And I won't be able to help you."

We were kids who thought anyone was fair game, especially guys who were crooks themselves. Who knew we had to be honest with dishonest people. Honor among thieves we found out later, was a big deal to mob guys.

The garbage wars of the late 1980s and early 1990s made me. Well, not made. I wasn't made, but was heading toward that mobster graduation day. I had done enough to make the upper level mob guys happy and I could tell they were grooming me for the next level. That promotion was what every want to-be worked for. All the hustling, errands, stealing, muscling and struggling were for one thing, to get a chance to be recognized and eventually "made" with the recommendation of another made guy.

I had been around sports and mob stuff all my life and now I had reached a fork between in the road between my two paths that was turning out to be a fuck in the road. I had been coaching for two years and we were building winners at Redemption, and at the same time I was having success with the garbage deals. We had crew up against other crews in a war for who would run the carting business in the Bronx and lower Westchester County and we were gaining ground and garbage each day.

The garbage wars went something like this.

We would pick an area where another carting company and the crew that owned it had customers and we would invade their territory. That meant putting our containers where the other guys had theirs. We would move their bins and replace them, or we would spray paint our company's color on the other guy's container and stick our decal on the side. It was like a game, but the game sometimes turned nasty.

One of our guys was caught doing some work on one of the other crew's containers and the shooting started. Bullets were flying all over the place and he called us to come and help him. A bunch of us got in a car and went down to the north Bronx neighborhood about 10 minutes away where the problem had started and found ourselves in a shooting gallery. I got clipped in the leg and my cousin got hit in the side before the shooting stopped and their guys took off. No one was killed, but we made our point and they backed off. A week later, some of the top guys met and settled the beef. We got control of the area and I was another step closer to the next level.

Being the devoted coach I was, I got patched up at the local emergency room and got to Redemption to coach my basketball game the next day. The wound was more of a surface cut, more of a burn than a hole because the bullet got slowed down by hitting a large container before it hit me. But I was limping noticeably and every time I walked past one of the kids he would ask me what happened.

"I tripped on a basketball and fell on my ass," I told one player, hoping he would leave it at that.

"I slipped on a patch of ice in the parking lot and sprained my ankle," I told another player, thinking they wouldn't pursue the interrogation if I made light of it.

But my kids couldn't or wouldn't ever let an opportunity to rag someone, even a coach, get away anything that easily.

"C'mon coach," Sean said. "You know you hurt yourself getting out of bed, because you're so old that you can't see in the morning and you fell over your cat. You're like that old lady in the television commercial who says. "I've fallen and I can't get up." Or did you have a late date and when you tried to get some, the babe kicked you in the balls?"

After five minutes of stupid questions and wiseass remarks, I replied again, this time with a story they might listen to.

"I got shot, okay? You wanna see the bullet hole?" I whispered faking a look around so no one but the team could hear me. Me and some of my friends were out hijacking a truck at the airport last night and I took one in the leg when the security guards spotted us. Too bad we had to kill the poor fuck. And that's what's going to happen to you if you flunk out of school and can't find a job. You'll grow up to be felons who steal at night and have to coach asshole kids at a dump like this during the day."

Sometimes the truth is so unbelievable that it works better than a lie. The kids looked at me, looked at each other in kind of a "is he bullshitting us?" look, and then they smiled, and then laughed. I still don't know whether they believed all or part of the story or just chalked it up to, "Hey, Coach is crazy," like they did most of the whacky things they saw or heard me do.

Anyway, they dropped it and never asked me about it again. The leg got better in a few days and it was forgotten. I think the rumor did get around the school that I had been shot though, because I caught some of the students and few of the teachers looking at me funny when I limped down the hall. Their eyes would go to my leg, back to my face and then they'd look away. I guess it made a good story and fed the fantasy some of the Redemption people had that Coach V had a mysterious other life.

But as time went on over my four years at Redemption, I found it more and more difficult to keep my stories and my appointments straight. My business activities would often collide with my practice and game schedules. If I had something run long at the Javits Center, I would have to call ahead and ask one of my assistant coaches to get the kids to a game where I would meet them instead of me running to the school and then with the team to the Bronx or Manhattan. Sometimes I would miss a practice completely and I'd hear about it the next day from the AD or a parent.

The kids and coaches didn't mind, but the school administration and the parents started getting concerned late in my fourth year when I was late for several games. I didn't enjoy my other "job" much anymore either. The game of crime wasn't as exciting or fulfilling as the coaching, and as time went on, I began fanaticizing about what it would be like to "resign" from my mob activities and become a full-time coach. The thrill of the "big score" that I remember having as a young guy coming up was almost completely gone by my second year at Redemption. I got a bigger thrill out of helping a kid become a better player or finding a way to beat a team we shouldn't beat. Planning a game was much more satisfying than planning a heist.

In planning a heist, 90 percent of the thrill was when you came up with a good idea for making the score, but you were always afraid someone would rip you off for the scheme and do it before you could. But when you did have a good deal you almost always had to tell the guys on top, the captain, who would give the okay. Sometimes you just did the job and turned over the score. Most times, when you were an up-and-coming guy like me, they kicked back down a portion of the money or some of the product you hustled.

One summer, when I was still in the entry level of my gangster career, a guy I knew from the old neighborhood who was a night watchman at Woodlawn Cemetery in the north Bronx, told me about some expensive stain glass windows they were bringing in for the new mausoleums they were building. When it came to crime, anything could be stolen, cars, trucks, earth movers, even small airplanes would disappear at Newark Airport. The bigger the object, the bigger the score, unless of course it was gems or money or drugs. Good things can come in small packages.

Well, this watchman saw a chance to make a few hundred dollars by taking a short nap in his security car while someone, me and some friends of ours, quietly removed the new stain glass windows, imported from Italy from the site where they were going to be placed in the mausoleum. I was psyched for this. Stain glass could be worth thousands and it could be resold in sections or as a whole.

So, I told my guy Ronny, who told Tony "Cigar" Paterno, the big boss. Paterno like the idea of the valuable glass being available and gave the okay. But the watchman said he was going to be away for a week, so we had to wait until he got back. I was okay with that and while I waited, guys started talking about the job.

"Hey, Tommy V is gonna get some kind of imported glass that's worth thousands," Johnny Mack told a couple of guys who were playing pool at the Capri Club, a social club in the Bronx where the crew hung out. "It's at some cemetery in the Bronx."

I was not happy to hear guys talking about the score because it hadn't happened yet and I didn't want it to go wrong. It could have been that Cigar mentioned the job and it got out that way. But I was sweating because now I had to make this thing work. Just as I was ready to leave the club I heard Cigar yapping in his back room office.

"What?! What?!" he said with that rough, high-pitched voice we were always afraid to hear, the voice that snuck out from his lips which were always locked around a cigar right in the corner of his mouth. "Where's he gonna get it? Where's the glass? In a cemetery? Fuckin' kid!"

"Oh Shit," I said as I walked around the pool tables to get a closer look at the back office. "Cigar is pissed about something."

"Get the kid, get Tommy," Cigar yelled.

I strolled into his office, which was filled with pictures

of Cigar with people like Frank Sinatra, Jerry Vale, Sammy Davis Jr. and a other celebrities, all surrounding a big picture, you know the one, of Jesus, with that sad look on his face, just about ready to die on the cross. That picture was the centerpiece of Cigar's neat office, just behind his big chair and desk. It was like Jesus was the founder of the company and Cigar was the CEO. The picture always struck me funny being there. Sinatra and the others looked at home, but Jesus looked out of place. He looked like he was not happy being on Cigar's wall. Not happy at all.

And Cigar was not happy either. He jumped up and leaned over his desk to talk to me. His cigar was just a stump now and the tobacco juice was leaking out from the corner of his mouth. He looked like Edward G. Robinson on crack. Yeah!

"What the fuck is wrong with you Tommy?!" he yelled. "Where are you getting this stained glass from?"

"It's a new shipment to Woodlawn Cemetery, Cigar," I answered in my most authoritative voice. "An easy deal. We just go in, stroll past the watchman who's our guy and pinch the glass. There's maybe four of five sections of glass worth $10,000 each. There's no problem."

"No problem!" Cigar said as he climbed onto the front of his desk and practically came out of his shoes. "No problem? It's a cemetery you fuckin' mope. It's sacrilegious to steal from a cemetery. What's next? Are we gonna go into the church and take the basket after they pass it out at Sunday Mass? Are you fuckin' crazy?"

"No Cigar, I just thought...." I said as I felt myself backing up. "No good?"

"What do you want to do, get me sent to hell, you fuck?" Cigar yelled. "We're religious people. We don't steal from God. What is our fuckin' thing coming to when we got kids who want to steal from a cemetery? No, no, no!"

"I'm sorry Cigar; you want me to get the stuff before

they take it off the truck, maybe on the road?" I asked trying to figure out a solution to this unexpected surge of religious fervor from the Bronx's top mobster.

"I'll kill ya Tommy, ya fuck!" Cigar yelled back. "No stain glass, no stain glass. I'm not gonna ever have one piece of heisted stain glass with a picture of Virgin Mother or the baby Jesus on it on my head. "Forget it. And next time you have a fuckin' great idea make sure it don't include nothing that can get us tossed into hell. Get the fuck outta here."

I was glad to get out of there with my life. Cigar forgot the incident the next day and smacked me on the back when I did a nice job straightening out some problems at the parking garages the next week. He even gave me an extra $500 just for cleaning up a problem with a guy who owed him money. He wasn't a bad guy. He was just an old murderer with odd morals.

But it always surprised me when mob guys would talk about God and church like they were saints or something. They would talk about respecting family and God one minute, and then lie, cheat and steal the next minute.

Some of these wise guys, including Cigar and guys he came up with, would whack a guy on Saturday night, chop him up into meat-market pieces over pizza, then spread the pieces around the New York metropolitan area salvage yards or swamps. Then they'd go to breakfast at a local diner and right over to 10 o'clock Mass on Sunday morning.

Those Hail Marys and the Our Fathers must have been tough to say just hours after sending some guy to hell without a chance to do an act of contrition or even utter a prayer. But these guys were able to get the words out, genuflect and walk out into the Sunday morning air without flinching.

Fuckin' unbelievable.

Was I capable of being like that? Could I ever be like that? I never wanted to find out, so I stayed away from the whacking side of the business. There were enough guys out on the street who would do those jobs but I wasn't one of them.

CHAPTER 11

I said, Lord be merciful unto me: heal my soul for I have sinned against thee. Psalms 41:4

Dr. Brendan Levine knows more about me than anyone alive, but if it weren't for doctor-patient trust that protects both of us he might wish he didn't. Doc has been my primary physician for about 11 years, dating back to the months leading up to my second divorce.

I'd always been a hothead, a character trait that came in handy in business—especially when someone needed to be straightened out. I could handle myself with my fists and did some bouncing in clubs and enforcing when sharks wanted their loans called in. But at the age of 30, with a young daughter and a five-year marriage on the rocks, I began experiencing panic attacks and fits of rage.

After years of drinking, doing whatever drugs were available to party with, and generally abusing my body, I could feel something was wrong. Even the slightest stress made my heart feel like it was pumping out of my chest, although when I played ball I could still run and play the field. I did what most guys do then they reach their middle 30s and feel fat: I started to exercise, work out at Bally's. You know, try to get in shape. I seemed to be getting stronger, but I couldn't beat the feeling of weakness that came over me when I was under any kind of pressure.

I told Dr. Levine about what I was feeling and he administered a bunch of stress and blood tests. The initial diagnosis was high blood pressure from anxiety and stress. Drugs followed, and Valium became my most helpful crutch. I took the prescribed dosage, and when I felt pressure rising up from my stomach to my chest, or when I had an argument with my wife, I just popped another Valium. Running to a big basketball game? Pop, a Valium. Problems with a collection or a guy who was outta line? Pop, pop, two Valium. A fight at home? Pop, pop, pop, three Valium. It got so I made my own mental chart. Small hassle: 1 pill. Medium sized problem, 2 pills. A big problem, 3 pills.

I've learned since that more than one mobster found his anonymous way into therapy. Why not? In prison they stick you with a shrink first thing; someone to help you figure out what motivates antisocial or violent behavior. The sessions get the inmate out of the daily grind of prison life and can help a guy learn to deal with someone besides his fellow criminals. Once a guy is released, he might look for help with personal problems. But unlike "The Sopranos," I don't think many mobsters gave their Dr. Melfi details about their crime connections and affiliations.

The one or two times I was held over in Bronx County Jail—twice for drug possession with intent to sell and another time for an assault on a guy who was mouthing off in a club we hung out at—I had a few sessions with the psychologist. You got free coffee and donuts if you went to the group therapy sessions, so I was in. The doctor asked about anger, childhood trauma, feelings of rejection and fear—things I thought everyone had.

"What are some of the things that make you angry,

132

Tom?" he asked me one afternoon.

I looked up from my glazed donut and saw 12 pairs of eyes looking at me; eyes that showed pain, loneliness, fear, and anger. I didn't feel very comfortable answering. "I get angry when I see something that's helpless getting hurt, like an animal," I said without thinking. "And when people try to make me out to be a fool, that really pisses me off. If I see someone trying to bullshit me, I can explode. I've smacked guys for things like that. Cutting me off while I'm driving and then flipping the middle finger at me. That shit makes me crazy."

"Why do you think that bothers you so much, a stranger disrespecting you?" the Doc asked. "Who cares if someone you don't even know says or does something stupid?"

"I care," I said in a quiet tone. "I fuckin' hate people who try to get over on me or think they can play that shit and get away with it. I don't know why; it just pisses me off."

Later, Dr. Levine tried to make me to understand that my reaction to insults or disrespect from strangers came from my distant relationship with my father, who never seemed to approve of anything I did. Doc said that down deep all I wanted was for people to like me, but because I experienced insecurity with my father's love, I lashed out when someone showed disrespect or tried to belittle me.

"Your anger comes from the fact that you felt unloved as a child," Levine said during one afternoon session after I related how I blew up at my wife when she called me a "jealous idiot." She had been talking to a guy in the neighborhood, standing on the corner and flirting. I didn't know why, but it reminded me of how my father would talk to women and flirt, and then come home and abuse me, my mother, and my sister, calling us names. Seeing my wife flirting with another guy really hurt, so I confronted her and made her come home with me. When we got back to our apartment, I slapped her and told her she was disrespectful. She called me a "jealous idiot," which made me even madder.

My anger always seemed to surface in my personal life, never on the field or at work. I found out early in my mob career that I wasn't a guy who could beat the shit out of somebody and enjoy it. I wasn't the antisocial type who could whack someone, cut them up, and then go out to dinner or a ball game. I had to collect, enforce, and sometimes beat up people, but I never liked doing it. I was like a soldier who went to war because he felt obligated to defend his country; a guy who preferred peace, but could do damage if called upon. I think the difference between me and the hit man types was that I cherished life. Even when I was down I had that little spark—the spark that came from childhood baseball games when you just enjoyed being alive and running and playing. I could still recall the innocence of childhood; not much, but enough for me to pity an injured animal and have mercy on a guy I had to beat the shit out of. I didn't trust or like most people, but I knew enough pretty good people to believe not everyone was a fuckin' deviant mobster, rat bastard, or cutthroat cheatin', lying fuck. However, when I was drinking, that little empathy I possessed would disappear. I could be dangerous when I was out of control.

After one such drinking binge with friends during my late teens, I first experienced what turned out to be a panic attack, although I didn't know it at the time. Uncle Mario asked me to pick up some money from a fellow named Pinkie, a small-time bookie who owed us about $500, plus the interest, which was $50 a week for three weeks. I spotted Pinkie in a park near my apartment building and waved at him. I was still hung over from the night before.

"Hey Tommy," Pinkie said as he crossed the street to meet me. A short Irishman with long hair wrapped in a pony tail, Pinkie wasn't the kind of guy who'd fight, even if you owed him money. He always employed a slugger, or collector, to get his money. Pinkie wouldn't hurt a fly; he preferred to talk himself out of trouble.

"Pinkie, what the fuck?" I said. "You owe my Uncle Mario five hundred bucks and the fifty dollar vig, three times. What are you doin' shirkin'?"

"Nah, Tommy, I'm just short right now," Pinkie said. "Give me a break, will ya?"

"It's not me, Pinkie," I answered. "My uncle's tired of waiting. You said two weeks and it's been three and you didn't pay the vig. Let's go. I'm not in the mood to hassle with this."

"Ah, Tommy, you cranky fuck!"

Before he could complete the c-k sound in the word f-u-c-k, I reacted to a sudden urge of panic. It was like when he started the word "fuck" I was being squeezed into a small, dark closet with no air. Even though it was a perfect sunny day in the Bronx, I suddenly felt trapped. I don't know what happened. I kind of blacked out, unable to breathe. But when I opened my eyes, there was Pinkie, lying on the sidewalk with a broken nose and his head leaking blood and me right next to him, like someone had knocked me out.

"Hey, what's going on," a voice said.

I looked up and saw a city bus driver and four other people looking down at me and Pinkie.

"Did you guys get hit by a car?" the bus driver asked.

"No, I got hit by him," Pinkie said. "And I don't know what the fuck happened to him. He just fainted."

I was embarrassed and confused. It seemed I'd bashed Pinkie a few times without any warning, and then just toppled over.

"I fell," I said to the crowd as I got up, not really knowing I'd passed out. "We were fighting and I fell. Get the fuck away from me, all of you. I'm all right."

"Here Tommy, take this $200 and leave me alone,

135

will ya," Pinkie said as he held a bloody handkerchief over his nose. "I'll get the rest to Mario tomorrow. You're crazy, man."

Without confessing any mob-related sins, I told Dr. Levine about the origins of my panic attacks, the constant nightmares, arguments with my wife, and my anger problems. I just told the doc that I had conflict about career-related things and needed to resolve my anger issues. He helped me with my medications—at least I thought it was help—and he was a good listener.

I always covered up a lot of fear and insecurity by justifying them as "pressure" at work. I don't recall being consciously afraid of anything after the age of ten. As a kid, I had typical fears about the boogeyman, someone breaking into to the house and killing me in my sleep, and Russia dropping a nuclear bomb on the Bronx. We used to hear those air raid drill sirens on Saturday afternoons in 1962, during the time of the Russian missile crisis. We had air raid drills in school, where we heard the siren or bell and had to duck under our desks and cover our heads with our hands. For a five- or six-year-old kid, that seemed like a good way to defend ourselves. The teacher would say, "If you jump under your desk, put your hands over your head, and don't look out the window, then the atomic bomb can't kill you," Sure! Then we'd all troop downstairs to the bomb shelter in the school basement until we heard the all clear. No problem. We were all so scared of Russia and the threat of atomic bombs that after awhile we accepted the fact World War III was coming. The Communist threat, and air raid drills, and talk of a nuclear holocaust became so common to us that we learned to forget about the bomb and worry about more intimate threats—like Fat Vinny Altamori, the biggest kid in the neighborhood, who could cause a guy more damage than any imaginary atomic bomb. Whether you hid under a desk or put you hands over your head, Fat Vinny was a real threat. I feared him for sure.

136

Fear is like the color of your eyes and skin, you height, weight, blood type and other genetic characteristics. You don't get to pick what you look like or what fears you will host. They just come to you at different times of your life from out of nowhere, like a bad dream that wakes you up screaming and sweating. And when you go back to sleep, it returns—again and again, until morning. When we're young, we understand our fears a little better because they're simple. You get a beatin' by your father; you fear the belt. You almost drown in the Bronx Zoo Lake trying to catch one of those big white swans with your stupid friends; you fear the water. You get smacked by Fat Vinny on 187th Street; you stay away from 187th Street. Your grandma dies in front of you and your brother dies in Vietnam; you fear death and God. But, by the time you're 15 or 16, your rational and maturing mind allows you to go swimming in deep water, even at Orchard Beach, and you get bigger than Fat Vinny and beat the shit out of him, and your father has to look up at you, so the thought of him whipping out his belt doesn't have the same effect.

At the same time I was getting past those childhood fears, I began having periods of insecurity that started with just an uncomfortable feeling and grew to episodes of near panic, for no apparent reason. My ability to ignore pain, fear, and even my own deep feelings came with a price—panic. During these anxiety attacks I couldn't breathe, with deep pain right in the middle of my chest, right around the heart. As Dr. Levine explained it: "A panic attack is a sudden surge of overwhelming fear that comes without warning and without obvious reason. It's far more intense than the feeling of being stressed most people experience during difficult times."

The first time it happened I was on my way to a Sunday morning softball game in the summer of 1985. I'd just grabbed a cup of coffee at the local Dunkin' Donuts and parked my car in the lot near the field where we played our league games. Before I could dial the radio to WFAN sports talk and get set to read the Daily News, it hit. First I felt warm, then hot, and then I started having trouble breathing, like someone had taken a hose and sucked all the oxygen out of the car. I opened the windows, all four, and tried to catch my breath. Nothing. Then the fear hit me. I was going to die from a heart attack or respiratory failure right there, with my softball uniform on, in my car on a Sunday morning with no one around. A 35-year-old former athlete with no real health problems, I would die from some kind of attack that I didn't understand. I started thinking about my daughter, my mother, my life, all the things I'd done wrong, and all my failures. I was sweating so bad my hands slipped off the steering wheel I was clutching with in both hands. Then, just as fast as it hit, the attack disappeared, like someone had let the air out of a balloon, I started breathing again and the chest pains lessened. When I opened my eyes, three or four of my teammates were looking through the windows, wondering what the hell I was doing. I guess they thought I'd fallen asleep.

"Hey, V, what the fuck?" our shortstop Joey Bastone said as he reached through the driver's side window to grab my arm. "You look like you seen a ghost. What's up?"

"V, are you all right," our pitcher Lefty Resigno asked as he jumped into the front seat. "You scared the shit out of us. We were calling you and you didn't answer. Want to go to the hospital or something

"I don't know what happened," I answered, grabbing at my chest. "I just had trouble breathing and got all sweaty. Maybe I'm drinking too much coffee. I think I'm okay. Just give me a minute and I'll come over to the field."

The guys left me alone and I took a long drink of water before climbing out of the car to get some air. Within a few minutes I felt fine. The attack seemed like a bad dream, when you think you're dying in a dark and lonely place or drowning in a cold ocean and all of

138

sudden you're awake and okay in your own bed.

It took five visits to the doctor and a load of tests for them to tell me I'd experienced a panic attack or stress-related trauma. My crazy mixed-up life had finally caught up to me, and every fear and anxiety I had been able to bottle up since childhood was manifesting itself in a way I never expected. I spent the next 10 years trying to stay one step ahead of those attacks that would come with no warning and for no apparent reason.

Dr. Levine's answer to the panic attacks was Valium, which became an alternative to panic and as familiar as a breath mint to me. If I couldn't feel it, it couldn't hurt me. And Valium is good for taking away your feelings.

CHAPTER 12

I will say to God my rock, why hast thou forgotten me? Why go I mourning because of the oppression of my enemy? Psalms 42:9

The guy just wouldn't shut up.

He started ragging my players from the opening tip and by halftime I wanted to go into the stands, tear off his rat-bastard head off and flip it to the referee, who was no better because he wouldn't stop the guy.

"White trash, Yonkers trash! Retards!" This punk kept it up like one of those drunken Yankee bleacher bums who'd never stop ragging, before they stopped selling beer out there at the Stadium. Even the other fans were getting sick of this guy.

Redemption teams got little or no respect from anyone as far as I could see. We would travel to an opponent's gym—some of the smaller ones were like cages—and have to put up with wise ass kids and asshole parents degrading our players. I guess they looked at us as the bottom of the CHSL barrel. Or maybe they didn't like the mix of street kids we had. Some of these schools were elite parochial schools where the kids

140

thought of Yonkers as a ghetto of failures whether you were black, white or in between.

But we would get respect, one way or another. I wouldn't let my kids be treated like shit. We always acted with class. I expected that much at all times on and off the court, on and off the field. But there were times when enough was too much. And even I had to control myself, to be a lesson in dignity for my kids, the refs, the fans and anyone else who were there.

It so happened Lorusso, the sports writer, was covering at the game. He didn't cover all the games in person and usually I'd have to call in the score and give him some info on our games. I didn't like calling in, so I was always glad to see the guy. Except this time, when I ran out of patience.

"Hey ref, what are you deaf?" I yelled. "Tell that guy up there if he doesn't shut up I'm going to come up there, rip off his head and pull out whatever brain he might have left."

"Okay coach, cut it out," the little Irish ref said.

That ref never liked me. I guess he envied my clothes or haircut or manicures; he was probably a retired teacher who counted every penny of the fifty bucks he got to do a game. He never gave my kids a break or a call, always chatting and bull-shitting with the big school coaches and telling me to stay off the court when I wanted to yell instructions. He was a real idiot, the kind of guy I would smack in the head and leave sprawled on the sidewalk if he were working in my business.

But this was Catholic school sports, and I respected the games and the people involved. I never got a technical foul called on me in three years on the sideline and never got tossed from a baseball game after three years in the dugout. I could deal with almost any problem between the lines or with people in the gym.

But this time I'd had it.

My Italian blood was boiling like a pot of my mother's pasta sauce with the lid on. After a couple of pleas to the refs and a few cold-blooded stares at the home crowd and that rat-bastard fan, I was done.

"Stevie Wonder could see what this guy's doin' and you're running up and down like a weak sister, ref," I yelled. "Tell that guy to shut up, get out, or face me."

I wasn't going to do anything to the guy. I didn't need the publicity or a trip to the can for assault. But I wanted to make a point that we weren't going to visit a school and be embarrassed or intimidated.

"That's a T!" the little idiot ref said as he whistled my first technical foul.

As long as I had one, I figured I might as well make it two and get ejected before I killed somebody.

"If that guy was talkin' about your mother, you'd do something, right ref?" I said.

Before I could turn around and sit down, the whistle blew and Irish ref's fat, freckled face was in mine. His neck was red, his belly was extended about a foot, and his red-hair comb-over fell over the side of his face.

"You're gone, Vitale," he yelled. "Go for a walk!"

The gym was as quiet as a funeral home where an unpopular guy is laid out and no one shows up visit. All you could hear was one of my players saying, "Coach is going to blow his cool, watch this." But I knew I couldn't do anything to hurt my team or my coaching rep. In a moment where I would have used violence or the threat of violence in my other world, I just had the amazing ability to stay calm. I could always stay calm on the field of play. I felt comfortable being there, no threats. Mob work came with a constant threat and always made me feel on edge. But sports, whether I was playing or coaching, presented such a great atmosphere that I would never do anything to spoil it.

So, I just took a deep breath and turned to my team."Beat these guys," I said. "I'll be watchin' and I know you can do it."

I walked right past that squat little asshole ref and headed across the gym with my Italian designer shoes making a distinct sound against the wooden floor as I strolled across the gym. The echo of my footsteps seemed to quiet the crowd—and the guy who was causing all the grief yelled, "Good-bye, coach!" in a nasty whiny voice.

I lifted both arms high over my head, flicked the middle finger of both hands, and sent a final message as I walked into the locker room. This was the first and last time my two lives—the coach and the mobster—nearly collided. I think I would have killed the guy if he'd been in front of me. I threw garbage cans, papers, chairs, anything I could find around that back office. Every few minutes I would compose myself and check out the game through the eight-inch square window in the door leading to the gym. I could imagine what people were thinking when they saw my big head, red with rage, staring through that window. I must have looked like a caged animal waiting for his raw meat. Back on the court, the Redemption fans in the stands had to be restrained from attacking the guy. When I saw that, I smiled. I knew he was done. I saw the fuckin' coward run out of the gym a few seconds later and disappear.

My team was a little shocked at first to see me lose my cool during a game, but they'd seen the veins on my neck bulge during long practices. After laughing a little and then huddling with my assistant coach Bobby, they got back to the game and pulled it out for me.

Lorusso wrote about my angry episode and it seemed like my reputation traveled. Refs got a little more respectful and we started getting some calls. Respect never comes easy, but we gained some with each dribble, each basket, each win.

On the baseball field it was a little different; we won a lot, and that brings instant respect. But we still had our days.

During one postseason playoff game later that school year, Jason Mendicino was pitching a great game against our rival Blessed Mary. The Crusaders were our toughest competition for a couple of years in both baseball and baseball. Because the kids from more affluent families, that anti-Yonkers prejudice would leak out once in a while.

It started in the third inning.

"Hey Jason," a parent yelled. "I hear your batting average is higher than your SAT scores."

Jason was a man among boys and this pin-point control was working that day. We were up 3-0 and the kid was hitting corners. He was a right-handed stud, big upper body, not tall, but big. He had legs like a football player and the back of a longshoreman. He was 9-0 or something like that and Blessed Mary couldn't touch him any time he pitched.

"Hey Redemption, you guys know you'll be working for our kids someday, right?" a lady yelled.

Yeah, it was a lady. Some fuckin' mother of one of their players or some other motherfuckin' fan actually yelled that. I couldn't believe it. I almost had the urge to go over to the crowd and start swinging a baseball bat. But out of the corner of my eye I saw Lorusso the reporter walk over to the group of fans and lean over the fence begin talking. He looked really upset and was waving his hands the way Italians do when they can't find all the words necessary to make a point. He later told me he threatened to quote their remarks in the paper if the taunting didn't stop and that he'd quit his job right there and start swinging himself if he heard another word.

It seems these people didn't have a subscription to the newspaper, or maybe didn't have the ability to read or just didn't care, but Lorusso's warning didn't stop them. They just kept it up, like a bunch of drunken sailors.

"Hey Jason, what's your probation officer's name?" a guy yelled and the crowd behind him laughed.

Now the Blessed Mary players and coaches were squirming a little because Jason was staring at their bench, back at the crowd, and then back at the bench. It looked like he was trying to find the face of a player that matched the face of the parent who was yelling.

Then it got real quiet.

In the bottom of the sixth inning, we played seven, up 3-0, no one on base, two outs, and Jason found his perfect moment for retribution. Jason turned away from the plate to look at center field, rubbed the ball in his meaty hands, smiled at the infielders, and turned to the crowd of hecklers. He took off his cap, tipped it to the crowd, and smiled. Then he turned to face the batter, the Blessed Mary catcher, the biggest kid on the team

Jason shook off the signs three times, and you could see the batter getting a little edgy. He wound up and in almost slow motion turned his hips, lifted his leg, and fired a pitch into the backstop about two feet above the kid's head.

"Ball!" the umpire called.

No one moved. Even our guys were a little scared. And the hecklers mumbled something about the pitch.

Jason just smiled.

The next pitch was closer; this time the batter had to jump a foot in the air to avoid being hit it the ankle.

"Ball two," the ump said.

I think that ump figured out what was going on, and being a Yonkers guy himself, he smiled behind his mask. He was going to let Jason take care of business. He was going to let those stupid-ass parents and fans learn a little lesson.

The next pitch was the biggest breaking curve ball I ever saw in high school ball. Jason's curve was usually sharp and cutting, but this one came from the third-base line and landed a foot outside, curving over the batter's head. The poor kid dove backward against the backstop, slid down the fence, and landed on his fat ass in the dirt.

"Ohhhh!" my kids yelled as they jumped up off the bench. "Stay in there, batter!" someone yelled.

The batter, to his credit, dusted himself off and got back in the box.

"That's ball three," the ump said quietly. "Count is 3-0." The next three pitches were out of some kind of a baseball movie. Three pitches, exactly the same, in quick succession—each about 90 miles per hour, and Jason had never been clocked on a speed gun at more than 85. Now, in the sixth inning, after about 70 pitches and a thousands taunts, this kid was hitting the glove at 90.

"Strike 1, strike 2, strike 3, batters out!" I remember the umpire saying.

The batter never took the bat off his shoulder. He was expecting to get a pitch in his back, but Jason's retaliation was a mixture of fear and skill. Jason smiled after the third strike was called, but instead of walking back to our bench on the first base side of the field, he took a detour and walked slowly to where the Blessed May fans were seated in beach chairs.

"Nice day, huh," Jason told the group as he took a sip of one fan's bottle of water. "Not bad for a guy with a higher batting average than his SAT. Thanks for coming, thanks for the water, and have a nice day."

Where I come from, respect is a big thing with teenagers, and even bigger with adults. Respect meant knowing who you were, what your responsibilities were and keeping order. In the mob, there were bosses, captains and soldiers. And there were coaches, captains and players on a team. Respect meant being a good player and doing what the captain asked. You worked hard, played smart, and obeyed the coach and you might be a captain someday if you showed leadership abilities. I taught my kids to respect the game and the other team. I believed the opponent made you a better player by testing you. If he was better, respect him. Then would go out, get better, and beat him. Even when you whacked another team, you should do it with respect. Be a good winner and a classy loser. But other teams and coaches didn't always see it that way. There were way too many assholes who were glory hounds or front runners, chest-beaters when they won and excuse-makers when they lost. The fans, parents, and school kids who backed those teams were the worst. They didn't know how to enjoy the games and back their teams without disrespecting their opponents. I hated that shit. It was loser shit and we always wound up beating those kinds of teams because they had no heart.

We got ragged in almost every gym, especially after we won our first championship. And some of those Bronx baseball teams would have chants on their benches that would infuriate us, especially when they did it in Spanish. My kids weren't above some ragging of their own, and there were times when I thought we'd be brawling before the game ended.

We kept it cool, though—most of the time. Trey Walton was the only African-American player on our team for the four years I was at Redemption. We did have a 7-foot all-American transfer from Oak Hill Academy, the national powerhouse prep school who enrolled in the spring of 1995. But he had some attitude problems and an asshole street agent using him, so he moved on before I could straighten his ass out.

By the time he was a senior, Trey looked like a Greek god, cut and solid. With his shirt off, he looked more like a tight end than a basketball player. Trey grew as a player and a man more than any other kid I coached in basketball. He lived way down in the Bronx, so it took a lot for him to get to school in Yonkers and back home at night after practice. There were many nights when he'd be the last guy in the van after a game or after a practice, so it got to be sort of a ritual, me taking him home. Race was never an issue with me when it came to coaching, but we were brought up to stay separate from other races, and that meant some kind of prejudice was built in. When it came to sports, athletes never seemed to have a problem playing with all kinds of people. It wasn't a problem for me at all; I never had friends who were black or Hispanic, but I never had many friends who weren't Italian, period. Coaching Trey and getting

147

to know him was an education for both of us. The defining moment in Trey's basketball development came in a two-game span during his junior year.

Trey loved to dunk a basketball. What kid wouldn't if he could? Once he found out he could do it, the big guy didn't hesitate, in practice or in a game, to slam one down. One handed, two hand over his head, tomahawk, whatever. If he found some space over the rim, he was gonna jam it. I had no problem with the kid dunking, but I warned him about showboating and doing it in a game.

"Trey, you miss a dunk in a game and make us look stupid, I'm gonna break your legs so you can't ever dunk again," I'd say.

"Don't worry C-Coach," he said with that big smile. "I'm the man. I'm the king. I ain't gonna miss."

Trey was like most teenagers; he listened, nodded, and then did whatever moved him. A great dunk made the girls quiver, the fans stand up and rock the house. and the opposing players respect you, so it was too tempting a prize for the kid who had the ability to pull off all those factions in a single, ferocious motion.

We were down by a point with two minutes to play in a game against Scanlan, a team we should have beaten. Trey got his opportunity to make the ESPN "Play of the Day" tape and he embraced the moment. Joey hit the big guy with a nice pass moving toward the basket between two defenders and Trey rose up, reached back extending his right arm full length, and slammed the ball toward the basket. The problem was, the ball didn't cooperate. It hit the front of the rim, rebounded about 10 feet above the basket, and came down in the hands of a Scanlan player. I nearly jumped out on the court and strangled the kid.

"Trey, what did I tell you?" I barked at him after calling a timeout."You wanna look good and pose out there? Sit on the bench and think about it. You might have blown the game because you want to showboat. Sit your ass down!"

We recovered and beat Scanlan, but Trey was really shaken by the public humiliation of missing the dunk, followed by the further humiliation of me reaming him out. But Trey was a better player for it. He learned when and where to do things on the court and concentrated more on rebounding, playing defense, and thinking about what he could do to make the team better.

There's was one incident when Trey reached his limit. This kid was easy going and always smiling, even during a ferocious game. We'd just beaten Bishop Foley, a team from the Bronx, and Trey had been in a game-long beef with one of their players. After the game, while we were leaving the floor and going out to locker room, Trey ran up the corridor where the teams dressed, ripped off his shirt, and stood in front of the Foley locker room calling out the whole team. He stood there flexing his arms and beating his chest, saying, "C'mon dogs, let's go!" None of the Foley players would take the invitation, beating it back to their locker room. Everyone was screaming and yelling behind Trey, and when I saw the commotion I went nuts.

"What the fuck are you guys doin'?," I yelled, pushing my players back so I could get to Trey. "You wanna do something, you don't pose and stand there yelling at those fuckin' cowards after the game. You're in a game and you got a beef, do what you gotta do on the floor. We don't talk. We act. I want you guys to respect your opponents and I want them to respect us. But if they don't, you don't wait until after the game and make a big play with fans other people all over the place. You do your shit in the game. Be men. From now on, you got a beef; I don't want to see any bullshit like this. C'mon dogs? What is that?"

Trey looked embarrassed. He knew I was talking directly to him and he was a little scared and a stunned that I was screaming at him. He put on his shirt and led the team back to our locker room. I was always proud when my kids demanded the respect they deserved, but I didn't want them to start mixing the stuff they saw on the street with what they did on the court. We earned respect over my four years at Redemption and it came from the way we worked, the way we prepared, the way we competed, and the way we won, with class. We weren't gangsters "handling our business" by brawling with the opposing teams. We handled our business like men and earned everything we got.

Right before Trey graduated in 1996, he called me over one day after school to tell me he wanted to thank me for what I'd done for him. "Hey coach," he said, "I'm going to remember all the stuff you taught me when I go to Vermont next year. You know, about respect and competition and having class when I play. And I'll also remember you took the time to take me home after games and talk to me about different things. You and me aren't a lot alike, but you're all right for a crazy, white Italian dude. I'll come back and watch you coach, okay?"

"Okay, big man," I said. "And make sure you find some brothers up there to keep you company. I won't be there to watch your back."

CHAPTER 13

Know ye not that they which run in a race run all, but one receiveth the prize. So, run that ye may obtain.
Corinthians 9:24

Hoosiers we weren't.

But Redemption's Catholic High Schools Association state basketball championship was just as much as miracle as the championship won by the tiny Milan, Indiana basketball team that beat larger-school teams and inspired the Hoosiers movie.

Gene Hackman played the troubled coach that had screwed up his career by hitting one of his college players and was looking for another chance to do what he loved. The small out-of-the-way Indiana school gave him a chance and he made the most of it.

I could relate.

Maybe it was fate, or luck, or a combination of both, but when we loaded our school van and headed for the campus of Fordham University that frigid and windy Saturday morning in March 1995 to play for the Class C Catholic Schools title, our hopes were a lot bigger than our chances. The defending champions, Regency High

School, might just as well have been the Knicks. They were big, fast, and had two Division I prospects on the team. We were lucky if we could get one of our starting five a scholarship to a D-II college. We had no size, no rep, no bench and little or no hope.

But we had heart and balls and my kids were basketball smart, and like I always said, "Give me five guys with balls and brains and I can win against almost anyone. Well, almost anyone."

We'd been knocked out of the playoffs early in 1994 and it was a painful learning experience. The kids were so happy to have won a few games along the way that making it to the 1995 title game was gravy. We wanted to see if we could go another step and claim some hardware for the school showcase that boasted dozens of trophies from the 50s, 60s and 70s, but none in the last two decades.

The '93-'94 season taught us valuable lessons about preparation and concentration.

Our baseball teams were different in character than the basketball teams. Baseball players have to have some skill to play the game and we had a few guys who were pretty good. The rest of the team was made up of an assortment of types. Some were good athletes with limited experience playing upper level baseball but could use their athleticism to get things done and the others were just kids who had reached their full potential and just weren't very talented. I'd coached at all the lower levels and I had learned to "manufacture" a good team by using the skilled and unskilled in positions where they could be most effective. If a kid could play the field and wasn't a strong hitter, I'd get him to bunt, hit the ball to the opposite field and take pitches to work a walk. If a kid was a strong athlete but didn't have much experience hitting, I'd teach him to look for fastballs he could hit and stay away from off-speed or breaking balls. With a little magic, some smart maneuvering and four or five talented players, we produced wins. Unlike the

152

basketball teams, which I coached toward the playoffs without caring if we won all our games, the baseball team won a lot of regular-season games. We were 54-15 over my three full seasons as coach and didn't lose a playoff game winning three CHSB championships.

The 1994-95 Emeralds boys' varsity basketball team made it to the Class C final with a mediocre 12-10 record, a banged up center, a short bench and a lot of attitude. Sean, who played his ass off during the three-game playoff run, wrecked his right ankle and had to be taped from his big toe to his thigh just to get him out onto the floor. I thought about not playing him, but when I asked him if he was ready he gave me a look I'd seen at mob meetings when one wise guy was being screwed over and wanted satisfaction. That look that said, "Don't play me and you'll be sorry."

"Sean, you gonna be able to go?" I asked him just before I gave my last-minute locker room talk. "We can put Trey in the middle and keep you on the wing so you don't get banged around or you can sit and be ready in case we need you. What do ya think?"

"I think you should start your locker room talk, Coach," Sean said looking me directly in the eye. "I think if you try to play with me on the bench you might prove that you have more balls than brains. I think these guys expect me to be out there, no matter what. And I think it's time to stop thinking and start playing."

I didn't say a word, because it was obvious this kid was going to play whether I put him in the starting lineup or not, and I wasn't about to restrain him on the sideline. If he was ready to play, then that was the way it was going to be. I gave my pre-game talk, but it wasn't the typical hype job. We went over the two previous regular-season games against Regency, which we lost by 10 and 12 points, and then I told the kids that they were already winners and this game was a test to see whether they could be champions.

"You're a winner when you give it all you have and

lay your ass on the line for your team," I said. "You've already done that 20 times this year. This time, you're gonna have a chance to be a champion. That means you take everything you know, everything you want and everything you dreamed and focus it on one 32-minute climb to the top of the highest mountain you can imagine. You can't stop for water, food or rest. You have to push until the pain becomes part of the thrill of the climb. And if you get to that mountain top, you'll know that not all winners get to be champions. And no one will be able to take that feeling away."

The kids were looking right at me and believing every word. When we left that locker room for the Fordham University gym floor, I knew Sean and the rest of the guys were ready for more than just a basketball game. They were ready to prove themselves in front of their world and I knew that this basketball game was their chance to own something to be proud of for life.

We recited the Lord's Prayer and went to work.

I never went to the floor with my team for the pre-game warm-ups. I stayed in the locker room getting myself ready, going through the game plan, talking to my coaches, or just relaxing before I had to spend a couple of hours at the edge of my seat coaching focused like a cat stalking a bird. And I wanted my players to be responsible for themselves, with the captain, Sean, leading the warm-ups. I always arrived on the floor about five minutes before tip-off.

As I walked down the ramp to the Fordham gym floor, to my left, just behind our bench, I could see a row of guys in dark jackets, some with ties, looking at their playoff programs, eyeing the crowd and pointing to my players as they went through their warm-up drills. I recognized them immediately as Ronny's crew and some of their associates and I'm sure the other fans in their section, people dressed in Saturday morning sports-type outfits there to watch the four championship games, might also have noticed that this row of

154

characters seemed a little out of place. It wasn't that they were dressed so differently, it was just that they looked more like the cast of the "Goodfellas" than Catholic school sports followers. They had big heads, big arms, no necks, and Florida suntans in the middle of March. Two of the guys were holding unlit cigars and another had sunglasses on and was looking over the top of them to see the floor. The most amazing thing about their presence at the game was that it was before noon, when most of these guys would normally just be waking up. A night game I could see, but Saturday morning?

I tried to focus on the floor and not look directly at the guys with the idea of going straight to the bench, but that didn't work.

"Hey V," a voice boomed out in a typical across the street Bronx greeting. "How's it look?"

I turned and looked at the row and my eyes went directly to Ronny "The Kid," who sat at the end of the row of guys, like a captain or a row monitor making sure his boys behaved. Ronny smiled and gave me two thumbs up. I could see his pinky ring flash as he wiggled his hands.

I nodded. "Hey fellas! We're good. We're ready." I smiled, nodded my head again, and turned back to the team. I was a little shaken to see the guys at the game. A few of my gangster friends had come to games before and I would see one of two in the crowd at different tournaments, but never in such an obvious show of unity. It was like I was being "made" or like they were there to show they approved. I was actually proud that they would come. I think now that maybe they were all a little jealous that I had another life—something good and pure—a "thing" of my own. Maybe they all wished they could have found a place in life, even just for a short time, where they could be that person they were meant to be, instead of some aberration of human existence – predators, thieves, killers and committed to a life that led nowhere. Maybe they just wanted to share my sanctuary

155

for an afternoon, just like the millions of sports fans who go to games to watch athletes, wishing they could play children's games into their adulthood.

The game horn sounded signaling the start of the Class C title game and I snapped out of my momentary lapse into self-analysis to get my guys onto the floor. I hadn't noticed that the crowd was enormous, about four thousand people there to see the CHSA playoffs that included a game with St. Raymond's and Rice for the Class A title. St. Ray's was ranked N. 2 in the nation and Rice No. 3. Rice's top player was the legendary Felipe Lopez, who had made Sports Illustrated magazine and was headed to play at St. John's University. That game was slated for 4 p.m., but fans had to buy tickets to the earlier games to get in for all four. Part of the deal was to watch our small-school Class C game, which most people weren't that interested in. Most of the fans were milling around talking, going to the concession stands and going in and out of the gym to the rest rooms.

The Redemption fans, who were always there to support us, and the Regency fans, also known to be very loud and into their teams, made up about one tenth of the crowd and most were seated directly behind their respective benches. The other fans, most who had come to see the larger schools battle for championships, checked the scoreboard occasionally through the first half of our game but seemed to be waiting for the next game to begin. But the crowd's disinterest would turn to avid attention as the game moved into the second half and our underdog team stayed in the game against the top-ranked Regency kids. Sean's sprained ankle was my fault. I'd worked him hard in practice the week before the game, pushing his buttons after he dogged it on a flat-footed rebound attempt. I challenged him to work harder because these practices were important, telling him, "Sean, we're waiting for our leader to show some inspiration out there. What are you, tired or something?"

On the next rebound following my mini-tirade he

went up hard, as if to show me he was not slacking off. He snatched the rebound from a teammate, but when he landed he stepped on someone's foot. His ankle bent like a door hinge, buckling his leg and scaring the kid he stepped on. He recovered quickly and despite the slip and obvious pain he limped back on defense looking right at me with those steely, blue Irish eyes glaring. I felt terrible. During the warm-ups for the title game, the Regency players may have thought that Sean's limping around in warm-ups was part of some kind of hype and psyche-out, but he was really hurting. He could hardly get his sneaker on in the locker room. We taped the ankle and Sean shoved it down into his high tops, tightening the laces so the ankle wouldn't move too much. Mannion never asked out of any game during my three years with him. He was a tough son of a bitch.

But getting Little Sweet Pea ready for the game was more of a problem. After we won our semifinal game Tuesday of that week, I told the guys what the practice schedule for the upcoming week was and when we would be playing Regency for the title. When I said, "We meet here Saturday, March 13 at 9 a.m. for a team meeting and to pack the van with game time 1 p.m.," Joey turned white as a ghost.

"I can't play the game if it's on the 13th Coach," Sweet Pea said with a stare that made me believe he meant it. "No way." The little guy who never backed down from anyone in the street or on the court and had to be restrained when opposing teams played dirty, was scared shit of something, so scared that he didn't mind sharing his fear. "The 13th is my unlucky day," Joey began. "When I was little I was hit by a car on the 13th and my grandmother died on the 13th and I fail every test on the 13th and ...."

Joey went on and on for what seemed like 10 minutes, reciting episode after episode of unlucky days stories that all ended with "on the 13th." He got so worked up, I started to believe him. The rest of the team

157

started out laughing at Joey's list of 13th terrors, but soon felt his anguish and seemed stunned at the horrible coincidences he was detailing. I was about to tell the kid to stay home when he got tears in his eyes talking about his Grandma. But life is tough and then you die I always said. I knew we couldn't play the game, or win any kind of game for that matter, without Joey at the point. But I didn't want the kid to dread what should be the biggest day in his life and the lives of his teammates, so I told him to get some rest after practice and then went to work devising a plan to counteract Joey's fears and superstition.

I needed something that would get Joey to believe he could play and not have something fall on his head. At a planned point during the following day's practice I waited for Joey to make a good move and hit a nice shot and when he did I whistled the practice to stop and yelled at my nervous point guard, "Hey Joey, you hit that shot just when my watch hit on 3:13 I said. "That can't be bad luck."

Everyone on the team looked over at their floor leader and waited for a reply. But Joey just shrugged and went back to practice. Fifteen minutes later I did it again. I waited for the kid to make a nice pass and yelled, "Hey, Joey, that pass came right on 4:13. I thought 13 was bad luck." The kid started to get it. He started to realize what I was doing. He began to understand that the 13 he was worried about wasn't the only 13 on the calendar or on the clock. I think more than anything though, Joey realized I was concerned about him and really cared about his problem with a childhood fear he had never faced. After the fifth time I mentioned the time and his ability to beat the clock and the number 13, he kind of smiled and relaxed. He was focused and really in charge of the team over the next couple of days and when Saturday the 13th came, Sweet Pea was the first kid to arrive at the school parking lot at 8:55 a.m. "It's our day Coach," Joey said as he jogged up to the van. "We're gonna kick some ass today. It's a beautiful day for it, too. Start up this bus and point it to Fordham."

Playing at Fordham, just a few blocks from where I grew up on Arthur Avenue, was a dream come true. As a kid I used to sneak into the Fordham campus with my friends to play football on the plush grass of the Rams football field, so it was magical for the game to be there. I was home and we had a chance to win our first basketball title.

We stayed with Regency's big scorers by double-teaming the ball when it got anywhere near their two big guys. We played great defense as usual and Sean limped back and forth, making 12 to 15 foot jumpers and passing off to Trey and Nicky inside for easy baskets off the back door and pick-and-roll. We were up by three with four minutes remaining, so I put the offense into a weave. Three guys in a passing weave at the top of the circle, moving the ball while the clock ticked off second by second toward a win. There was no 35-second clock in the CHSA in 1995, so holding the ball and shortening the game wasn't unusual for an underdog team. The method helped a coach to deal with a more talented team, keeping the score down to give us an opportunity to win in the late stages. We milked the clock, stalled, moved the ball and took a 50-49 lead late in the game. When Regency finally realized time might be running out, they fouled us to get the ball back. But we had three months of intense free throw practice under our gym shorts and the fouls played right into our plan. We made 6 of 7 free throws, both ends of two 1-and-1 bonus chances because they were over the foul limit and in the penalty. They couldn't get good looks at the basket in the final two minutes and we held them off for a 56-52 victory.

The post-game locker room was filled with reporters from the New York newspapers, some who had never covered us before, and a couple of cable television teams jammed in to interview the kids from Yonkers who had upset the Regency team from Manhattan. I blew off a couple of reporters and waited for Lorusso to come over. It was like a superstition with me, to talk to Lorusso first because he was the only reporter that covered us when we sucked. Now that we were winning, I owed him the first interview and I always saved my best quotes for him. After a few minutes I saw Lorusso's bald head above the other people in the locker room and waved him over.

"Well, Coach, you gotta be a little surprised and really proud of the team," Lorusso said as he held out a hand to shake mine.

I grabbed the guy and hugged him with both arms and said, "We never thought of ourselves as underdogs Danny boy. We knew we could play with anyone in our class and now everyone will know who the Redemption Emeralds are."

"What was the biggest factor in the win Coach?" Lorusso asked as other reporters gathered around behind him to steal a quote.

"Heart and balls, Lorusso, heart and balls," I said pointing to my chest. "And you can quote me or edit me. It's still about heart and balls. These kids don't quit. They don't let me quit. I love 'em."

The next day I picked up all the New York newspapers to read the reports. The Daily News had a nice game story, so did the post and even the New York Times had a short piece following the reports on the bigger schools and how St. Raymond's had upset the high school phenomena of the year Felipe Lopez and his Rice High team. When I got to rack with the Yonkers Daily Herald, I had to blink to be sure what I was seeing wasn't a mirage. There, on the front page of the newspaper, filling most of the page, was a big picture of team celebrating, tinted in green for the Emeralds and a headline that read:"REDEMPTION SHOWS HEART", and in smaller letters in a sub-head,

"Emeralds upset Regency for Class C title."

I bought about 20 copies of that newspaper. I wanted to hand one out to every person on the block and read the headline like one of those old-time newsboys, "Extra, extra, Redemption wins championship!"

But that wasn't my style; I didn't even tell a soul on the street. A few guys who I knew from the neighborhood passed me on the street and said they had heard we won and congratulated me. But I acted as if it wasn't a big deal and just smiled. I got a cup of coffee and a bagel and I just sat there on Bronx River Road on a bench with Sunday traffic going by and held the newspaper, staring at that headline to be sure it wasn't a dream. It was like I had seen my own children do something heroic.

"Heart and balls," I said to myself with a smile. "Heart and balls."

Emeralds take Class C title

BRONX, N.Y. – Basketball fans from the New York City area gathered around press row to ask, "Where's Redemption High School from?" after the tiny school from Yonkers upset favored Regency High School of Manhattan 54-49 in the CHSA Class C championship game at Fordham University.   Trey Walton led the Emeralds with 18 points and 12 rebounds and Emeralds' captain Sean Mannion, visibly limping on a sprained ankle throughout the game, delivered 14 points, including four in the final minute of play. Redemption will play for the CHSA state title this coming Saturday in Schenectady.   "We wanted to prove that we were a championship team, not just a good team," Walton said. "To be the best, you have to beat the best. Now, we're the best in the area and we want to go the next step to the state title."   The Emeralds, who had 12-10 regular-season record before winning four straight

161

playoff games, led by six with four minutes remaining then put on a dribbling and passing clinic to keep the ball out of the hands of the Regency offense.

"I'm proud of the way the guys stayed in there against a strong team to win the title." Redemption coach Tommy Vitale said. "These kids stuck to the plan and overcame injuries to win. Winning here in my hometown of the Bronx was a big kick."

CHAPTER 14

In all these things we are more than conquerors through him that loved us. Romans 8:37

Winning isn't really important in high school sports until you get to the second season.

My baseball and basketball teams did okay during the six regular seasons I coached at Redemption, but my goal was to keep the kids doing their schoolwork and getting better as a team while preparing for the playoffs. Playoffs are the Nirvana of high school sports.

We worked all year for the playoffs. I didn't have the luxury of a deep bench in either sport, so my basketball players had to be in shape to play a full 32 minutes, and maybe more. My baseball teams weren't deep either, so I made sure I taught the basics to every kid just in case we lost a guy to injury. I taught them every trick I ever learned and made up some new ones just to be sure we were always prepared for anything.

My basketball practices were like Marine basic training, highlighted by the constant "suicides." Suicides are a coach's way of seeing how long and how fast a kid can run before he throws up. The team would line up on the base line at one end of the basketball court and sprint to the foul line and back, to the half court line and back, to the foul line across the court and back, then to the opposite end line and back. The suicides drill is torture. It burns your lungs, legs and arms at the same time, as the body screams for oxygen, but it gets you in shape to run for 32 minutes. They say. "What doesn't kill you makes you stronger". In our case, what didn't kill us, gave us a killer instinct.

Hard work makes you tough. And my kids were tougher than most.

We ran lay-up drills, rebound tap drills, weave drills and then finished up with some full-court sprints before diagramming and running through our plays. I could tell by how we practiced that first week of my first basketball season that we would be tough, if not talented. The kids had that inner-city edge, the ability to extend themselves to prove they could do it. That kind of arrogance that tells you, "I'm gonna do this to show that fuckin' coach that he can't beat me."

When I did encounter a "dog" or a "prima donna," players who didn't have a team-first attitude, they complied or they were gone. There was this one kid, Donny Garrigan, who was one of our best players and had his own little crew or two of three on the team who followed him like little puppies waiting for a bone. He could have been a strong team leader, but it was all about him and his game. No matter what I told him, he had another idea about what he wanted to do when he got out onto the floor. I put up with Garrigan's crap for a while because I thought he'd come around to my way of thinking, but he was stubborn. One afternoon at practice, the team was screwing up almost everything I had taught them the day before and Donny boy was the instigator. It was time to establish which of us was going to be top dog, which of us was going to run the team.

It was no contest.

"Hey Donny," I said, whistling the practice to a stop."Get your fuckin' stuff and get the hell out of my gym. You're not going to play my game, you're off the team."

The rest of the kids, many of whom had grown up playing with Donny on recreation and club teams where he was always the top player, stood there with their mouths open ands stared at me as if to say, "What are we gonna do without Donny? He's our best scorer. What the hell are you doing, Coach?"

Donny paused for second, looked at me like he was surprised, then just laughed and waved a hand in my direction like he thought I was bluffing, kidding or just trying to shake up the team. "Right, Coach! I've been here for three years and I'm not quitting. What's the big problem?"

"That's right," I said. "You're not quitting. You're fired. So, get your shit and your fuckin' sucky attitude, put them in your gym bag and get the fuck out." Donny may have been a jerk, but he did have enough street smarts to know I wasn't kidding. He packed up and walked toward the gym exit mumbling something about, "You'll see. You can't do this to me." Just as he got to the doors where he thought he was safe, he turned and said, "My father's gonna come and talk to you about this and I'll be back on the team tomorrow. You'll see."

Donny was a man of his word. His father came in just before practice was over the same day and asked if he could talk to me. The guy looked just like his son, rough Irish looking guy who was a plumber or electrician or something. He had a big smile on his face, like a politician trying to set someone up for a deal. But the smile didn't last long.

"Hey Coach, how's it going?" he said. "I'm Donny Garrigan's, Donny's father. I heard the kid messed up and you threw him out of the gym. What can we do to straighten it out? The kid wants to play."

"I'll tell you what you can do," I said, talking loud

enough so the team could hear me. "Tell your son to come back tomorrow, apologize to me and the team for being a selfish fuck and then maybe I'll take him back. He's a ball hog, a stupid player and a "Me" guy, which I won't have any of on my team."

Garrigan looked stunned and tried to recover some of his pride by standing up to me. "Hey, Coach," he said. "You just got here and maybe you don't know how it goes at Redemption. My kids all played here. I played here. It's our school and you can't just come in like you own the place and cut kids. It's not gonna happen. And you can't win without my son. He's the best player you got."

That was it.

Now I knew where the kid got his bad attitude. His father had been pampering him since he was a little CYO player and everyone had been bending over backwards for the kid along the way. This was the first time the Garrigans were faced with a real coach who wouldn't back down. "Hey, Garrigan," said, this time with more emphasis. "You tell your kid to come back and apologize like I said and I might let him back on the team. But you never tell me what I should do as a coach. No parent is going to dictate to me who is going to play and when. This is my team unless the school decides to fire me. So, let's get it straight right here."

Garrigan had more pride than brains. He refused to have little Donny Jr. apologize, so he took the kid out of school and enrolled him in another Catholic school over in New Rochelle. I had made a stand to save my team and it cost me my best player. But, there was never a problem with discipline after the Garrigan incident. We didn't win many games that first season, but we learned to play as a team and I know the other kids gained respect for me. It was about "team" after that. We also worked hard on team defense and team offense. Some basketball players think that because there's only one ball in the game, it should belong to one go-to guy who

166

is best suited to put the ball through the hoop.

I didn't have a Michael Jordan or Kobe Bryant to take over a game, and even if I did, that wasn't the way I thought you won games. I believed you played as a team and that would make you five times more effective than if one guy was slam-dunking the ball or blocking 25 shots.

Our practices were loud and the language we used couldn't be found anywhere in the Catholic or any other bible. There were a more than a few "assholes", "motherfuckers", "cocksuckers" and "fucking beautifuls" coming out of that gym each afternoon during basketball practice and on the practice field during baseball season. I'm not going to try to make excuses for my approach like I was using the language to motivate. Words like shit, fuck, asshole and cunt were part of my vocabulary, words that had effect and could accent a moment. While growing up, I heard the language of the streets in the streets and adopted it because I thought it worked.

Obscenity is used by mob guys all the time because the violence of the language is directly associated with the impending physical violence. It's no stereotype, the language you see in "Goodfellas" or "Casino." These guys, even the ones with some kind of education who could string together three- and four-syllable words, preferred the four-letter variety as a verbal warning that violence or retribution could be meted out as quickly as a "fuck you."

Not that every day included a brawl or a whacking, but we used the threat of violence to deter the need for violence. Just like when we were kids, the threat of your father beating you was more than enough to keep you honest. And I adapted to language of the streets like most kids do. I heard Italian spoken at home from my grandmother and aunts and uncles, but not enough to really learn it or use it. I heard English, or at least Bronx English, spoken in my home and at school, so that's the

167

primary language I spoke. When you're a little kid you may hear a curse now and then at home depending on the way your parents talk. You hear the language of the streets more in the schoolyard where kids seem to practice all sorts of sinful behavior just to see if they can get away with it, and you perfect the lingo as you grow toward being a teenager, when imitating grownups is the mark of complete rebellion. In my neighborhood, cursing helped to communicate anger, excitement, fear, happiness, almost any emotion in a few simple words, getting right to the point of the matter.

So, English was my first language and Fuckin' Cursin' was my second. Puerto Ricans down Southern Boulevard, Zips off the boat from Italy and Albanians who were moving into the neighborhood didn't need a translator to understand a good flow of curse words. The simplest of English language phrases received immediate translation in my brain on their way out of my mouth. I never said, "Look at that fool." It was, "What an asshole, motherfucker that guy is."

I never said, "Don't you owe me some money." It was "Where's my fuckin' money, you prick?"

I never said, "Look at that lovely young woman. It was, "What a nice piece of ass."

Yeah, my mother would slap me and tell me not to use language like that when women or priests or people I just met were in the room, but after a few years of working the two languages—one for regular people and one for "offended" people—I just gave up and used the language that worked everywhere. I even talked to my cat and dogs the same way.

"Lady, you fuckin', cunt cat, stop scratching the couch."

"Blackie, you rotten, motherfuckin' dog. You shit on the carpet, you fuck."

One afternoon at Redemption, my hoop practice got so loud that one of the brothers in the rectory next door came into the gym and asked to speak to me. He was a

168

very meek and intelligent kind of guy who taught religion and English. A nice guy I guess, but a little bit of a pussy, not like some of those older Irish and Italian priests who were hard asses, who took a drink or two everyday and smoked cigars and did, well, whatever else priests do in the privacy of their rectory.

So, I was surprised Brother Dominick wanted to talk to me. I walked over to where he was standing and said hello.

"What's up Brother Dominick, I said my nicest Catholic school voice. How's your love life?"

The young priest didn't seem to like my attempt at humor, so I recovered quickly and said, "How can I help you?"

"Coach, I hate to bother you during practice, and by the way, the team is really doing well and making us all proud. But we can hear you screaming up in the rectory, in the sanctuary and across the street at the elementary school. It sounds like a bar brawl in here and even though we understand that you need to yell a bit, could you possibly watch your language a bit and keep the yelling to a minimum?"

"Sure Brother Dominick," I said. "I didn't realize we could be heard in the rectory, the sanctuary and next door at the elementary school. I'm just trying to get these fuckin' hardheads....., excuse me, stubborn gentlemen, to get these drills right. We have a playoff game Tuesday and we have to be ready. We look like shit... I'm sorry; we look very disorganized right now. We'll keep the fuckin' noise; I mean the level of noise, down. Sorry."

"Thank you Coach," Brother Dominick said in that quiet voice he had. "If Monsignor has people from the parish come in and complain, we'll have a problem and I don't want to be the one responsible. In the future, try to use some more appropriate language when instructing the boys instead of talking like a fucking longshoreman, okay?"

My jaw dropped.

Brother Dominick just smiled, turned, and walked away.

My basketball and baseball practices were producing more and more wins on the baseball field, where we didn't have as much competition as we did in basketball. We won the Catholic Schools Class C baseball title in 1993, 1994 and 1995, rolling over the smaller school league. With pitchers like Jason Mendicino and Ricky Lopez, all we had to do was score a few runs, play decent defense and depend on the arms we had.

We beat Scanlan for the title in 93 and again in 94 and then Blessed Mary for our three-peat in 95. Baseball was my real love and teaching the game was another thing that came easy to me. For some reason I had good intuition about people, seeing things about them from their body language and the way the moved. It was a good gift to have in my business, being able to tell things about people. I could almost always judge if a person was a cop, a wise guy, an easy mark or a guy too tough to mess with.

Athletes have a way of showing how they feel and how they are going to perform. You can see it when a pitcher is moving around the mound, whether he's feeling good about his stuff. And you can tell when a batter is uneasy in the batter's box, when he doesn't think he can hit a certain pitcher. All those things are subtle and you learn to translate them over time. Mechanically, there are lots of things that reveal what a person is like. Confident people walk a certain way, like they know where they're going. And people who are strong and determined have the ability to move their bodies to go along with that confidence. The mechanics of a person tell you if he's strong, weak or able to handle things.

I could break down a batter's personality and swing in just a few minutes. Where his hands were, what his batting trigger was, where his best hitting zone was. Once I saw the swing I knew if a kid would be able to handle a pitch and if he couldn't, I could often fix it with some corrections and some hard work. Some kids were stubborn and stayed with their natural swings because they had some success, but others, those who wanted to improve, would listen.

The more I coached, the more I realized I had a gift for getting the most out of kids, whether it was pushing them to do their schoolwork, which I hated as a kid, or giving them the confidence to hit a baseball. But coaches, even on the high school level, are also ego driven. There are a lot of coaches who coach exclusively for themselves – to be the center of attention, a leftover from the days when they were stars themselves.

The person who gets all the praise for the team's successes and cops to the cliché, "we didn't have talent this year" when they don't win. You know them right off the bat. They talk a lot about themselves and say things like, "my kids are very coachable" or "we were very prepared" and very often forget to mention the names of their players. And there are also the coaches who genuinely want to help their kids succeed and don't care about their won egos, always taking a back seat and never taking credit. Those are the coaches that say, "Jimmy played his ass off" or "my kids gave 100 percent", and are always talking about the players.

But the best coaches, the ones who are consistent winners and have the ability to prepare their kids for college and beyond, are the coaches that have big egos and even bigger hearts. They want their kids to succeed at games as well as in life and they want to be able to say, "I helped make that kid a better man or woman."

The high school coaches I saw growing up at Yonkers schools, guys like Tony and Donny DeMatteo and John Volpe, they all had the recipe for success. Even professional coaches and managers like Pat Riley and Phil Jackson, even the humble and mild-mannered Yankees manager Joe Torre, maintained that balance

171

between satisfying their own egos and the success of their players and teams.

For me, each practice and each game was a passion play incorporating my search to relive those simple childhood joys of playing the games and how much of those joyful experiences I could convey to my players. When I was coaching, I was like a parent sharing new experiences with a young child; the first taste of ice cold watermelon, the first baby footstep from dry hot sand into the refreshing cool ocean tide, the weightless thrill of a park swing as it rises and falls, a first visit to Yankee Stadium.

Is a parent selfish or egotistical for wanting to be present when his child takes that first step? Does a father gain any personal satisfaction from seeing a child ride a bicycle on his own? Hell, yes. The coach – the father – bursts with pride when his child achieves because he is seeing himself again, innocent and able, without sin, and with the chance that the son or daughter will not make the same mistakes he made. "That's my kid. A chip off the old block." "That's my player. I taught him that swing or that blocking technique or that move to the basket."

Ego? Sure. Thrilled to see the kid's success? Definitely.

The perfect coach is like a good parent. And I had achieved the perfect balance over and over again in my fours years of coaching. This gift I had for teaching kids was the most selfish and unselfish thing I'd ever done. It was for me. It was for them. I'm sure that's the way Tony and Donny DeMatteo, John Volpe, Pat Riley, Joe Torre and many other coaches and managers felt, too.

At least the good ones.

CHAPTER 15

Ask and it shall be given you, seek and ye shall find, knock and the door shall be open to you. Matthew 7:7

Religion wasn't for me.

I played softball on Sundays and that's the day most churches played their games. So unless I was going to be Jewish and give Sabbath Saturday to the Lord, you weren't getting me into church.

But, God was something or someone I could not really ignore—like a feeling someone is following you, an identity inside yourself, a spirit that moves your flesh and bones. I knew I had a soul because I cried when my brother died, and when my grandmother died and when my chance of being a pro baseball player died.

But it—God—could easily be shoved into the background. I ignored the idea enough so that I could justify what I did to earn a buck. I saw "our thing" as a church or sorts; a government, a movement or a cult, an organization that demanded commitment, honor, dedication and reverence. Like the blood sacrifice of the Old Testament, "our thing" required a sacrifice of self and the ability to keep an oath to—well, a bunch of guys who shared power.

Mob guys are like priests or senators or corporate captains. You have an order, a rank, a place to call your own, and but instead of doing good to earn favor with god, a "soldier" can move up in rank depending on his ability to erase the accepted morality. God can be there, in ceremony, weddings, funerals, baptisms; but only as a ritual replacement for your own altered conscience.

So, coaching a bunch of Catholic school kids, working around nuns and brothers and priests, standing in the sanctuary and passing those statues of Jesus in the school hallway each day, served as a temporary substitute for my lost faith in God. While I was coaching, helping kids avoid the traps I had fallen into and providing a positive motivation as an "educator" of sorts, my heart had a chance to pump good blood, while in my other life, bad blood still flowed.

Then I started to read my press clippings a little deeper than a first read. Somehow, the perception this reporter Lorusso had of me was beginning to define who I was—at least while I was at Redemption.

"Vitale inspires his kids to get their schoolwork done or they sit," *Lorusso wrote in one column. "His hard-nosed practice sessions, both on the baseball field and basketball court, demand excellence from the tiny parochial school's athletes. A former New York Yankees farm hand, Vitale imparts his unique and sometimes abrasive edge, and his competitive drive, to his young players. Part father figure, part big brother, part rascal, the upstart coach without any past coaching experience has given a spiritual boost to a church-school athletic program that was in need of a resurrection. Vitale is a missionary of success to an adolescent band of willing disciples."*

"Damn! That's good."

After a couple of months I started to believe my press and felt that I was experiencing a transfiguration, or at

174

least a transformation, from a dark-side gangster type to a sanctified savior to a bunch of kids. I didn't sound any different, didn't look any different and at times could still be a hard, insensitive, corrupt man. At the same time, I would say things like, "Hey, Trey, make sure you don't disrespect that teacher," or "Hey, Nicky, watch your attitude and treat that girl right."

I think the responsibility of leadership was making me a kinder, gentler person. I knew that personality adjustment would never work on the "job," but it fit in perfectly when a kid needed some advice or looked like he was troubled. I could feel their pain, relate to my own experience and administer just the right dose of love; love I wished I had received when I was young. Other times, when the mood was wrong or I saw something that pissed me off, like an administrator provoking a kid, I would revert to the guy who handled problems with focused anger. Man, was I feeling schizophrenic. The funniest thing was that I liked having a spiritual aspect to my coaching, not just the fact that we played in the shadow of The Cross, all those relics and statues and things hanging around the school and the church, but the idea that to be a winner you had to have a motivation that was pure. For the team, no "I" in team, one for all and all for one. That shit ain't shit. It's a reality in sports.

Before each game we made sure we represented, you know in the street the kids would use the term represent. In the mob, we used the words "oath of loyalty" and "Omerta" to the death to motivate us. As a team, we would have a pre-game locker room talk where I would lay out the game plan. I'd use every motivational trick I could think of, including putting a number like "45" up on the blackboard and telling the team that if we held the opponent to "45" we'd win. Or "I'd put up "55" and say if we scored 55 against their defense we'd win.

Having a number or something like that to focus on

really helped get the kids into the game and most times the number came out right. Before one semifinal playoff game, and I knew we would need a good game to beat this one team from the Bronx, I really got going in my pre-game, telling the kids the other team didn't respect them and they'd have to go out and earn it.

"You guys are going to be nothing, losers, if you don't leave your guts out there on that floor tonight," I said. "I don't care if we win because we can't control fate, but we're not going to get bounced from the playoffs because we didn't break our asses out there. We're in our fuckin' house, our gym, where they can't come in a rule us. You guys are gladiators, soldiers, warriors, and we are going to fight for what's ours. Am I right?"

"You're right V," the kids yelled back.

"Are we fuckin' warriors?" I yelled.

"Yeah, Coach!" they responded.

"Are we gonna kick ass?" I yelled.

"Yeah, we're gonna kick ass," the team answered.

"Well, let's fuckin' go out there and give them a Redemption ass-kickin," I yelled.

"Yeah, yeah, yeah," the team screamed as they joined hands in a circle. "Team, team, team, team, team!" the guys chanted as they jumped in that circle with their arms over each other's shoulders like a huddled football team before the Super Bowl.

And just as they reached a fever pitch, I pointed to Sean and said, "Sean, lead us in the Lord's Prayer."

. It always worked. Focus, fever, then the Lord's Prayer.

You could hear a pin drop in that locker room as Mannion, in his Yonkers-Irish accent started praying the only prayer most of these kids knew.

"Our father who art in heaven, hallowed be thy name......" The whole team bowed their heads and followed Mannion. ".....Thy kingdom come, thy will be done, on earth as it is in heaven. Give us this day our daily bread and forgive us our trespasses as we forgive those who trespass against us. Lead us not into temptation, but deliver us from evil. For thine is the kingdom and the power and the glory forever. Amen."

I couldn't or wouldn't ever say I was a religious person, and I hated the hypocrites who prayed and then went out and committed every sin in the book. But somehow, in the locker room before a game, prayer seemed as natural as chalking up the Xs and Os, as right as going over a defense, as right as huddling together and jumping up and down to a chant of "team, team, team."

That one locker room experience, before what would turn out to be a 55-45 semifinal victory taking us into the championship final, was like a tent meeting in some Bible Belt town where everyone gets caught up in the spirit and people get healed, fall down when the preacher lays hands on them and the whole town gets saved.

We weren't a "religious" team even though we were from a Catholic school, but we had a spirit that came from somewhere and when we called on it, it always seemed to get us through. The Emeralds won their first Catholic Schools area title in 1994 and I can honestly say that the Lord's Prayer we said before our games helped get us there. I believed.

My last Redemption baseball team, in that spring of 1995, capped off the most amazing six months of my life. I was happily married for about three months, still in that honeymoon stage, and we had won the state basketball title in March and started the baseball season a week later. We rolled through the season with a 16-2 record and ripped through Scanlan and Spellman in the first two rounds of the playoffs. Melissa was seeing me at my best, a winning coach that had a bunch of kids that loved me as their coach.

My panic attacks were almost non-existent as my wins mounted, but there was pressure from Ronny and the crew because I wasn't doing much business-wise. I was kind of living on my savings and hoping something would change for me – either a big score a big

177

coaching opportunity – I didn't know which. We rumbled into the best-of-three championship series against our friends at Blessed Mary. They had a good pitching staff but we were ready for them.

We got a strong pitching performance from Jason, who hit about .500 that spring and was like 8-0 on the mound, and took the first game 3-0. The second game was a tight one, with us trailing in the sixth inning. Our pitcher Andre Figueroa kept us close despite a bunch of errors that could have been attributed to a nervous group of guys who wanted that third straight title. Down 4-3 in the sixth, with runners on second and third, Blessed Mary's pitcher Mike McDonald hung a curve to our third baseman Justin Cerrone, who was a really good looking kid, a model or actor type, but not a great hitter. That curve was a gift from God, an answer to prayer. Justin waited on the break and served the pitch into right field where it dropped, scoring both runners for a 5-4 lead. We held on to win and I found Justin near the mound as parents, fans and players converged into a big human pile of celebration.

"I waited on it Coach," Justin said with that smile and personality that would eventually take him to an acting career after high school. "I was struggling, but I did what you said and just kept my eye on the ball and waited."

It was a feeling I wish I could have frozen for eternity, like an oil painting of a great victory on the battlefield that you might see in a museum. The scene was out of a feel-good movie, with all those faces, the seniors I coached for three years, my daughter jumping up and down, Melissa standing there so pretty with a big smile on her face, and the parents, each of them coming up to me and thanking me for helping their kids become winners.

That moment was what I used to dream life was all about. It was a moment of winning, happiness, satisfaction and peace.

But like that first time I went to Yankee Stadium, that

sparkling bubble was about to burst. I was overwhelmed with joy yet I just couldn't fully accept it. I stood there -- with all those kids that I had coached, their family and friends, celebrating around me -- and I felt like a stranger. It felt good to be the reason why these people were happy. I felt good that I could do something that good. But would it last? I feared it wouldn't.   It didn't.

Emeralds three-peat

NEW ROCHELLE – Justin Cerrone's two-run single in the sixth-inning provided the winning margin yesterday as Redemption high School of Yonkers won it third straight Catholic Schools Class C baseball title, sweeping the best-of-three series with a 5-4 victory over Blessed Mary in a game played at Salesian High School.

Cerrone, a third baseman, slapped a single to right field, waiting on a curveball, to deliver the game winner. "I'm just glad to have been able to help out," Cerrone said as he greeted family members after the game. "We always play as team and even when I wasn't hitting much, Coach V trusted me to do my part.

Redemption, which finished the season with a 16-5 record, is the first team in school history to win three straight baseball championships in the modern Catholic School League era that began in 1956. "They're all great," Redemption coach Tommy Vitale said when asked about the championship. "You never know when it will be your last. So you try to enjoy it. I'm more excited for the senior kids I've playing for me for three years, because they wanted this. They wanted to go out winners."

CHAPTER 16

Humble yourselves in the sight of the Lord and he shall lift you up.
James 4:10

State champions?

No way!

Redemption had won three Catholic High School Association area baseball titles in three years and we had just put the finishing touches on a 65-63 comeback victory over Blessed Mary to win our second consecutive CHSA Class C area basketball title. The CHSA includes Catholic high schools in New York City and the surrounding suburbs, so even though we were a Class C school with about 400 students, the titles were still something to brag about.

But now we were headed for another shot at the state championship, which meant playing the upstate representative from Buffalo. We made it to this game in 1994 and had our asses handed to us along with some gas and toll money so we could to make it back home from Syracuse, where the game as played, to Yonkers.

Beating top-seeded Regency High School at

Fordham University in front of a big crowd in March of 1994 shocked the parochial school world. The kids were on such a high that they never showed up for the state title game against Nichols Catholic. But being away from home to play basketball was a strange experience for them. They thought it was a party. They thought their young bodies could endure anything after the practices I put them through for three months. They would find out quickly that staying up most of the night would produce a payback during the game the next day.

We got shellacked, 64-38 and it wasn't because the other team was that good. It was because we just weren't ready to play in a big game. It was because we left our game in the motel room and at the local bar I dragged them out of the night before. Well, they showed up, but they were all hung over from partying the night before the game, and, well, beer, pizza and three hours sleep doesn't translate into baskets and rebounds. I found them at a local bar near our motel and I could tell by their faces that they weren't going to be good for shit at the 11 a.m. tip-off.

On the bus to Schenectady, the 1995 team seemed more than a year older and more than a year wiser. We still had all five of our starters from the previous season and these kids weren't thinking beer, they were thinking about last year's embarrassing performance. I made sure they remembered.

"Hey, Joey," I said as I stood in front of the bus supporting myself by holding onto a seat on each side of the aisle. "Want a beer?"

My point guard, "Sweet Pea" Larkin, was a tough little guy with quick hands and a competitive personality, a gym rat type who loved playing any basketball game he could find—in the local park, down in the black neighborhoods of south Yonkers, on an AAU team or in a pick-up game he might spot while walking home from work or school. He always had a new pair of basketball shoes, Air Jordans or some other top model, even when he was broke he'd find a way to "buy" some new shoes. His shaved his head every day I think and had a confident bop when he walked. You'd think by the way he talked to other players, led a team and dealt with referees that he was 6-6 and not 5-6.

"No Coach," Sweet Pea answered as he looked up from a Sports Illustrated magazine with Duke basketball player Bobby Hurley, a Larkin-type guard, on the cover. "Maybe after we win."

That was it.

Sweet Pea had a game face on all the way to Schenectady and he made sure none of the others were goofing around either. Sean, Trey, Nicky, Billy, the other seniors had their Walkmans on or were sleeping or reading Rap magazines. I could hear the rhythms of Tupac Shakur coming out of Trey's headset as he mouthed the words to the rapper's newest album.

Shakur would be shot and killed later that year in September I think and I remember thinking about Trey when I heard about it. Trey loved Tupac and would always argue about music with me. Because he stuttered a little bit when he was excited, I'd love to get him going. He'd say, "C-Coach, you g-gotta listen to this, it's dope poetry and it talks about the plight of the underclass in America."

"It's just poetry for dopes," I'd say, laughing at Trey's attempts at evaluating music. "Let's see if this rap crap lasts as long as Ole Blue Eyes. That's not music. It's a bunch of kids talking shit."

"Coach, Ole Blue Eyes, who's that?" Trey would answer even though I told him about Frank Sinatra a million times. "Is he one of you relatives that sing at weddings?"

"Yeah, he's a relative," I answered. "And who's Tupac, your long lost brother from the old country? He's lucky if one of his rap crap gangster friends doesn't smoke him in a drive by. Don't all those rappers carry Uzzis in their baggy pants?"

182

Trey would go at it with me for a few minutes, then waved a hand and put his headset back. He'd listen to Tupac or Biggy or one of those other thousands of rappers and that would get him ready to play. I got used to the kids' music; didn't like it, but I got used to it.

I guess I understood a lot about the rap world, a street culture of gangsters and gangster wanna-be's fighting for attention and turf. The only difference between the mob and gangster rappers was they were peddling music, sex and dope and the mob dealing in gambling, prostitution, garbage and dope. Not that different, except in the cultures. We were Italians who had "believed in family and honor" and this new gang mentality and culture was more fractured, the product of broken homes and broken families in the inner cities of America. When you think about it, these kids had plenty to be angry about. Their violent and reactive personas made their world harder to control or for most Americans to understand.

Unlike the rap generation gang bangers, we Italians gangsters were "businessmen" and America had gotten used to our methods, even embracing what we offered: drugs, alcohol during prohibition, and gambling. Gambling became so mainstream that our stranglehold on it would diminished when individual states realized how much money could be made from what was once considered an illegal vice. State numbers, lotteries, casino gambling, they even gave the poor Native Americans, who we nearly eliminated completely in our own holocaust called "moving west", casinos of their own. With each new state-backed gambling enterprise beginning with OTB in the 1970s, we lost some of our business on the street. Where old ladies used to play the numbers at the local grocery store, now they were standing in line at the corner deli, drug store and stationary store to drop a dollar or two on the daily number, lotto or scratch off tickets.

By 2000, most white America's kids had embraced

183

Hip Hop and Rap as "their" music and despite the efforts of some to label these inner city black and Hispanic kids "outlaws," they took on a romance of their own and after 20 years of rapping on the door of society, they are as easily accepted into mainstream society, if not more accepted, than the mobsters we came to know and love through James Cagney, Edward G. Robinson, Humphrey Bogart and Michael Corleone with his lovely Italian-American family success story.

So, Trey, Tupac, Sweet Pea, Bobby Hurley, Sean, Billy, Nicky and me were ready to take on this Buffalo-area team, Trinity Catholic, a team we knew very little about, except what we read in Lorusso's preview.

Trinity Catholic may be Redemption's worst nightmare," the story read. The guards Jared Beekins and Caron Russell are both good shooters with the ability to get their own shots, the 6-2 pair towers over Redemption's Joey Larkin and Billy Nitkowski who are 5-6 and 5-9 respectively. Trinity's inside players are 6-4, 6-5 and 6-1, and the 6-1 player; Josh Reynolds jumps like he's 6-10.

Redemption counters with its best weapon, heart.

The Emeralds, all but laughed at last year, took the CHSA title in an upset and even when the team was shunned again as defending champs, getting a No. 3 seed in this year's playoffs, they set out and again upset the favorite Regency at Fordham earlier this week.

Sean Mannion at 6-2, Trey Walton at 6-3 and Nicky Bruno at 6-2 are blue-collar workers who have overcome bigger players to win big games. Larkin and Nitkowski have high basketball IQs and have been able to outwit opposing teams, expertly enacting their coach Tom Vitale's always inventive game plans.

Look for Trinity to win by 10, but don't count the Emeralds out, especially if the Lancers get into foul trouble.

Lorusso always did a good job scouting out the other teams we had to play for his sports section previews and

I spent time during the week grilling him for whatever he could tell me. This time I had an idea of how to deal with a bigger, but slightly slower Trinity team. And Lorusso always gave us a chance to win, even though he often thought we didn't have a shot. The week before, in his preview of our semifinal game against Regency, he said, "I give the Emeralds a fighter's chance, but Regency is too strong. In fact, if the Emeralds can pull this off, the rag-tag bunch of shaved-head hoopsters can shave my head at center court in their gym."

Lorusso looked good bald.

The team couldn't wait to find the reporter after the victory and even though we had celebration party planned that week, all they could talk about was "shaving Mr. Lorusso's head."

The local cable station heard about it and sent over a reporter to capture the event for the evening news. Lorusso couldn't have backed out of this if he wanted to, first because he had written the challenge in his column and second because the cable sports guy had mentioned it on his show like 10 times before the game. The guy's word was good. He showed up before high noon, greeted by a bunch of the students waiting in the parking lot. The whole basketball team, most of them with shaved heads themselves, had already decided how the haircut would be performed.

"We're each gonna take a turn with the clippers, Mr. L," Sweet Pea said. "And no one's allowed to shave the beard."

Lorusso, who had a serious case of male pattern baldness and was losing a lot of his hair, anyway, seemed like the perfect candidate for the Michael Jordan look. He'd already trimmed his full beard down to a goatee and never hesitated, taking a seat on the chair the kids provided right at center court on the Emeralds' logo.

""A free haircut is all I wanted," Lorusso said as Sean, Trey, Nicky and Billy surrounded Sweet Pea to watch the

185

first stroke of the clippers. "I knew you were gonna win. I made the challenge just so I could save the $15 my barber charges me for a haircut.

"Well, Mr. L, maybe you won't doubt us after this," Sean said. "When you go out into that frosty Yonkers air this afternoon, you'll remember the Emeralds are for real."

Each player took a swipe with the shears as the whole town watched on television. The kids used Lorusso's head as their trophy, and anyone in Yonkers who didn't know we were champs knew now.

"I'll see you guys next week after you visit Schenectady to play Buffalo and get beat," Lorusso said as he rubbed his Yul Brynner hairdo. "In a week, I'll need a trim."

There would be no second haircut because Lorusso acknowledged his mistake in a follow-up column.

"It seems the Redemption Emeralds are better basketball players than barbers, as is evident by my new look," Lorusso wrote. "Any team, or reporter for that matter, that may underestimate their ability to overcome the odds, is in for a rude awakening and a bad hair day. Don't even count the Emeralds out this weekend when they face a Trinity team that is 20-2 and an obvious favorite. I made that mistake and it cost me what was left of my thinning head of hair."

We learned a lot from our first visit to the state championship game in 1994. It was the first time many of the guys had been on a road trip away from the watching eyes of family, teachers and the brothers. These kids were no strangers to having a good time. They drank, smoked a little pot and goofed off with their friends in the neighborhood like many high school kids. They chased girls and even caught some. They were not innocent Catholic school kids by any means.

We learned a valuable lesson at the state championships, a lesson we would use the very next winter when we defended our CHSA Class C title.

Everyone considered our first CHSA championship a fluke because we beat the favorite, Regency High school, an elite academic school that only accepted top students who had to pass a test to get in. Beating Regency put us on the basketball map in New York, but staying on the map was going to be difficult. The next season it was our old friends at Blessed Mary.

The Crusaders beat us in both regular-season games, two wars that really proved we could play at a high level when we applied ourselves. But Blessed Mary had some talented players, a couple of shot makers and big kid who could rebound and run the court. We always had match up problems with faster teams, but we were in such good shape that we always outlasted even the quicker, more talented teams.

We wiggled and waggled our way through the first three rounds of the playoffs, and then we were set to defend our title at one of the local colleges, where we would have to manage a big court against Blessed Mary. The big games were my meat. I loved the pressure because I had been in so many tough spots in my business that I had nerves of steel and a poker face.

My kids were like me, all nerve, and willing to play anyone. So, against the book, I always scheduled a few teams early in the year that I knew we couldn't beat; teams in the bigger-school Class A league that had more talented, more skilled and faster kids. I wanted to test my kids, even lose a few games, just so they would be tested and ready for the playoffs. While other teams padded their schedules with games they could win, we never backed down from a chance to play a name team, just to get the experience.

The method, which some parents and other coaches disagreed with, worked.

We played the 1995-96 CHSA Class C final at Iona College in New Rochelle, a tough defensive battle with my guys hanging tough against Blessed Mary's two top guns, Steve Serbita and Keshon Smart.

Down 67-63 with less than a minute to play in the game, Trey used his long stride and leaping ability to drive across the lane and scoop in a layup to make it 67-65. Sweet Pea stole the next inbound pass jumping in front of a Blessed Mary player and I called time out.

"It's right there for us," I said looking into a huddle of exhausted but confident kids. "This is our fuckin' championship, ours! Let's play smart, find the open man and get a hoop. Its five guys out there and anyone can make it happen if you're in the right place. Let's look for the guy with the best shot and win this thing."

When we came back on the floor, Billy Nitkowski, who was our fourth or fifth option most times but always ready to spot up for a 3-pointer, was left wide open. Billy took a pass from Sean Mannion to the left of the top of the circle behind the 3-point arc, paused, looked for an outlet, and didn't see anyone more open than he was. He set himself, rose up and calmly hit the 3 like he was shooting hoops in his backyard. We had a 68-67 lead and I jumped out of my designer loafers. They were forced to foul to get the ball back. We made a free throw on the next possession and held on for a 70-67 victory.

I don't think I've ever been that excited about any win, baseball or basketball—not until the next week and the next game that is.

After beating Blessed Mary in that come-from-behind thriller, we were poised to take another shot at the upstate champs. But this time we would be ready. It was the most memorable game of any kind I've ever played in or coached at any level.

I'm not kidding.

This was the type of game that they make movie out of, a come-from-behind, overtime, big-plays-by-little-people game that had the opposing team, coach and fans shaking their heads. And me, I just stood there and smiled most of the time, turning to look at Lorusso at the press table once in a while to see his reaction. He would smile back, shake his head and go back to his game notes. I couldn't believe my team was even in this game against a power like Trinity, and Lorusso looked like he just couldn't wait to write the big upset story if we could pull it off.

We stayed in the game through three quarters, but faded in the fourth; trailing by 15 points, yes 15 points, down 78-63 with less than six minutes remaining in the game. From that point, the game unfolded into a foggy fantasy for us and some kind of horrible nightmare for the Trinity team. Their guys couldn't hit a shot for almost three minutes. My guys, in great shape with two years of running suicides, showed me 10 sets of the biggest of balls I've ever seen, pressing, pushing, slashing and shooting their way back a basket at a time, a free throw at a time, a defensive stop at a time, until we were within four points with less than a minute to play. I called a timeout after Sean made the score 80-76 with 55 seconds showing on the clock.

"Well, we proved we could play with the best," I told the kids as we huddled in that Schenectady gym full mostly with Trinity fans. "We'll go home with our heads up no matter what." "We're going home with the trophy, Coach," Sweet Pea said. "We have 55 seconds left and we're gonna die out there if that what it takes."

I always thought after we beat Blessed May that we could win the state championship with some luck and the right breaks, but when we were down by 15, I just wanted the guys to go out strong with some pride and not just fold. Now, I felt just like Sweet Pea. We were here. We had 55 seconds left. Why not win? What sealed the deal was when I glanced over to the Trinity bench and saw their kids with their heads down, sucking wind. Even their coach looked shocked and winded. How could his team, ranked No. 1 in the state poll for our school size, be struggling against the team ranked 6th? A small team with a short bench and no reputation for winning titles against a perennial winner with kids who looked like they were headed for the Los Angeles Lakers.

Then something happened that gives me chills to this day every time I think about it. I got those goose bumps that jumped up all over my body and I could feel every hair on my head stand up. Just before we broke our huddle, I glanced over to the Trinity bench again and spotted their head coach, a nice black guy with a winning smile who I met before the game for a few minutes. He was looking right at me. He was just staring at me like I was a ghost or he was having a déjà vu moment. He had a look on his face as if to say, "You got me. You got us." It was eerie. He was looking at me instead of talking to his team. It was like he knew the outcome, like he'd seen the future and knew what was going to happen. That look reminded me of guys I had seen who were in line to get whacked or were on their way to do a 5-year stretch upstate. Like there was no place to go, no place to hide. Just stand there and take it.

I looked back at my team. We put our hands together in the huddle and yelled, "TEAM!" in unison. We went back on the floor in a sprint and Trinity slowly walked back to meet us. They had lost two of their starters to fouls and they looked like their coach—beaten.

But it wouldn't be that easy. We stopped them twice; three missed shots from out near 3-point land by their top guard, and got a beautiful pick-and-roll basket by Trey. Then another amazing thing happened. Nicky had fouled out, so I looked down the bench and couldn't decided which of my bench kids had the balls to get up and go out and play. So, I asked them, "Who wants to go out there and make some plays for us?"

My reserve, reserve, reserve guard Matty Bell, whose father was the girls coach, jumped up and ran toward me like he'd been waiting his whole life for that exact moment. I liked that he was ready and wanted to go in, and he was the only guy who answered the call, so in he went. Matty made a steal on the inbound play and just like you saw in "Hoosiers," hit two free throws, cold off the bench, to tie the game at 80-80. "I just wanted to be in there," Matty told me later. "I just wanted to be part of it."

I never saw a kid more excited to be part of a team, and it was that attitude I spent four years teaching my teams. The idea that we were in this thing together, like a family. And when I needed it most, all through the playoffs, it was there. Matty proved you don't have to be a star to be a winner.

My guys nearly fainted when Matty's second free throw dropped through, but with four seconds remaining Trinity still had a final chance to beat us in regulation. They in-bounded the ball and tossed it up past the mid-court line. But the pass hit one of their players on the top of his foot and rolled harmlessly, almost in slow motion, out of bounds, right into their coach's hands, as the buzzer went off. Their coach looked up, with that look again, and tossed the ball to the referee.

Overtime!

It was all us. Trinity was spent from the frantic fourth quarter and you could see they weren't focused as overtime began. I told my kids, "Here's where all those suicide drills, all that running in practice and pushing you to the limit that made you hated my guts, pays off. We're in shape and they're over there looking for an oxygen tank. I don't think they can run up and down the floor for another three minutes. Let's go out there and take what belongs to us."

The guys just smiled at each other and huddled up to one more, "Go Redemption" yell, before going back onto the court. I felt like a father watching my children graduate to adulthood. They started the game looking like baggy-pants, pimple-faced kids and now they looked like men, warriors on the way to defeating a giant enemy, confident and proud.

We scored twice early in the three-minute overtime

session and they had to foul us to get the ball to try to cut the lead. We made our first two free throws, took an 86-80 lead with less than a minute to go, and then held the ball for the final 25 seconds of the game. When that buzzer went off, the buzzer that signaled our state championship, I walked right over to the Trinity coach to shake his hand.

"Great game coach," I said. "Thanks for the game and good luck to your kids. They're a good team."

He smiled, shook his head again and said, "That's the most amazing thing I've ever seen in all my years of coaching. You and your guys have a lot of heart. Big time heart. We had the horses, but you guys had what it takes to be champions."

State champs?

No problem!

Emeralds Best in State

SCHENECTADY, N.Y. – Yonkers has a state basketball champion.

Not since the 1930s, when a version of a state basketball championship was contested with teams from various regions invited to participate in a tournament, has Yonkers has a state basketball champion.

That changed yesterday afternoon when the upstart Redemption Emeralds of Yonkers, two-time and defending champions of New York City area CHSA Class C, recovered from a 15-point fourth quarter deficit, then raced past heavily favored Nichols Catholic School of Buffalo 86-80 in an overtime thriller played at Richards High School.

Coach Tom Vitale, who has led the school's baseball teams to three straight New York City Class C baseball titles, added the school's first state championship to his handful rings. The Emeralds, who had four of their five starters score at least 10 points led by Sean Mannion and Trey Walton with 18 and 17 respectively, shocked the

192

crowd heavily populated with Buffalo-area fans.

"I have to credit our ability to play as a team no matter what circumstances or opponent we are up against," Vitale said. "This is the best performance I've ever seen from one of my teams because the kids showed heart, discipline, courage and an attitude of never giving up no matter what the score."

Larkin, who joined fellow seniors Mannion, Walton, Billy Nitkowski and Nicky Bruno in their return to the state championship game after losing last year, agreed with his coach.

"We're just a good team that plays as a team," Larkin said. "No one guy is more important. We got help from everyone on the bench, too. We proved Yonkers has what it takes and that last year's championship was no fluke."

CHAPTER 17

A gift (talent) is as a precious stone in the eyes of him that has it. Proverbs 17:8

About the time I was establishing myself as a winning basketball and baseball coach in 1994, my parallel criminal career was hitting a high note too. My boss Ronny was giving me more and more important jobs to handle, collections from unions, the docks, garbage negotiations, etc. Ronny was a good guy, as wise guys went, pretty fair and honest and not a hog. You earned for him, you got paid. You had a "family" problem or a problem with your real family; he really took an interest and tried to help.

Ronny told me being married and having kids was the way to live, and warned me about screwing around with whores and other women who were just after money and got their kicks being around "the life". He told the big bosses about what good things I was doing all the time, and even though they knew me through my Uncle Mario, who was a made guy and later a boss, it helped to have a captain front for you, especially after having so many problems in my younger days. Ronny lived in a nice suburban house with his wife Jeannie and his kids and always kept a low profile. He wanted to do business like "our thing" was "a business". He had style and was gaining power with each new deal he made.

Ronny told me I was one of his main guys and that he was pushing me to be made sometime soon. In 1994, after we won our share the garbage territory and had things going pretty good, it looked like I would be the first "made" coach in the Catholic schools league. The thought of moving up to a position of power should have made me excited and happy, but it gave me a funny feeling. It was like I had two women that I loved, one of them sweet, beautiful and kind and the other hot, sexy, dangerous and tempting. I wanted both, but I knew that one would kill the other and I knew being made would force me to quit coaching.

"A made guy can't coach basketball," Ronny told me the afternoon of my wedding to Melissa. You're looking for problems as it is, being in the paper every day. Get a hobby, like playing cards or going to the track, if you're looking for a way to relax and have fun. The "life" doesn't allow us to be like other people. This thing of ours is a full-time job."

There it was again.

Ronny was right. After all, how many mobsters have you heard of that had another career on the side while they were involved in gang activities? There was that guy Dion O'Bannion, Al Capone's rival in Chicago during the 1920s and 30s. O'Bannion was a florist and a mobster. Capone supposedly had a laundry business and the Gambinos dealt in the dress business in New York. Other guys had "legitimate" businesses like garbage companies, construction corporations and even video, pizza and grocery stores. But those businesses were fronts, or covers for the mob stuff. No one, especially the feds or police were fooled. When Capone had O'Bannion whacked, he had more flowers in his funeral than any other mobster, celebrity or politician ever had at their funeral. But there weren't too many wise guys with professional or other occupations. Hobbies maybe, like Capone loved opera and Bugsy Siegel loved the movie business and wanted to be an actor, but you never heard of a mobster being a teacher, or a photographer or an accountant. Having a real job interferes with the whole concept of being a mobster.

So, when Ronny warned me about how coaching was taking too much of my time and energy, he was predicting an eventual problem. And he was warning me about how dangerous it might be. I think he allowed me to keep coaching because he saw what it meant to me. Maybe he was thinking he had something special inside himself too that was hidden by "the life" and just didn't want to ruin it for me. But my two lives would collide soon after that talk with Ronny.

We were all out at the Shore Club on New Rochelle's waterfront for my third wedding in early 1996 just before the basketball playoffs were about to begin. Melissa had convinced me that we should get married after just six months of a hot affair. I was doing well financially and thought marriage might help me turn my life around, settle me down. Me and Melissa said our vows on a warm March day in the gazebo near the water on the beach of the Shore Club just before sunset. We invited about 100 people, including family and friends, just people who were very close to use. My daughter and Melissa's daughter were flower girls. Melissa looked like a Barbie doll, a beautiful 5-foot, 1-inch Barbie doll decked out in a fashionable short, white cocktail dress. When we set the date for the wedding we didn't expect that my basketball team would go as far as it did, winning our first Catholic Schools championship, so we had to postpone a honeymoon to Florida and instead spend the next day driving 100 miles to Glens Falls for the New York State Federation basketball tournament final being held that Sunday.

The wedding drew an interesting assortment of

guests. The list of attendees included people from very different worlds colliding in one place, my wedding. The reporter Lorusso was there. I invited him because Melissa had gotten to know him and his kids at games and liked the things he had written about me. I liked the guy too. He had gotten to be a like a friend, or as close a friend as I could have had in a reporter. I guess I always wanted him to see the good side of me, so he wouldn't look for the bad side. Lorusso sat at a table with some of my coaching friends and guys I played softball with.

At another table, there were eight guys, no women, which was an unusual seating arrangement at a wedding, but not unusual for these guys. There was Ronny, my boss, "Big Ben", the capo, Junior, one of the top buttons in the crew and four other associates I knew. The picture of that table was a collector's item. Eight wise guys bearing gifts. I took Lorusso over to meet the guys because he kept asking kidding me, asking me who they were, and if I thought any of them wanted to dance.I told Lorusso that they were business associates of my Uncle Mario, who was in construction and they got me a lot of work doing renovations and other construction contracts.

"A lot of broken noses over there, Coach," Lorusso said. "Why all men at the table? Are they like a gay glee club or something?"

"Come on over with me and I'll introduce you," I said. "They all know you."

"Know me?" Lorusso said with a surprised look on his face. "I think I would remember these guys if I knew them. Are you sure I know them?"

"I didn't say you knew them, I said they knew you," I answered. "They're some of your most faithful readers. They read your newspaper; you know the stories about Redemption."

"Oh," Lorusso said. "Can they read?"

I shot Lorusso a look and he kind of looked down at the floor because he knew he might have offended me by goofing on my friends. He may have had a few glasses of wine and forgotten he was a journalist for a second. It was funny though. These guys looked like an assortment of gangsters off a movie set, except for Ronny, who looked like a stockbroker or lawyer. They had no necks, shiny suits and tans. Their hair was slicked back with mousse or cut close to the head and they each held an unlit cigar, waiting for the right moment when they would all go outside on the terrace and smoke.

"Gentlemen, this is Danny Lorusso, the sports editor for the Herald," I said as we reached the table. "Mr. Lorusso, this is Ronny Capelli, Sal Trumbo, Mikey Resigno, etc, etc, etc. They're friends of the family."

"We're like family to Tommy," Ronny said as he stood to shake hands with Lorusso.

Ronny's hands were smooth, manicured and tanned. You could smell the Calvin Klein on him, just a scent, not too strong.

"I like the stuff you write," Ronny said. "You tell a good story and you're treating Tommy right. How's the team doing?"

"It's a good team," Lorusso answered with a smile. "But the coach is the real story. He's got those kids, baseball and basketball, playing like winners. He's a good coach. He could coach college, even pro I think. Coach V has a unique talent. He's a good leader. He makes his players better. You guys should be proud of him."

It sounded like Lorusso was presenting my resume, but he didn't realize which job it was for. Ronny was nodding with each comment like he was saying, "Yeah, he's a good leader, he's talented, he has charisma, he should be "made."

"Yeah?" Ronny said. "You think he's that good?"

"Could be, with the right school and right situation," Lorusso answered. "Redemption doesn't have a program that pushes sports like St. Raymond's or Rice. If V coached a major school he would go from high school to college in a couple of years. Believe me; I've seen a lot of coaches and he's as good as any of them."

My face and neck were getting red and my tuxedo was feeling real tight. I felt like a young kid standing there while my mother was telling my boss how good an employee I was.

And then Ronny said something I couldn't believe. Maybe he was just being conversational or wanted to keep Lorusso believing I was just a coach. But he said something that stunned me.

"I think you're right," Ronny said. "I think he was born to coach. He has a gift. I've seen his games a few times. It's like he belongs on the bench. Keep up the good writing Lorusso. Hey, don't I know some Lorussos, Mikey? You got any family in construction Lorusso?"

"No," Lorusso said. "My family's in oil, fuel oil. You know, Grandpa came here from Bari on the boat in 1918, delivered ice and coal and then later he got into fuel oil. Lorusso Fuel in Mount Vernon."

"Yeah, that's it," Ronny said with a smile. "I know Lorusso Fuel. Good family. If you ever need anything let Tommy know and he'll give me a call. You know, Yankee tickets, Broadway shows, a deck built in your back yard, let me know. I like what you've done for Tommy. I usually don't like newspaper guys, but you seem okay. Hey, do you know that prick Lupica. I hate that guy."

"No, don't know him," Lorusso said. "Nice meeting you guys." Lorusso shook hands all around the table and went back to his table. The wedding went off without a hitch the rest of the day. Lorusso asked me about my "friends" a few times in passing over the next couple of months, but never pursued it much further because I would always change the subject when he brought it up. But that wedding marked a collision between my worlds that would have repercussions over the next few months with Lorusso, Melissa, Ronny and the crew and my coaching career playing big roles.

Ronny "The Kid" was a musician of sorts, played guitar

in a rock band when he was in high school around clubs in Westchester like the Crazy Horse in New Rochelle and the Limelight over in Mount Vernon. He was pretty good some guys told me, even thought about going to music school. Sometimes when I would call him on a Saturday or Sunday morning, he would say, "I'm in the garage playing my guitar, call me back later" and it would strike me funny that he sounded different. Sort of like happy, like quieter and calmer, like the music was his escape from "business."

The Kid was always telling me about bands and music he liked, like the Beatles, Bruce Springsteen or Eric Clapton, not like the older mob types who were obsessed with Sinatra, Dean Martin, and the more "modern" Four Seasons, Dion and the Belmonts and Jay Black and the Americans. I think music was Ronny's real love, like my coaching. I often think he would have been much happier if he had chosen music as a profession. Music was another one of those connections to the "good" side of life that even mobsters couldn't resist.

I loved "The Boss" and all his albums, had them all. I think I must have gone to 40 or more of Bruce's concert during the 1980s and 90s. We'd do anything to get tickets and we'd get four or five of us and go out to the Meadowlands or wherever he was playing in the area. Two of my favorite moments in life happened at Springsteen concerts.

The first was when we got seats in the first row of the second tier mezzanine at the Garden in 1987.

Bruce's guitar player Little Stevie, who wound up playing a mobster on the HBO series the Sopranos 10 years later, was off doing his own thing at the time and wasn't backing up Bruce with the E Street Band on the tour. So, when we sat down in our seats we nearly went crazy when Stevie showed up and sat right behind us. We turned around to talk to him and he was great, talking about the concert, the different tunes Bruce was going to play and Bruce himself. And to top it off, the

200

middle-aged lady sitting with Stevie, who was talking about Bruce like she really knew him well, finally introduced herself as "Bruce's mom." Me and my guys talked about that concert for months – for years – after that.

The second Bruce incident was a double winner. It was 1989 and he was playing the Meadowlands, where we knew some guys who could get us in to good seats. We got seats upstairs, but with our friends in security, got down onto the floor of the stadium after paying off an usher or two. We'd never pay for tickets. We always knew a union guy or a security guard who would open a door and once we were in, we were on our own to find a good spot. I used to see all kinds off wiseguys at Bruce concerts.

After years of going to ballgames and concerts for free, I wondered if anyone was paying to get in. Me and my friend Vinny, who was a big Bruce fan too, got seats in the eighth or ninth row from the stage and we were in our glory. There was some other band on before Bruce and just before he was about to come out, we looked in front of us, a row ahead, and saw this short woman with a great body dancing to the music and talking to her friends. When the hot blonde turned to the side to look around at the crowd, we realize it was Dolly Parton. I couldn't resist the opportunity to at least say hello, so I tapped her on the shoulder and she turned around, showing me those big, beautiful blue eyes and of course that magnificent chest. She smiled and said hello in that thick, high-pitched southern drawl, then agreed to give me an autograph. She signed a piece of paper I had in my wallet, "To Tom, a great fan, Love Dolly."

Before I could thank her, there was a crowd of people moving toward her to get autographs. The ushers pushed people back and tried to give her some room to hear the concert without being bothered. Some guy that was sitting behind us yelled out some stupid remark about her tits or something and I turned around, grabbed the guy and pushed him away so the ushers could grab him.

"Thanks, Tom," Dolly said when I turned around. "You're a gentleman."

Dolly left about an hour into the concert while the lights were still low, but as she was leaving, she stopped next to me and gave me a kiss on the cheek and thanked me again. I was stunned and thrilled. A kiss from Dolly Parton at a Bruce concert. She was really sweet and I still have the autograph.

Music was always a big part of my life as it was for a lot of guys we hung with.

All of the older mob guys had their favorites they would go see for weekends in Atlantic City. Las Vegas or Florida, where they would spend time gambling and seeing the shows. The older guys loved the music from the 50s and 60s and didn't really appreciate rock 'n roll. Some of us younger guys would rag the older guys and call their music "golden moldies" or "non-stop doo-op." You could tell how old a guy was by the music he had on his car stereo or what they played on juke boxes.

CHAPTER 18

In God have I put my trust, I will not fear what flesh can do to me. Psalms 56:4

Living on the edge—straddling the fence—can be as exciting as it is dangerous. It's like walking a tightrope, knowing you have some control of a dangerous situation. But even one of the Flying Wallendas high-wire act, I think it was the old man Karl, missed once – just once – and he paid for it with his life.

When the excitement of being young and impetuous passes and maturity tries to force its way into your life, decisions must be made on whether to live on one side or the other. Like Dylan said in his rebirth album when religion took him over for a decade, "You gonna have to serve somebody. It may be the Devil or it may be the Lord, but you gonna have to serve somebody."

Everyone from Jesus to Hitler, from Gandhi to bin Laden, from Mother Theresa to that Texas mother who drowned her five children in a tub, has faced those moments of decision between the black and white of life. Jesus chose the help of a higher power—his father—to fight off his 40 days of temptation, and offered a sacrifice of love that has been the basis of faith for over 2000 years. Hitler chose the dark side and his maniacal choices led to the loss of millions of lives and the fear that it all might happen again if the devil has his way.

I could clearly see the edge from the roof of my Bronx River Road apartment building. My four-year fantasy at Redemption was coming to an end and the choices seemed limited. I didn't know if I wanted to die or just fade away someplace where no one knew me and I could start my life all over again. It would have been so easy to just slip off the edge down eight stories onto the sidewalk–splat! But my mother and sister and daughter, and now my players, would have to endure that horrible after-death experience. As much as I wanted to die, I still had the will to live. Baseball games and basketball games flashed through my head as I sat on that ledge. Winning baskets, championships, post-game celebrations, passed through my mind like old silent films, the ones that flicker like Charlie Chaplin movies. My life flashing before my eyes had a lot of losses, but there were some wins. Wins I could still feel. I would try to stay alive for just the chance of one more win.

There was a big celebration back home after Redemption won its first-ever state basketball title. We qualified for the New York State Federation Tournament the following weekend, which invites champions from parochial, private and public schools to compete for the honor of being the best team in each division. We had a bye in the opening round, then lost the Class C Federation final to a Liberty Lutheran team from upstate Troy that had a 6-11 center we couldn't deal with.

When we got back to Yonkers after the Federation tournament, the mayor and city council invited us to city hall to present us with a proclamation for winning our state title. The school planned a party and everyone came out to celebrate our historical victory. I should have been in my glory, but I laid back and made sure all the kids got the credit for what they had done. Each of them spoke at the victory dinner and when I got up to speak I thanked everyone at the school and made a public promise that the school would have to keep or risk embarrassment if it didn't.

"Redemption hasn't had the respect of the high school basketball community in Westchester for years and these kids have brought credit to a small school that no one expected to win a league title, much less the state championship," I said. "We want to thank the school for all of the support the last two years and I know the kids will be proud to wear the championship rings when they receive them later this year."

Principal Rella squirmed in his seat a little, but then a big smile crossed his face when he realized I was forcing his hand for a reason. Everyone applauded and the team looked shocked at the idea that they would be getting rings. Rella seized the opportunity and stood to address the audience.

"We're a small school and we don't have a big budget for sports and other extras," Rella told the crowd of parents and boosters. "But Coach Vitale and his boys have given us something to be proud of for years to come, so we'll find some way to get the appropriate jewelry by the time the school year ends."

My players rose to their feet and went crazy when they heard Rella's promise, on the record in front of everyone. I just looked at the principal and gave him the "thumbs up" sign.

By the end of the 1995-96 school year, with a combined five baseball and basketball titles won over the three previous years, things were unraveling for me. My Clarke Kent identity was cracking and keeping my other business separate from my coaching was so stressful that my therapist had me on more Valium to help relieve the anxiety. I guess the residue of guilt or the fear that one of the kids or parents or teachers or priests would find out about my other life was getting to me. My temper flared more often and I suffered more anxiety

205

attacks. And now Lorusso, who'd nominated me for his newspaper's Coach of the Year honors in basketball and baseball, was asking too many questions about me, looking for new angles on my life. He'd done so many basketball- and baseball-related stories, that I guess it was inevitable he wanted to give his readers more insight into the coach who came from nowhere to win titles at Redemption.

But Lorusso didn't know about my mob ties, the Monsignor didn't know, the public didn't know and the kids didn't know—at least until my fourth year when some of my more street-wise players started to suspect I wasn't "Joe Job" and had some other things going on that might not be on the up and up.

It was one winter afternoon when I got my "garbage connections" to make a pickup at the school that Joey asked some questions about what I did.

"Hey Coach V," Joey said as he walked into practice that afternoon. "There's a load of garbage on the ground outside where the team van is. It smells and cats and birds are eating at it. What's the deal with that?"

"I don't know, Sweet Pea, but I'll see what I can do to get it out of there," I leaned over to pick up the phone on my office desk.

"What are you gonna do, ask us to go out and clean it up and make it part of a practice drill, like when you made us sweep the gym floor 100 times?" he cracked.

"No, you dope! You guys would probably screw it up and throw each other into the compactor and I'd have to get a whole new team of knuckleheads. I'll call a guy and get it done."

Ten minutes later, four guys from KC Carting, Co., with four shovels and a big container truck pulled into the school lot. Within minutes they had the place cleaned up and an empty container in place. Joey must have told everyone on the team about it and the news spread that "Coach V snapped his fingers and some garbage guys ran over to clean up the school lot. The coach must have connections."

It got a little tight about then, with all the talk about my ability to get things done and people kidding me about the guys who came to watch some of our games, but I managed to get by with a few white lies. I told the kids I had a friend who owned the carting company and he wanted to help the school by cleaning up the garbage. We left it at that. No one really knew what I was involved in.

Other schools were now becoming interested in me as a coach. Baseball coaches at the larger schools were asking me to come over as an assistant coach, with the promise that I would take over for them when they retired. I got the reputation for being able to handle tough kids, a quality that many older coaches needed in an assistant. The other Yonkers coaches read the paper too and they were asking, "Who is this guy who had two teams winning at Redemption?" "How the hell can anyone get those teams to win anything?" and "Why is this guy getting all the ink in the local paper?"

A few people remembered me from my days growing up in Yonkers schools, but my high school sports career was so short that I never established a rep there. I had never coached outside of neighborhood baseball teams and was a part of the coaching fraternity. Because I'd been able to keep my mob business quiet over the years—never was arrested for any organized crime activity or associated with any known member that could be proved—few people knew what I did for a living or made the connection between the small-time Catholic school coach and his "other career" job. Except the "guys."

"Hey V, we saw the article about the game last week. Nice job!" one of the guys from Morris Park said one night at an after-hours place. "You got a nice little crew over there. Real "organized" if you know what I

207

mean. The Capo Coach, huh?"

I was proud to hear this guy mention my success. It seemed the fellas had been reading the newspaper stories and were getting a laugh out of the fact I was playing this double life. But my boss Ronny was concerned, to say the least. Ronny was one of the youngest captains in the family, a rising star with a low profile and a businessman's mind. He liked talking about world events, politics, history and sports. Everyone I knew liked sports. The Kid, as we called him, went about his business like a lawyer or an investment banker, but he could be dangerous.

The story goes that Ronny got made after a series of mob killings and a power struggle for territory in 1989 and 1990. The Gambino and Genovese families were in a tug-a-war over construction and window installation contracts in the mid-70s when the mob made millions in new construction in the NYC area. When things got tight and some mid-level guys started talking about the window scams—selling wholesale to builders at elevated prices—Ronny "settled" more than a few problems, and potential witnesses either stopped talking or stopped living.

Ronny was sort of a street legend – feared by anyone around organized crime circles -- because he was being credited with at least six hits during his rise on the street and never even got pulled in for questioning once. He was like a silent and deadly force. Even in a supposedly secret underworld, where a loose word could get you dead, word spread when a guy was making his bones by killing for the mob. One of Ronny's reputed victims was a former bookie, Nicholas "Saint Nick" Bocelli, who weighed about 400 pounds and added on a pound or two every time he passed a deli or a bakery. "Saint Nick" disappeared from his quiet Bronx Gardens home one evening and hasn't returned or appeared anywhere else since. The talk was Bocelli had been working for the feds and was turning state's evidence on the window jobs disappeared from his quiet Bronx Gardens home. He was supposed to be in hidden away until the trial began, but he had a girlfriend out in Throgs Neck and snuck over to visit her one Saturday. "Saint Nick" and his vintage, black 1967 Fleetwood, which was the only car with room enough to hold the fat slob, were last seen parked in Ferry Point Park, located in the shadows of the Whitestone Bridge on the Bronx side of bridge. All the police found were 16 empty White Castle burger boxes and a large vanilla shake cup with Saint Nick's prints on them lying on the ground near where his Caddy was last seen. That's 5,000 pounds of car and 400 pounds of Saint Nick, recently filled with White Castle murder burgers, disappearing into thin air.

"At least his had a good last meal," Ronny joked when the Daily News ran a story about his disappearance. "He probably begged whoever whacked him to let him finish off the sack of burgers before they let him have it. And where, oh where do you dump a load like that?"

Even if Ronny didn't do Saint Nick, he was like most mob guys and didn't like a rat, especially a fat rat. Ronny was all business and never seemed to make a mistake, especially with "his" people.

"V, this coaching thing can be a problem," Ronny said after we won our second baseball championship. "What happens if you get busted and then the papers have big stories about what you're doing? That shit would be bad. We'd look like we were using the church or something. As long as you keep it quiet, it's okay, but be careful."

Keep it quiet?

We had just won another baseball championship and we had a basketball team for the next season that I thought could win the CHSAA title with the right amount of luck. Lorusso was asking people from Yonkers if they knew me from my high school days and working on a profile story on me that would detail my lifestyle and history. He met my new girlfriend and my daughter from my second marriage a few times, but that's all he knew about me.

According to Lorusso's stories, I was a construction company owner who loved coaching, nothing more. But the guy seemed to want to find out more about me to fill in some of the gaps about my life. It was fuckin' driving me crazy that he might find that one person who would say, "Tommy V? Yeah, he's a mob guy. Garbage, unions, gambling. What's he doing coaching?"

The day finally came when I had to make the choice I'd been avoiding since I was a little kid. Good and evil have subtle boundaries that can be maneuvered when you're a kid. A white lie, stealing some baseball cards from the corner store, beating up a kid, cursing. Temptations were expected and falling once in a while was no real sin.

But life decisions were tougher once you found a niche, especially in a life of organized crime. Having an alternative like coaching presented a polar extreme. Choosing between the possibility of coaching and becoming a "made" guy was like choosing between buying a house in Alaska or Florida, eating a big steaks every day and becoming a vegetarian, being a heterosexual and being gay, or choosing heaven or hell as a final retirement community.

Ronny helped me make my choice one early morning on a stroll near Yonkers Raceway.

"V, this thing with coaching has got to go if you wanna stay with me," Ronny said. "You had a good run, but I'm into some heavy action and I need my guys to be with me 24-7. We're moving up, moving in, and taking over some big things. I know you can be a big-time leader and we can build a strong crew with you. The coaching thing, it's gotta go."

I felt like I just got whacked, and the look in Ronny's eyes told me that if I said or did the wrong thing this morning, they'd be looking for a new coach that

210

afternoon because I'd be feeding cows underground somewhere in the Catskills within the day. I was stuck and I knew I had to do something.

"Ronny, you know I'm a loyal to you," I said. "I'll do whatever you say. But I don't know if I'm ever gonna be able to forget coaching. If I could, I'd erase most of my life, all the mistakes and things that happened to take my shot at baseball away. That's the only thing I ever loved. And coaching is the only thing I love now. I don't know if I can love this "thing" and this life the same way."

Ronny didn't say a word. He just put his hand up and turned and walked away. I saw him get into his gold Mercedes and drive off. For the next week I was in an anxiety-induced daze. I coached the baseball team practices and we won twice, but I just kept seeing Ronny's face, his hand raised up telling me to stop talking. I thought," if my life was a mobster movie, I'd be a dead man.

Things began to change after that early morning meeting with Ronny.

The headline on May 2, 1996 read:

Garbage Haulers Indicted

YONKERS -- Seven men and five companies with suspected links to organized crime were charged with conspiracy to control the garbage hauling industry in Westchester County and other New York City suburbs through threats, extortion and bribery over a period of 20 years, the article read.

The Feds from the U.S. Justice Department, the FBI and the Internal Revenue Service came down heavy on all my bosses in the summer of 1996, and I wasn't even touched. The Justice Department hauled everyone with an Italian last name in for questioning, but because I wasn't a known associate and had kept myself out of any legal trouble, all they could do was ask me about my relationship to gang members. I told them I knew some of the names they had as friends or acquaintances from the neighborhood and had a construction business and some relationships with garbage haulers and other guys, but not related to any criminal activity.

I don't know why, but the DA seemed to think I wasn't a big player. They kept asking if I could offer help in fingering any of the big players. Maybe they thought I'd turn. I'm sure they knew I was involved in some way, but they didn't have real proof or evidence on me. I never talked business on my home phone, cell phone, or on any other phone, doing all my communicating outdoors in parked cars, malls, restaurants, etc, where you couldn't get bugged.

The indictments came down hard. They alleged that "we" beat up other garbage haulers, burned trucks and other equipment, and even bribed public officials and union officials to gain hauling contracts and gain more territory.

The accused, including Ronny, Mikey and the big boss Tony "Cigar" Paterno, were accused of using intimidation and bribery to ensure that legitimate companies were kept out of the industry.

No kidding.

What's new?

The violent incidents included fires set to vehicles and property in 1990 and 1991 when we were just beginning to get into the carting wars. The wars with our own groups lasted until 1994 and 1995, and then we moved in and pushed out the legit haulers by offering the best rates. After we took over, the rates went sky high.

The indictments listed charges such as obstruction of justice, tax evasion, and antitrust violations against the individuals and their companies. It was the beginning of the end, at least for about 6-10 years, for Ronny and the other bosses. A conviction could mean up to 100 years in jail and big fines. A few of the guys went to jail and are still serving time, and most of them lost property, cars, boats, and a lot of things they couldn't account for with the tax people. I wasn't touched.

My anonymity and the fact that I had a reputation with coaching made me tough to nail. I had come within weeks, maybe even days, of being present at meetings that would have connected me with all the other carting guys.

Not being "made" saved my ass.

CHAPTER 19

For all they that take (live by) the sword shall perish with the sword. Matthew 26:52

The one thing you learned early in my neighborhood is that most people have a healthy fear of mobsters. In fact, that overwhelming fear and the resulting benefits are probably why many street toughs opt for a career in "the business."

The mob built a reputation for violence since the first "Mano Negro" or "Black Hand" took a foothold in Lower Manhattan in the early 1900s. Word of mouth spreads quickly when people are scared. The Italian Cosa Nostra (Thing of Ours) in America replicated the Sicilian ancestral Mafia using murder and threats of violence to seal its organization's power from the first days. That power spread to all of the major cities in the United States by the 1950s and maintained its strength by reputation. Other crime groups from Attila and his Huns to Hitler's Gestapo right up to the modern day street gangs used fear as a way to gain and keep territory and power.

So, when people found out you might be associated

with a mob family, word got around and those people feared you. I could go into almost any restaurant in New York and get the best table, or I could get tickets for a Mets or Jets game because I was a part of a crew and everyone wanted to stay on my good side. Smiles, gifts, good seats, and a kind of fearful respect came with the ominous legacy the mob earned over the years. And I was just egotistical enough to enjoy it. My lack of success in school and the abrupt end of my baseball career weren't the only reasons I fell into a life of organized crime. The "life" had a certain glamour, a sinful allure that attracts people like me who enjoy tempting fate without regard for the things most other people consider valuable – their family, their friends, their lives.

My third wife Michelle once asked me why how I could enjoy coaching young people and be so successful at it—a trait she found attractive—while being a criminal at the same time. I think she was impressed by the power of my mob persona at first, and then she realized that even the slightest attachment to the mob made me an unfit husband and father because business came first on almost every level. And some of my players wondered about it too, even if they didn't really know about my business.

One late winter afternoon after a game at the end of the 1996 basketball season, I was driving Trey back home to the Bronx when out of the blue he said, "Hey, Coach V, why don't you come coach at the school full time, like as a gym coach or teacher or something? I know it don't pay much, but you're really good at it, better than most of the other brothers and teachers. You really have a way of making kids listen. But you'd have to stop cursing, I think."

"Nah, Trey," I said. "I'm no teacher. I just love sports and I like coaching. What would I do, go back to college for four or five years and become a teacher and get a job teaching at some school and make, what $30,000 a year? I can't do that. I got a business and big deals going on all the time."

"What kind of business do you do better than coaching? Shit coach, you're the best around at baseball and basketball." Trey looked out the window as we passed the Orchard Beach exit on the Hutchinson River Parkway. "I think you made a bad career choice, my man."

Bad career choice was right.

As I looked over at this big, black, smiling basketball player who was headed off to college and a career of his own someday, I was suddenly jealous. I felt all of my unfruitful teen years rush across my mind and couldn't remember anyone ever sitting with me in a car or anywhere else and talking to me about college or a career. My father was gone by the time I started screwing up in high school and my mother didn't know how to get me to even go to school without crying and yelling at me every morning. My teachers gave up on me, and for good reason, by the time I was 14. And I didn't have a coach like me, who was willing to break heads and kick ass to make sure his players got their schoolwork done.

"What are you thinking about Coach?" Trey asked me as we reached his house.

"I'm thinking you should get that Spanish homework done, get some sleep, and be ready to practice hard tomorrow, dog," I said. "And don't stay up late jerking off and thinking about Halle Berry. You gotta graduate and get out of the ghetto so you won't be a janitor someday."

"Or a businessman who should be a coach, like you?" Trey said as he shut the door behind him and lowered his head to look in the window of the car. "Coach, you talk about what we should do. Use all our talents and become something someday—but look at you. You should be coaching and teaching, not hustling garbage containers and union dues. Hey, we know you're a big man in your business, whatever it is, but

216

you're a better coach, Coach. 'Nuf said. I'll see you at school tomorrow."

As I drove back to Yonkers I wondered if Trey and the rest of the kids had guessed what I was involved in and this conversation was part of some scheme they'd cook up to let me know that they knew. I felt like a teenager who'd just been lectured by my father. I knew Trey was right, just like I knew Lorusso was right – about me being a coach. My conscience had always been easy to control and I'd become a genius at denial – justifying my lifestyle and making excuses for my choices since losing my brother, my son, my baseball career. I even justified my life to my wives and children, believing that earning and supporting them was a good enough reason to stay in the life. But now, with my daughter Vanessa getting to the age of understanding and always asking about what I did, and now Trey questioning my choice of careers, I was running out of good answers. Being successful as a coach proved I was more than a hustler, a mobster, an underworld character out of some gangster movie. I had a life that meant something to a growing number of people and I didn't know what to do about it.

As I reached home that dark February night, Trey's face and voice coming through the frosty, half-opened car window came back to me.

I knew one of my lives had to end to save the other. But which one?

Later that year, when my ties with the family business were slipping and we were all being investigated by one law agency or another, one of those "golden moldie" guys found me early one cold morning in December as I was coming home from a local diner. I'd just parked my car in the garage of my building and heard the unmistakable click of Italian shoes as they walked closer to me. I'd learned long ago to deal with the fear of being ambushed or jumped by enemies or friends, so I wasn't afraid—just curious about who this fuckin' morning crawler was. It could have been one of the

217

tenants of the co-op on his way to work, or someone's boyfriend on the way home after a staying over at some bimbo's apartment. We had more than a few ladies in my building who were busy, if you know what I mean—and I knew from first-hand experience who entertained "company" and who didn't. Or it could have been a mugger. We'd experienced a few burglaries over time, but I put the word out on the street that whoever robbed the place or hurt anyone in my building would be tracked down, killed, cut up, wrapped in 15 separate garbage bags, and left in places so deep and dark that even the worms wouldn't be able to find the body.

But it wasn't a tenant or a visitor or a burglar. It was a button guy named Frankie Fusili, a guy we called "Foggy" because he wasn't too swift in the brain department, but also possessed the keen ability to appear out of nowhere without making a sound. He was the idiot savant of stalkers, which was a skill necessary to be a good hit man. That ability allowed Frankie "The Fog" to complete his appointed task, whether it is petty theft or murder for hire, without being seen. He was a short guy with a body builder's physique. And no matter if he was wearing an Armani suit or blue jeans and T-shirt; The Fog always wore a Yankee baseball cap.

"Hey T," Frankie said in a daytime voice, not trying to be unheard. "What's up?"

"What's up? Frankie, it's 5 a.m. We're up. You, me, and the milkman, that's it. Are you lookin' for me?"

"No, I'm not lookin' for you. I know where you live. That's why I'm here, to see you" Frankie said.

I didn't know if he was being sarcastic or just so dumb that he thought he needed to explain that he was sure that I lived here. But Foggy had a serious sound in his voice, so I just laughed and said, "What's up, Frankie? Did Ronny send you?"

"I'm not saying who sent me," Frankie answered. "Some people told me to give you a message: That if you aren't in business with them anymore, you should go away and stay away from any lawyers or government guys. Some government guys are asking everyone to come in and answer questions, and these guys, I think you know them good, say go away or don't talk to lawyers. Am I saying it so you understand?"

I understood perfectly and I could sense these weren't the opening remarks that might come before a whacking, because there are no opening remarks to a whacking. If you're on the spot, the button or the guy doing the work just does it. Sometimes if you really got someone angry, you were made an example of and they did things like torture you before they killed you. But mostly, as far as I knew from things I'd seen and heard, when you got whacked, you got whacked. Then, maybe they'd cut you up to get rid of you.

Frankie wasn't there in my garage to whack me. He was there to warn me. For some reason, Ronny and the others were going to let me walk away from the business as long as I went quietly and didn't make a move toward any law enforcement people. Believe me, if I'd even talked to a cop or the D.A. they would know five minutes later. Frankie repeated his message slowly and deliberately as if he were getting paid by the hour, then he patted me on the back. He was so close to me I could smell the calamari he'd eaten for dinner. The brim of Yankees cap was down near his eyes and he had on a leather jacket and jeans with a black T-shirt that read "World's Best Father" in white lettering. I looked at his cap, his eyes, his shirt, and then his shoes as my head drifted down to the concrete garage floor where I noticed a big oil spot near my foot.

When I looked up five seconds later, Frankie "The Fog" was already 10 feet away, back turned, walking down the driveway to the street. I was still alive, but I had been warned. "Go away and don't talk to anyone."

With all the heat coming down on the New York City families, it was easy to move away from the crew. I knew they couldn't tie me by any taps because I never talked on the phone about business, never, ever. I always met guys outside or in a place that couldn't be wired. I guess I was lucky enough to not have been mentioned. Guys would use references like "the kid from Tibbetts "or "our friend from Bronx River Road" or "that associate from Pelham" when talking about someone involved. And a wise guy always knew not to mention anyone's name—especially a last name. It wasn't unusual to have a conversation like: "Hey, did you invite that guy from New Rochelle to the party?"

"Yeah, he's goin' to meet us there and he said he can have three large steaks to split up," the other guy would answer.

"Three?" Are you sure there's gonna to be three? I'm hungry," the first guy would answer.

"Yup, three. Real nice, fresh and double-thick," the second guy tells him. That short conversation could be about a crew stealing three SUVs, or steaks, and needing to chop them into parts that night in New Rochelle at a garage that was expecting the "fresh" recently stolen trucks. Japanese food might mean foreign cars, and so on. We had our own language and we changed the usage just about the time we thought the Feds would decipher it.

We were all shocked and couldn't believe it when we heard John Gotti's crew at the Ravenite Club, which was using an old woman's apartment above the club for their sit-downs and meetings, got busted. The tapes coming out of that apartment, with men talking about everything from whacking guys to construction scams to where money was stashed, were like confessions. Once the feds had those tapes, Sammy "The Bull" Gravano and the others were cornered. When they realized they were going down, they turned.I thought our guys were too smart for that, but the wires planted in the carting offices turned up enough information to get convictions on the garbage deals and other things, like bribes to city and county officials.

220

Anyone who tapped my phone would hear tapes of me in conversations with my mother, sister, my daughter, kids on my teams, and me calling in my games to the newspaper.

"Hi, Ma, how you feelin'? How's Aunt Mary? How was bingo?" or "Practice has been moved from 3 to 4 p.m. tomorrow, Sean. Be there and tell the rest of the team about the change."

Anyone listening in on my phone would have thought I was a coach, union carpenter, and divorced father—a regular guy who made sure to take care of his mother. Watching all the big guys fall was unreal, like the Titanic was sinking and I had a lifeboat all by myself. As long as I didn't get too close, the vacuum created by that sinking ship would not pull me into the giant whirlpool.

My only problem after leaving the coaching jobs and disappearing from my mob activities was that I had to look for other ways of making a living, and that took some creative maneuvering.

Reputed Mobsters Arrested

WHITE PLAINS – Seven Westchester residents alleged to have ties with organized crime and connections to two of the five New York crime families were arrested yesterday in coordinated early-morning raids by FBI and Westchester County police.

The Westchester men, who included reputed mob kingpins Bernie "Big Ben" DeLeo of Yonkers and Ronny "The Kid" Cappelli of New Rochelle, were arraigned in County Court on felony charges including, extortion related to the sanitation industry, bribery, money laundering, sports betting and loan-sharking. Each was being held on $1 million bond.

DeLeo and Cappelli join an ever-growing list of reputed organized crime members who have moved to Westchester County over the past decade, setting up house to appear to be legitimate businessmen.

FBI spokesperson Frank Killehan said the arrests came as the result of a 10-month surveillance and investigation that included telephone taps at several mob-owned locations in the Bronx, Mount Vernon and Yonkers

DeLeo, Cappelli and the others face up to 25 years if convicted on all charges, The men also may be charged in the 1993 murder of an associate Ray "The Ragman" Romano, who was found dead in the Throgs Neck section of the Bronx with three bullet wounds to the head.

CHAPTER 20

But I have prayed for thee, that thy fail not; and when thou art converted, strengthen thy brethren. Luke 22:32

I haven't burned all my bridges; I just never built any that were strong enough or long enough to get me to where I was meant to be.

Something always keeps me from finishing the deal. Something that haunts me like the ghost of Michael Jordan over the New York Knicks, who might have won a couple of NBA titles if "He" hadn't been there winning championship after championship.

Like something that keeps a great singer from having that No. 1 record, or a great painter from being acclaimed until he's been dead for 20 years and collectors pay a million dollars for one of his paintings. What's missing is the magic that made Elvis who he was and the Beatles, the Beatles. It's what pushes successful people over the top and keeps the rest of us wishing we were them.

But I think I know what my something is. I just wasn't prepared to finish the deal. I don't know why. Everyone else seemed to know, but not me.

You've heard it, "If you don't get your education, you'll be working dead end jobs for the rest of your life. Or, "You have to have a plan and stick to it to be successful," or, "Good looks and talent won't get you far if you don't put in the time."

Yeah, Yeah, yeah. I think those phrases were invented for me. Teachers, starting in junior high, my coaches, my mother, my sister, my friends, even my bosses in the mob have said things like that to me since I was a kid.

"You could be the best, or you could have it all, or with your talent you could do anything you want to."

But there was always that something.

Something fumbling during a possible winning football drive when you can see the end zone a few yards away.

Something that lies there waiting to get you, like ptomaine poisoning after a great meal.

For me, it was something that happened between the ages of 5 and 13, somewhere between being a little kid and growing pubic hair; somewhere between innocence and sin. It was what made me the person I was instead of the person I dreamed of being.

Something cut me off from straight As and a high school diploma and a college degree and a Major League Baseball career and a happy marriage and .... well. ... and success.

Sometimes I think I know what that thing is.

You know.

It was my father's fault for not encouraging me or disciplining me, or teaching me the right things, or being there for me. Or, it was my teachers' fault for not making me do the work or making school exciting and interesting enough, or being assholes that didn't understand I needed help. Or, it was my wife's fault because, well, she was a bitch who didn't understand me and she was selfish and she was, a woman. Or, it was my coaches' fault because they knew I had talent and

224

they didn't nurture it or help me get through school.

That thing made it impossible for me to succeed. That thing was going to kill me sooner or later, yet I couldn't figure out what it was.

By the time I started coaching at Redemption, I still didn't know for sure, but I was getting closer.

Knowing that "thing" was the key to clearing it out of the way. Like an alcoholic who admits he's an alcoholic or a drug addict who confronts his habit, or a wife beater who admits he's out of control, you have to admit the "thing" exists before you can deal with it.

First it was my rebellion against any authority that prevented me from getting a real education, then a wrecked knee that ended a chance to play pro ball. Then it was insecurity in my marriages that made me believe I wasn't going to be able to hold on to love.

Hey, I even let my desire to be a coach gets in the way of a potentially successful career as a gangster. Now there's a conflict. Bad guy lets good side get in the way of him being a bad guy. Even the angel and the devil on my shoulders couldn't get it right.

Near the end of 1996 it was getting to the point where I didn't know if I was coming or going. My therapist had me back on Valium because I'd have periods of extreme agitation and occasional anxiety attacks. As tough as I was, not afraid to bust up a guy, steal anything, any size, or stand up to guys who were the toughest people in the union or garbage businesses, I would have panic attacks where I couldn't breathe. I could take a full breath and still not get enough oxygen.

The Valium made me lethargic, but helped me stay in control while I was working or dealing with the crazy night owl work. During practices and games, I was content, but still anxious; worried that something bad was going to happen. My greatest fear was that I'd do something to screw up the coaching. My fears were realized in the spring of 1996.

I spent the better part of 1996 commuting between

the U.S. Attorney General's New York City office and at Redemption High School, detoxing from long hours of interrogation. The DA, a woman named Joanne Whitman, had enough information on my associations with Ronny and Big Ben and the family connection with my Uncle Mario to use it as leverage in trying to get me to turn on the crew I was working with. Sammy the Bull and a bunch of other rats had already started making deals to save their asses, turning on all the big bosses of the New York families and ushering in the final days of the hold we had on the garbage and construction trades. I was just one of a hundred guys they were questioning, but unlike Gravano and that Goodfellas asshole Henry Hill, there wasn't much on me. At least not enough to make me want to rat. What could they do— send me away for a couple of years for conspiracy or RICO convictions? Maybe a union thing or an extortion charge? It wasn't enough to make me a target, but Whitman and the other feds were trying anything to get guys to turn.

I must have spent 100 hours answering the same questions over and over again.

"Who was your supervisor when you were selling garbage routes?

"What is your relationship with Ronny Capelli or Big Ben DiLeo?"

"What positions did you hold at the Javits Center and who got you the jobs?"

I answered the questions as honestly as I could without giving any names, details of possible crimes, or revealing anything other than what I did on the job, how much I got paid, and that all my jobs were legitimate. I think I only got upset once when Whitman asked me about my coaching and whether the school knew I had ties to a mob family.

"What do you think the kids and the monsignor would say if they knew their coach was involved in questionable activities," Whitman asked. "How long do you think you'd be allowed to stay there, coaching kids?"

"Why don't you stick to the reasons why I'm here," I answered. "And leave the school alone. I haven't done anything you can prove and why would you want to hurt a bunch of Catholic school kids anyway. What are you, an atheist? Just stay away from that shit. Send me to jail if you want, but don't mess with the school or my kids. They have nothing to do with anything you're looking into."

Whitman was persistent, but I wasn't giving anything up, and after a few months of dragging me in and making me miss practices and even some games, she moved on to the next guy and kind of left me alone. I think she wasn't actually a bad broad. I think she realized there wasn't anything I could help her with and I wasn't worth the time and money. She had bigger fish to catch—and she landed a whole bunch over the next year.

But she did accomplish one thing with me; she got me wondering if I could get by at Redemption too much longer. After those interviews with everyone going in for questioning, guys started getting paranoid—even more paranoid than usual, with everyone whispering about who was ratting and who wasn't. The fact that no one whacked me was a minor miracle. I guess the big guys found out from inside information that I wasn't cooperating and gave me a break. But things between me, Ronny and the others were never right after that. It was just a matter of time before people were gonna fall—and fall hard.

The spring of my interrogation year, the baseball team was 5-4 and headed for a mediocre season, my first non-winning spring. But I thought I could get the kids going and teach them enough to get us into the playoffs and maybe a round or two. But the investigation, Melissa's neurotic behavior, my neurotic behavior, and being married to a woman with more problems than even me, was getting to me. I missed a few more

227

practices, and then was late for a couple of games. I looked bad. I felt bad. I had a short fuse and I was looking for a way out of my skin.

The athletic director Donna Spakowski didn't like me a lot to start with, or at least that's what my paranoid mind told me. So when she called me in to talk with her and the Principal Don Rella that May, I was really in a panic.

"Tom, you know we love you here and you've done a lot for the kids and the school over four years," Spakowski said. "But Mr. Rella and I feel you aren't communicating with us. You're missing practices and games and we can't depend on you. Last week the kids had to get one of the parents to drive the team van to a game. We're concerned about your commitment. Is there a problem with the job, the team?"

Without getting into it, I told them I was having problems at home and with my business, but I thought I could handle it if they'd let me work it out.

"I think I've earned another chance and I can get us through the season," I said. "I always put the kids first and if I'm not doing the job, I'll get an assistant to help me. But I want to stay."

"Tom, the parents are starting to complain about the way you handle the kids, the cursing and talking dirty to them, joking around about girls, sex and things like that," Rella said. "Maybe you should take the season off and come back in the winter for basketball."

I blew up. These fools who had watched me coach their kids to heights the school had never seen were about to take away the best thing in my life and I was powerless to do anything about it. But I knew the dream had to end and I had to get to a place where I could straighten out my crazy life.

"No, that's all right, I don't need this shit!" I screamed. "You people don't have a clue. I'm doing the best I can and I just need some time."

I didn't realize it but my voice was cracking and I was

sweating from every pore. The four years of double dealing and trying to hide things from people had taken its toll and I was falling apart. I would have cried, but I didn't have anymore water left in my body after perspiring so much. I could see Rella and Spakowski were getting a little scared, so I backed off and walked out of the school.

"Forget it," I said as I pushed open the office door. "I'll resign. I'm not coming back."

I left the school that April afternoon just before my team was supposed to meet me for practice, got into my car, and haven't returned to Redemption High School since—not even to pick up some of the stuff I left in my desk – pictures of some of the games parents gave me, newspaper articles, and even some changes of clothes I used to keep in my locker. Maybe they cleaned that stuff out and gave it to the Goodwill. I hope some homeless guy got to enjoy my silk shirt and my Calvin Klein underwear. I left my heart, my life, my chance to continue coaching, and my kids without looking back. I was exhausted after four years of deceiving myself into believing I could be a full-time coach, trying my best to make my kids winners, experiencing victory after victory and championship after championship.

I had no more energy.

Like a marathon runner who collapses after running 26.2 miles, my body, mind, and spirit were spent. If someone had asked me to pick up a five-pound sack of sugar I couldn't have done it. And with my mob affiliations slowly fading day by day, I had no more juice.

I was an out-of-work gangster and part-time baseball and basketball coach. I had nowhere to go but home. And home wasn't where my heart was either, with Melissa running to her mother complaining about my mood swings and telling her friends I was abusive. She hinted about leaving me and I hoped she would.

The one thing I felt for sure was relief. I'd managed to break free of the gangster life and didn't have to worry about being found out at school. But what would I do with the man I'd become? I was a popular and successful coach with no one to coach.

When I left the school that day, the trip back to my apartment took 20 minutes because they were doing some roadwork on the parkway and only one lane was open. I was so stressed that I felt like I was going to pass out. My head ached and I couldn't focus on the road. The traffic finally cleared and when I got home, I fell into bed like I was dead. Melissa had packed up, taken little Tommy, and gone to stay with her mother, so I slept for about 20 hours straight. It was like I hadn't slept in four years. The apartment was dark and lonely, the cat litter needed to be changed, and the hamper overflowed with dirty clothes. The only light I could see before I passed out was a trickle of sunlight leaking through the window shades. I hoped that ray of sunshine wasn't the last one in my life.

The next sound I heard aside from my heavy breathing into a pile of pillows was the phone.

I never answered the phone. First, because I thought for years it was tapped, and second I always wanted to let the answering machine tell me who was calling before I bothered to get it. "This is Tom, I'm not home right now, so please leave a message after the beep and I'll get back to you as soon as I can." I heard myself say.

After the beep I heard a familiar voice: "Hello Coach V, it's Danny Lorusso. I'm calling to get your comments about leaving Redemption. Rella and Spakowski called and said you just resigned. I hope everything's okay. I knew there was something going on, but I'm a little surprised at the timing. If you get this message before my 11 o'clock deadline, call me at my office. You know the number."

Beep....

"Oh shit," I said to myself. It was 8 p.m., so I had a couple of hours to decide what I wanted to do. If I called

Lorusso, he'd want to grill me about why a successful coach was quitting out of the blue. I'd never said a word about moving on and just the day before I'd reported a game and talked to him about how I thought we could improve our team that spring. I waited until 10 p.m. and then made the call, hoping he'd write something quick and short that no one would see.

"Lorusso, sports," he said in a familiar greeting. "What's up?"

"Danny boy, it's Coach Vitale," I said in a quiet voice I'm sure he didn't recognize."

Coach, is that you?" he answered. "You all right?"

I'd shared with Lorusso that my wife and I were having some problems and I thought we might break up, so he probably thought that was why I'd quit. He also knew I'd missed some games. While I was being investigated it got tough to make every practice and game, so I started calling in sick. But I wanted to make some kind of statement for the paper, so I cleared my throat and told him to write down my comments. "I've been asked to resign because of personal problems that have made it difficult to perform as coach," I said. "But I had hoped the school would allow me to work things out and stay. I think I've earned that right. That's all I want to say Danny boy."

"I'll call you next week and we'll have lunch or something," I said, not really meaning it. "For now, take it easy."

I hung up the phone before Lorusso could ask any questions. He called back a few minutes later and got to hear my answering machine message again. The story Lorusso wrote about of my firing/resignation appeared this way in the next day's paper.

Redemption High School baseball and basketball coach Tom Vitale abruptly resigned yesterday in the middle of the spring baseball season after administrators at the parochial school asked for his resignation.

Vitale's three-year baseball record entering this year

231

was 54-13 over three seasons. His team didn't lose a baseball postseason playoff game in three years, compiling an 11-0 record and taking three Catholic School League titles. His four-year basketball record was 45-50, but the over-achieving Vitale teams managed to upset two heavy favorites en route to winning both the 1994 and 1995 Catholic championships and the state title in 1995."

"We all have faults and we all make mistakes," Vitale said about his resignation. "But I tried to give the boys at Sacred Heart some pride in themselves. I made them do their schoolwork. Winning wasn't as important as getting kids, who I loved, to believe in themselves. I don't want to be anywhere where I'm not wanted. But I would welcome an opportunity to coach somewhere at the high school or college level."

School Principal Don Rella, who recently praised the four-year coach for his work with his players and the athletic program, said, "Mr. Vitale has done a great job in his tenure here at Redemption. It is with regret that we have asked him to resign. He had not been available to fulfill his coaching responsibilities over the past several weeks. We wish him God speed and hope that he finds another position soon."

The chance to coach again hasn't come—yet. I've coached some recreation baseball, but nothing permanent. I can never pass up a game in progress, whether it's Little League game on some tiny field or a high school game where one of my friend's kids or someone else I know might be playing. I stand on the sidelines talking about the game and critiquing the coaches' moves or coaching the game ahead a batter or two, an inning or two, in my own mind.

You gotta know when you don't have an aptitude or talent for a particular job, but judging from some of the people I've seen at work, many people don't ever get what their talent is or isn't. That goes for the impatient, frustrated people working as bank tellers or store clerks, who have an attitude about everything and never smile when they're serving you. And there are doctors with cold hands and colder hearts, the teachers who can't control a class and bore you to sleep, the plumbers who spend five hours on your clogged drain and have to come back the next day to fix it, and the singers who can't sing. That American Idol show proves the point. How many of those assholes who audition are unable to hear that they can't sing a fuckin' note on key?

I felt like an American Idol contestant every time I tried a new job or business after I left coaching and my mob job. It got so bad that one day when I was driving my mother to the doctor I had about 50 cents in my pocket and didn't know where my next paycheck, my next dollar was coming from.

"Look at those guys over there toweling off cars at the car wash Ma," I said. "They got more money than I do. At the end of the week, they're gonna take home a paycheck. I got nothing. I'm shot. I gotta get a job and start living again."

"Don't worry Tommy," she said. "Something will happen. You'll be fine. I'm here for you. As long as you're not in trouble and you're healthy, you can get a job."

Jobs don't come easy for a guy with no high school diploma or college degree, so I had to try to hook up with friends and friends of friends to find work after leaving Redemption. I was shunned by my mob associates, so there wasn't anything coming from them. If I'd been convicted of a crime and sent away, they would have helped me with some cash, but because I chose to move away from the business, I was like a stranger—and they were always watching to see if I was cooperating with the any law enforcement people.

I had some contacts in the food distribution business from my union days, so I managed to get an ice cream and desserts vending route, supplying stuff to restaurants, stores and hotels. I hooked up a refrigerator truck and built up a good route. I could still make my own hours

233

because deliveries were on order and not in the mornings when most of the other food guys delivered. It wasn't bad, but it forced me to keep a regular schedule, work days, and sleep nights, which had become tough for me. At the same time I was working in an after-school sports program teaching little kids to play basketball, baseball and soccer until their parents picked them up to take them home. That job was from 3 to 5 or 6 p.m. and it kept me around the sports scene.

I also did some coaching with a club baseball team, coaching 14- and 15-year-old kids. These kids weren't as dedicated as my high school kids, because the team was a summer recreation team and the kids would rather have been swimming, sleeping late, or chasing girls at the local pool. I missed coaching the high school level where the kids were in a more structured environment and responded better to discipline. I wasn't playing softball myself any more because it was just getting harder to recover from the muscle pulls and other nicks and bruises.

I used some of my old connections again and managed to get referred to a real estate broker in Tarrytown who helped me get my sales license. The broker gave me a desk in his office and three-person staff set-up on the Hudson River, where real estate values were high and prospects looked good. But it was tough for me to sit still and wait for customers, cold call looking for potential listings, or run around taking people to 50 different condos before they'd say, "Maybe we'll try the Bronxville or Eastchester area. We don't see anything along the river that's us."

I didn't mind the business of selling or renting property—I just didn't love it. And after all the shit I came out of, getting into another dead end job or business wasn't for me. I knew the dream of being a successful realtor was fading when I had to show some apartments to a couple from the Bronx who wanted to move to the suburbs. "We'd like something with three bedrooms, perhaps a co-op rental, near the river, with nice views, modern kitchen and bathroom—and perhaps a fire place," the lady said. "We can afford up to $1,200 a month."

When I answered, "Miss, you couldn't even get a modern bathroom in the suburbs for $1,200 a month, forget about a whole apartment," the woman said I couldn't be much of a professional if I didn't have access to the type of unit they required.

I looked at the two of them and realized there wasn't enough money in the world to make me want to deal with assholes like that every day. I was in the real estate business for less than six months.

I got the chance to handle some work in one of the local town recreation departments, and even though there was no money in it, I grabbed the opportunity. They knew my name from coaching at Redemption and, thankfully, not from my mob work, so I was a quick hire. I guess they didn't check too far back for a low-paying after-school job. I was coaching girl's softball in the spring and indoor hockey in the winter, making ten dollars an hour in the afternoons, but it felt good to be back working with kids. My paychecks, between $180 and $200 a week, got me by.

One afternoon on the way to work delivering ice cream, I stopped to pick up a newspaper and check the baseball scores. Before I could get to the sports page, I was paralyzed by the screaming front page headline that read: "Reputed Mobster Capelli Disappears."

I'd heard a rumor that Ronny had turned and ratted on the top guys in the family, but I didn't believe it. Now he was headed for a six-year term, maybe four years with good behavior, for extortion and related RICO convictions on loan sharking and construction and bribery, so he could have handled that, no problem. Since I'd been away from the business, I didn't know the top guys had found out that Ronny was skimming and not sending up the right amount of money from what his crew earned. I heard from a guy later that Ronny was made to disappear to send a message to other guys that you don't hold back what belongs to the main men.

"He's never gonna be found, never, ever," the guy told me. "Ronny was too smart of his own good. He had it all and got greedy, thinking he could take extra while all the indictments had everyone distracted and going to trial. But someone ratted on him and now he's gone."

I was stunned. I felt like I'd lost a family member. A real family member. I liked Ronny and he was always straight with me. But the guy was right: Ronny got too smart. He was always a step ahead of everyone and he taught me to be that way. "Never talk to people about other people or what you're doing," he would say. "You can trust yourself, but no one else. And don't be one of those guys like Gotti, who has to show himself to the world, be a big guy in the media. Be like the old timers, quiet, private, smart."

I guess Ronny wanted to be sure his family was taken care of before he went away. Even being a loyal guy, a good earner, and being willing to go to jail wasn't enough to save him. By 2004, Ronny "The Kid" Capelli had been gone for nearly five years. Not a trace. No body, no clothes, no car, no bank records of money being moved.

Nothing.

It was like he disappeared and went to visit Jimmy Hoffa. His wife still thinks maybe he went into hiding in Costa Rica or somewhere. He was smart enough to do something like that, but I don't think he'd leave his wife and kids, who he really loved. No. Ronny was a casualty of the treacherous and deviant world of the mob, just as I'd have been some day had I stayed in the game.

CHAPTER 21

If we confess our sins, he is faithful and just to forgive us our sins and to cleanse us from all unrighteousness. I John 1:9.

I called Lorusso early on a Saturday morning just about a week after I left Redemption. It was around 7 a.m. and his wife didn't sound too happy about the timing. I'd been up all night with a bad headache and needed to talk to someone about what was going on in my head.

"What's up Coach V?" Dianne Lorusso asked in a groggy voice. "Is something wrong? Is Danny supposed to be somewhere to meet you? Is there a game?"

"No, Dianne," I answered. "I'm sorry about calling so early, but I need to talk to the big guy? Is he in?"

"Yeah I think that's him snoring next to me here in bed. I'll see if I can get him up. He did a Knicks game last night and didn't get home until 1 a.m."

I had gotten to know Lorusso's wife Dianne pretty well over the years. Her kids were the same age as my Vanessa and they would sometimes come to our games with their mom and dad. The kids would play together and I invited them to our team barbecues so Vanessa had some kids to play with. I think Dianne had some kind of intuition about me. Even though her husband was a pretty smart guy and a good reporter, he was naïve when it came to the real world, having grown up in the protected Westchester suburbs in a religious family. Dianne was a street-smart Puerto Rican girl from Morris Park in the Bronx, a tough Italian neighborhood a lot like Arthur Avenue. You could tell she'd been through some tough times growing up. She didn't trust everyone and was protective of her husband. One time she even asked me about what I did and made a face when I wasn't too clear about my business. She probably knew guys like me growing up and had legitimate reservations about my lifestyle and my relationship with her husband.

I could hear Lorusso rustling the covers and yawning in the background. A few seconds later Dianne handed him the phone.

"What's up Coach," he said. "How the hell are you? What's the matter? Did your watch stop? It's like 7 a.m. You know I don't get up on Saturday until the kids ask for breakfast. What's the deal?"

"I'm a little tired," I said. "I'm not sleeping too good since I was bounced from Redemption. Listen, I'd like to talk to you about something important. Let me treat you to breakfast. How about 8 a.m. at the Argonaut Diner on Yonkers Avenue?"

"Yeah, sure, V," Lorusso said. "I'll see in about an hour. But if I'm late, get me a big cup of coffee and keep it hot."

Lorusso must have been really curious about what I wanted, because I got to the Argonaut in 50 minutes and he was already there, sitting in a booth drinking coffee and bullshitting with the diner owner about the Knicks game he'd covered the night before. When I got there, the owner said hello, gave me a menu, and left us alone.

"Thanks for coming DLo," I said. "What are you gonna eat?"

"I'm not hungry, V," Lorusso said. "I'll just have coffee and maybe an English muffin. By the way, you look like shit. What have you been doing? I called to see what you thought about the story I wrote on your resignation and you never called me back."

"Yeah, I'm sorry about that," I said. "I took the phone jack out of the wall and haven't talked to anyone for a week. I guess leaving the coaching job bothered me more that I thought it would. There's something I wanted to get straight with you before you heard it from someone else. Things are being said about why I left and I wanted to tell you the straight truth. Can we talk off the record? You know man to man, friend to friend?"

Lorusso had a strange look on his face, like he knew what was coming. And the fact that I asked him to keep my words off the record seemed to make him more curious. I think he was surprised that I said "friend to friend" because I'd never really expressed that kind of sentiment before. Lorusso had a lot of friends in the community. He was the type of guy who could write about you, whether it was positive or negative news, and still keep your respect. But because of my life and my "business," I always had to keep my distance. Now, as he sat there across from me with his English muffin and coffee, I sensed he'd expected this moment of revelation for a while.

"Shoot, V," he said. "Everything is off the record. Man to man and friend to friend. What's up?"

The words came out of me like they'd been waiting on the tip of my tongue for years. It was like going to confession with a priest you knew you could trust. The four years of Lorusso's writing all those good things about me somehow made it easier to tell him the truth. It was like he already knew about my other life and had been protecting my sanctuary at Redemption. I owed it to him to admit who I really was.

"D, I'm in a life or death situation here," I said. "I've been involved for a lot of years in organized crime

239

activities and that's the reason why the coaching thing fell apart on me. I tried to separate the two parts of my life and got away with it for awhile, but it got too hard to manage both, so I decided to quit."

Lorusso's face turned pale. He grabbed his hot cup of coffee with both hands and lifted it to his mouth, looking over his glasses at me. I could see the beginning of tears at the corner of his eyes, but I didn't know if he was scared shitless or just shocked that he'd misjudged me so badly. He took a deep breath and put the coffee cup down, shaking a little as he dropped it on the plate. "I did agree this is off the record, right?" he said with a forced smile.

I nodded yes.

"That's good, because I didn't bring my mini recorder or a pen and pad. I guess I can't write it down or record it, so there's no story. Hey, you're kidding right? Tell me you're kidding. Tell me I haven't come across the best story in the history of high school sports and can't write it. Tell me you're jerkin' my chain."

I didn't answer. I just looked down into my coffee cup and Lorusso knew I wasn't bullshitting him or playing a prank.

"I knew you dressed too well to be in construction," Lorusso said. "I never saw you with rough hands or dirty fingernails. And all those guys, your friends at the wedding and at the games, the guys with the Florida tans, no necks and cigars. Was that your crew?"

"Forget all the specifics DLo," I said. "I don't want to tell you anything that might get you in trouble or make it tough for you if I'm ever up on charges, which may happen soon. Let's just say I've been involved in some things you might have heard about. Garbage, loansharking, gambling, stuff like that. Some of my family, on my mother's side, are big guys. I got involved after my leg blew out in Yankee camp and I've been into this thing for about 20 years. I just wanted you to know, because I know you tried to do the right thing for me and

240

the kids. Whatever happens from here, just keep this shit to yourself. And don't go writing a fuckin' tell-all book when I'm in jail. If I get clipped or disappear one day, you can write what you want."

"Get clipped?" Lorusso asked. "What, are you going to get whacked because of the coaching? Are you kidding? Those guys that came to the games seemed to like what you were doing. Everyone did. You did a lot of good things at Redemption."

"I'm not getting whacked," I said, hoping it was true. "But the government is bringing us all in to investigate some things and from what I hear they have wire taps and other evidence that's going to shut down the garbage business. In cases like this, if someone rats, who knows who they'll blame? I just wanted to get clear of the kids and the school before this, but I couldn't leave. I loved coaching those fuckin' kids. Now, my people tell me I have to keep my mouth shut and stay away from any publicity. I was out there in the newspapers every day thanks to you, and that wasn't cool when all this started coming down.

"Yeah, I'm a great reporter," Lorusso said as he lifted his coffee to salute himself. "A mob guy coaching a Catholic school team—two teams—and I just go on writing about you for four years, nominating you for Coach of the Year and telling everyone all about the tough-guy coach who miraculously wins championships with a bunch of Yonkers knuckleheads. I'm like a blind man in the dark. What the hell was I thinking?"

"Hey, DLo," I said. "Don't be so hard on yourself. There have been a dozen feds trying to get something on me for 10 years and not one charge. What's one sports reporter supposed to do? No one knew what I was—not the church, the school, the kids, no one. You were just trying to do something good for some kids and I got the benefit. Hey, no one has to know."

"Right," Lorusso said. "This is all off the record, right. The problem is, what do I do when you go back to your

241

family and friends and back to work. Is that off the record too?"

"I'm quitting," I answered. "I'm getting out. Just let it go."

"Getting out is great," Lorusso said. "You're not going to coach again, right?"

"I'm talking about the "business," I said. "I'm out of coaching, but I'm getting out of the business, too."

"You mean you're getting out of the mob?" Lorusso said with a wide-eyed expression. "From what I hear, you can't retire from the mob. From what I always heard, they retire you."

Yeah, well I'm getting out," I told Lorusso again. "My bosses are all in big trouble and I don't know how long they'll be on the street. My Uncle Mario was a big-time made guy, so I have some friends making it possible for me to fade away. I just have to clear through the feds' investigation, keep my mouth shut, and stay away from friends and associates. I'm gonna be a man without a country or a family for awhile. I just have to find a legitimate way to make a living and I'm not used to that. Maybe I'll start a business or something. But I'll be staying away from things – and I won't be able to talk to you after this. I don't want anyone to think I'm giving you any information on the record, you know?"

"Okay Coach," Lorusso said. "I've been thinking about taking a job in South Jersey at another newspaper and moving my family to a quieter place, so maybe this is good timing. Maybe I can go into the 'reporter's without a clue' protection program for reporters who can't see a big story when it's right in front of them. Good luck V, with everything. And it's too bad you have to stop coaching. I don't know what kind of gangster you were, but you were a great coach with real potential. And that's on the record." He finished his coffee. "I'm gonna go now. Michael and Danny have baseball games this afternoon. Tell Vanessa I said hello and keep in.... well, maybe I'll

242

hear from you someday. But stay safe."

"Thanks for the good press," DLo," I said as he got up to leave the diner. "We had four great years at Redemption and a lot of it was because of you. You made the kids believe. You made me believe there was something good in my life. Take care of your wife and kids, and if you ever come across a coach or a kid who doesn't seem just right but needs some good press—well, you know what to do. I'll see you sometime."

Lorusso moved his family down to South Jersey about six months later. I saw his last column in the Daily Herald and I read it while I was waiting to apply for a job with a real estate management company. He wrote about all the good sports stories he'd covered and how much he respected the athletes and coaches he'd gotten to know. I hoped he included me as one of them.

But I felt like a real rat bastard for getting over on the guy for so long. I just never wanted him to know me as anything but a coach. He was a good reporter. I was just a better con man. But my conning days had come to an end.

CHAPTER 22

Old things are passed away, behold, all things are become new. II Corinthians 5:17

Waking up to an alarm clock at 7 a.m. is a revelation in itself. It's sort of like starting life all over again – getting up and going to school with everyone else, waiting for lunch in the cafeteria, dragging through classes and anticipating the end of the day when you can go home and have dinner and relax.

In my former life, I'd just be getting into bed at 6 a.m. after a night at an after-hours joint, partying or strolling around talking about "business." I've said it before, a thousand times: living the mob life was like being in a vampire. You're a creature of the night and build an aversion to sunlight because the dark is the best place to do business. You don't ever have any real friends you can open your soul to. And love is never really for sure.

Being a vampire sucks.

When you look in a mirror, you hope you don't see your reflection because you might not like what you see.

Going straight was like having a stake plunged into my black heart, and despite what you see in movies,

244

killing a vampire doesn't necessarily mean the "monster" is dead. In my case, that stake through the heart—the possibility of a new and better life—killed my desire for the dark side and left the good side of my heart still beating. The monster has slowly faded since I was ripped away from my "friends" and forced to choose another way of living. Guys I used to work for had disappeared, been whacked, or were being entertained by the federal prison system for long stretches—some for as long as 15 years.

There were even a couple of rats I knew about who'd opted to hide in the witness protection program with that jerk-off Henry Hill, who was the featured rat in "Goodfellas," and Sammy "The Bull" Gravano, who turned on John Gotti.

Don't get me wrong, I know now that I can't ever hope to completely justify the mob life, what it does to the world around it, and what I did to my world. But I could never have ratted on anyone to keep my freedom. I would have gone down myself before turning on someone else. I read about all these guys in all the five New York families who turned state's evidence to get shorter sentences or immunity. Immunity from what? These are the guys who did the killing, stealing, cheating and the lying, and then they want to get rewarded for ratting on someone who did the same things? I don't like talking about what I did, but I like talking about what other guys did even less. We're all sinners. I wish all the shit that happened would just go away. But each person has to live with his or her own sins. I'm not going to blame anyone else for what I did, my father, mother, Uncle Mario or people I met along the way. It's all on me, and I'm no rat. That's just the way I feel.

The alarm clock now rings for me along with millions of other nine to five people who make a living on the job every day. The radio is set to WFAN, the sports talk station and I hear Don Imus, a New York City radio talk show host I learned to like over the years because he's a

245

survivor like me. Imus went through bad relationships, cocaine addiction, and alcoholism and remained on top of the radio world for 30 years or more. This particular morning, he's ragging on some phony politician who's trying to make a point about the Middle East, but the I-Man keeps reminding the guy that we're over there making sure our SUVs have affordable gas. Imus does his morning drive show until 10 a.m. when the sports guys come on. I love listening to those clowns talk sports; mostly talk show hosts who never played the games they're talking about and criticize everything and everyone. And the people that call in—man what losers. The same few people, Richie from Flushing or Billy from Bensonhurst, calling every other day, looking for air time and probably daydreaming some producer will hear their ESPN-like banter and hire them to do a talk show. But I listen because the subject matter is still my first love—baseball, basketball, football—all of it still sucks me in.

My two dogs, Blackie and Lucky, two little rat terriers, jump up when I roll out of bed like they have jobs to go to, too. I've got to feed these little worms before I feed myself. They're pests, but I guess they're my family. I love animals of any kind. I don't even kill bugs when I find them in my apartment. I just pick them up and put them outside. I hate to see anything that's helpless being hurt. People make their own problems and get themselves into trouble, but animals are helpless. I love dogs especially. Dogs are loyal, even to a guy who has had such a hard time getting his shit together in life. None of my dogs ever asked me what I did for a living or how much money I made. They just return what you give them. You love them. They love you back. It's not that easy with people.

"Good morning Blackie, did you have a nice sleep?"

"Look at you Lucky, are you hungry? Is Blackie treating you right?"

The dogs jump, yip, yap and run in circles, like two

little kids who love seeing their daddy in the morning. I've always had dogs and cats. I wouldn't like living completely alone.

Breakfast is some grapefruit juice, two cans of Purina liver and kidneys, and a bagel or a muffin leftover from the day before. I get the juice and some bagel; the dogs get the Purina and pieces of muffin they beg for.

A quick shave and I'm out.

I'm working in north Jersey now, at a sports development center. After trying an assortment of jobs—the dessert route, selling real estate, and a floor restoring business, I finally landed a part-time job at a recreation department teaching little kids the basics of different sports. Imagine that, a street-tough type coddling little rich kids, teaching them how to hit a ball—for $10 bucks an hour, no less.

Some of the kids would cry when they got too hot on long, summer camp days or too cold during late fall after-school soccer or they'd just feel tired because their mommies or nannies weren't there to help them. But I would treat them like the bigger kids, tell them to "get tough" and "suck it up," and they liked it. "What's the matter, Tyler or Samantha or Lucas?" I'd say. "Do you think the big kids cry when they get tired? No, they don't. They just suck it up and play harder. Did you ever see Michael Jordan cry during a game? No? Well, then, don't punk out on me and get back in the game."

Those kids loved being talked to like that. All kids love a little kick in the ass. It shows them someone thinks they can do better. Kids shouldn't be coddled all the time. It makes them weak. It was fun watching the little suckers show me their games faces, and when one of them would finally get off a good kick or hit a ball really hard, they'd punch the air or mimic me and say, "Yeah, baby, I'm the man!"

The part-time job turned into a full-time gig at a YMCA; there's another match made in heaven, huh?" I went from a mob-connected Catholic school coach to a recreation leader at the Young Men's Christian Association. God became the best employer I ever had.

By then, in late 2001, I was almost completely detoxed from my meds and my past life. A few years out of the "life" and people forget you. Most of the guys I worked with had moved on, gone to prison, or were just nowhere to be found. Young wanna-bes come along with dreams of being John Gotti, and if you move aside and out of the picture, with your bosses no longer in power, you're forgotten.

I liked being forgotten.

Well, not completely.

Once in a while, when I went to a high school basketball or baseball game, someone would come up to me and say, "Hey, didn't you coach Redemption hoops and baseball back in the 90s?"

"Yeah," I'd say," "That was a long time ago. We had a good run"

"Why aren't you coaching now?" the guy might ask. "You were good and some of these coaches now aren't really doing the job. You should be coaching"

"If you hear of a job, let me know," I always say, knowing that most of the coaching openings go to certified teachers or coaches. "Find me some kids who need a kick in the ass and I'll take the job."

I worked at the YMCA for a couple of years, got my GED and started attending a local community college. Despite my years away from school, I managed to complete my associate's degree in recreation and then go to night classes at City College in New York to finish my bachelor's degree. Man, nobody in my "crew" ever had any kind of degree or even cared to try to go to school, so I was pretty pleased about being able to hang on and finish even if it took the better part of five years. By 2002 I had some paper on my resume and decided to apply for a position as a recreation coordinator in a northern New Jersey town where not too many people would know me. I didn't have much of a resume, at least

I had a degree in something A few white lies about my job background, a lot of stuff about my real coaching and sports career, the recreation and YMCA work, and a nice recommendation from a couple of reputable people I met along the way, and I managed to land nice job as a recreation coordinator.

"A nice job."

Man, that's something I thought I'd never say, except maybe after beating up a guy or lifting a nice haul at the docks or nailing down a cushy do-nothing union gig at the Javits Center.

Tommy V has a nice job.

Hey, it might even be called a career. Not career criminal, career loser, career failure, but career recreation specialist. The community where I work knows me only as a recreation guy who loves working with kids and is the guy to go to when you need help with finding a good field, open gymnasium, or a league for your kids to play in. But there are times when even the most obscure former criminal faces his past.

One afternoon on my way home from work back to Yonkers, I stopped in a local deli in New Jersey, just before I got on the Palisades Parkway. I wanted to pick up some cold cuts, fresh mozzarella, and other stuff for my mother. The deli owners were originally from the Bronx and had their own fresh tomato sauce and other Italian foods you used to be able to get only in NYC. They'd moved to suburban New Jersey in the mid 1990s and brought their food with them, even importing stuff from Arthur Avenue, like breads and pastries, from the old neighborhood's bakeries. The guy on line in front of me happened to turn around to tell me how great the sausages were and he did a double take like he recognized me.

"Hey, Tommy, what the hell are you doin' up here?" the guy asked. "The last I heard you left that coaching thing and most of the guys you hung out with were busted for some garbage thing. How the hell are you?"

I recognized the guy immediately as Richie Basile, a guy whose family owned a market in the old Arthur Avenue neighborhood. I couldn't lie to the man, so I told him I'd moved on to other work, left "the business" and was working in sports fitness. "I'm good Richie, how you doin'?" I answered. "How's your family? I'm not connected to that stuff anymore and I'm doing pretty good now."

Richie, who was never connected to any mob stuff but was around it most of his life like all of us from Arthur Avenue, looked surprised but relieved that I wasn't involved anymore. "That's great V," he said. "I remember you were a great baseball player and I think I heard that you were a great coach in Yonkers somewhere. It's good to see you're doing what you love doing. Some of those other guys never got anywhere. They had their time, but it all fell apart. There's no life in that shit. Good to see you, man. Good luck with the sports thing. I live right here in town, so maybe I'll see you around."

I was a little nervous that he might tell someone that a former mob guy was working at the local sports fitness center, but I had to let it go. What could I do? If someone found out I had that kind of past, it could be a problem, but I had to let it go. I felt better when Richie turned and came back to shake my hand.

"Good to see you V," he said. "I always liked you and knew you had a good head and a good heart. Peace, man."

I got my mozzarella, cold cuts, and some of that sausage Richie recommended and headed back to Yonkers.

So, the alarm clock rings for me five days a week. I drop by the local 7-11 for some hot coffee and a newspaper and I'm off to beat the morning traffic across the Tappan Zee Bridge. I don't even mind the morning glare splashing off the Hudson River, a sight I used to see coming home at dawn. I enjoy seeing the other commuters with their coffee cups and rolls, eating on their way to work.

My mornings are spent setting up sports programs and assigning athletic fields to different organizations, which is a lot easier than running with a crew of hothead mob types. The people I work with may not be glamorous, but they show me respect and I don't have to fear being blindsided by someone with a beef. The toughest challenge each day is to make sure all the kids are playing where they should be and all the parents are happy.

Most days are business as usual, but when 3 p.m. comes I'm always happy to see little kids running around, learning to play the games I learned on the streets of Fordham. These kids have it made; nice facilities, good fields, summer camps. I sometimes wish I'd grown up like them, with a silver bat in my hand. But I have to put that behind me. I'm learning to get past regrets.

Sometimes a kid will ask if I'm married and if I have kids. You know, kids think if you work with kids, you must have some of your own. I tell the younger ones yes and tell them that I have a daughter who's 18 and a son who's 8. That usually satisfies them.

But talking about family is still tough, because my daughter has kind of slipped away a little as she has gotten older. You know, teens don't need the two parents they live with on their backs and another one who they have to visit every weekend giving them more grief. My daughter just tells me to leave her alone when I try to offer advice about school or boys. I love her to death, so I don't push myself into her life. She has the right to make her own way without my long-distance parenting.

My son Tommy Jr. is the one I really miss, because he's grown up without me being there. His mother and I divorced when he was just a year old and she always busted my balls about custody and visitation. She moved upstate and made it tough to get to the little guy. But he's doing good. I have his picture on my desk at work

251

and my night table at home. He looks a lot like me.

I try to believe Tommy would be proud of me because I've changed my life and I'm doing positive things. Every time I see a bunch of kids playing or I'm running a baseball camp or kid's league, one of the little kids always looks like Tommy. And when I see one of them who has natural ability, I go back in my mind to when I was a kid and I hope my son loves playing ball.

I really hope my son gets to know more about my success than my failures. But I'm sure my ex tells him what a fuck-up she thinks I was. That's usually the case with break-ups. The kid always gets one side or the other.

I was watching the Sopranos one night. I don't usually watch that shit because it hits too close to home and I never liked the way the mob guys were depicted on television and the movies, except the Godfather, which is a classic. I sometimes think mob guys watch the Godfather and emulate the characters instead of the actors imitating real gangsters. Life sometimes imitates art. I knew a lot of guys who grew up wanting to be Michael or Sonny Corleone. But art could never really imitate the real mobsters' life, because you can't portray that kind of loneliness and emptiness with just words or on film. The life isn't as glamorous as we all thought.

But I looked at those Soprano guys and realized how much like me they were before I got into coaching; wise guys who didn't have a clue who they really were. They were men who believed that power, money, and the ability to steal was a badge of honor. Honor, my ass. The life is treacherous, dark, deceitful, jealous, anti-family and can bury any real talent a person might have. Underneath every mobster there's a kid who loved art, sports, math, politics, music or science, but buried that love because it didn't go well with a dark suit and dark glasses.

I lived that life, and believe me, it was no life. It cost me love, family, and any real friends who might have been scared away by my darkness.

252

I still have days when I'm lonely and feel like I've wasted my life, but at 45, with all the medical knowledge we have about staying healthy, I could live another 50 years, enough time to balance out my legacy. Hey, Grandma Moses didn't start painting until she was in her 80s and Hemingway didn't write his first successful novel until he was what, about 35? And Noah didn't build that ark until he was like 400 or something – in Bible years anyway.

Anyway, Noah was old and God told him to build an ark to save mankind and he didn't say, "I'm too old and who'll believe me." He grabbed onto his destiny and saved two of every living thing to keep the world running.

I'm not saying God has a plan for me, because I don't know yet if I really believe in God the way other people do. But I do know that something saved me from my own flood. Saved me from being eliminated from the world. I'd like to think I had the guts to change, the guts to realize I was headed for destruction, and that I determined I would save myself.

But when I look back on my days at Sacred Redemption, the times when I walked onto those baseball fields and basketball courts and felt like a king, I know I found a sanctuary just in time. I needed to experience a little bit of heaven to know I was living in hell. I needed just a taste of success and fulfillment to know that the joy of life was there waiting for me.

Was it a miracle, falling into that baseball job back then in 1992?

Or was it fate?

Sometimes I think, "Where would I be right now if I hadn't taken that coaching job? Probably in jail, or dead or wasted somewhere on medications visiting therapist after therapist, or maybe even in mental institution. Hey, don't get me wrong; I'm no saint and I don't go around preaching to people and telling them to repent and changed their lives. I'm still trying to get comfortable with this new identity I assumed when the old one got peeled away. I see myself as like Jonah, the guy in the Bible who tried to run way from God and got swallowed by a whale. After a while in that disgusting, stinking stomach, he got vomited out and landed in the place where God wanted him to go anyway. He was so glad to be out of that hellhole, he was happy to do what God asked of him. I don't think I'm ready to preach salvation to anyone. I'm just glad to be out in the light.

All I know is, my time place at Redemption High offered me a type of sanctuary, doing what I loved, expressing my gifts. It saved me. For what? I don't know yet. But I've built a part of that sanctuary inside myself and when that alarm clock goes off each morning and the old man tells me to "fuck it and go back to sleep," the new man slides out of bed and says, "I know I can do something good today. I know there's something good in me. I know it, because I've lived it every day for four beautiful years."

Ma died just after New Year's in 2005 after a two-year tussle with all kinds of terrible cancers and her passing added another punctuation mark to my life story. I still don't know if her death will cast a large shadow on me, be a question mark in my search for faith or just be a comma in my up and down travels with more highs and lows to come. I do know that with everyone I've lost, her loss has been the worst because Mama Rose was my patron saint, my best friend, the role model for anything good in my life.

The wake and funeral included the expected tears, sleepless hours and acknowledgement of my loss, but relief for Ma because she was in peace after a good but often difficult life. To no one's surprise, even the funeral mass held a Tommy V moment and a challenge to my renovated life. The mass itself was held in a small church near where we lived on the Mount Vernon-Yonkers border. As I've said before, the rituals of the church never appealed to me much, but I was present and willing to participate in the ceremonial mass because

254

Ma would have wanted me to. The priest, who didn't really know Ma at all and was appointed to do the mass, trudged through the service with very little emotion or enthusiasm, saying little about my mother and reciting the dry liturgy to the small crowd. Toward the end of the mass he asked family members – my sister Lorraine's kids had asked to speak -- to offer their thoughts about their Grandma. I hadn't planned to speak but after the kids said such beautiful things, I felt I had one last opportunity to tell people how much I loved my mother. As the organist began to play the next song, I rose and moved toward the alter podium just as the priest began to read another scripture. He spotted me and seemed annoyed.

"Excuse me, but I wasn't informed that another person was going to speak," the irritated priest said dropping the bible he was holding onto the lectern in front of him and throwing up his arms as if he were thrown off his schedule. "We can't all just jump up and come up here. What kind of funeral mass are we running here!"

I was embarrassed standing there in front of everyone in that near empty sanctuary and a little pissed at what he said. When I moved to return to my seat several members of the family urged me to go forward. They were all shocked that this supposed representative of Jesus had been so abrupt and rude. I ignored my red face and growing anger, walked to the altar, stood at the podium and said, "I hope they have angel hair pasta in heaven because Ma won't stay if they don't. She was my best friend, a friend to anyone who needed her and she will make heaven a better place."

Then I waved my hand at the asshole priest, who was now sitting and fuming, waiting for me to finish.

"I hope that didn't take too much time," I said sarcastically and sat down.

My mother would have been proud. She was always telling me to hold my explosive temper and to be careful what I said. I took my place behind the casket as they carried Ma out of the church and didn't even turn to glance at the priest. And I didn't need to straighten the guy out because as I leaving the church I spotted my aunt and my cousin reaming the padre out, blasting him for his insensitivity and rude remarks.

"What do you have a lunch date or something?" my aunt said. "Are you in a hurry? That was the worst thing I've ever seen a priest do in any church at any function. This family was hurt by what you did. And don't show up at the grave sight for that ceremony or I might push you in.!"

I felt a great sense of satisfaction as they lay Ma to rest at St. Mary's that morning. I could proudly tell her, "See Ma, I didn't smack the guy or even get angry. Maybe her death made me understand that her life was spent trying to make me into a good person and I wasn't going to dishonor that love by doing anything stupid. I could even feel some of the stress of my life leaving my body as I said good bye to Ma. She was leaving me in body, but leaving a part of her loving spirit with me.

I've had a lot of experience with pain and never wanted to face it until I realized there was an alternative. Ma's death, although it left a big space in my heart, made me want to be more like her, She was helpful, caring, not judgmental and a haven for me and others in trouble. Just a saint.

Hey, I sometimes think, maybe someday I can be a sanctuary for someone else, like my Ma was for me — some confused, scared kid who needs help, a person who may need some guidance, or even my own children, if they ever choose to reach out to me again.

Hey, who knows? I may even get another chance to coach. It could happen. It happened once before. And after all, a coach is what I am.

That's one thing I know for sure.

About the
Author

Danny Lopriore is a veteran newspaper reporter, editor and columnist who has covered high school sports and news for several daily and weekly newspapers in New York and New Jersey since 1989. He lives in Westchester County, N.Y. with his wife Dianne and three of their five children. "Seasons in Sanctuary" is his first book.

CPSIA information can be obtained at www.ICGtesting.com
Printed in the USA
BVOW032044230113

311442BV00001B/17/A